BOTH SIDES OF THE FENCE 2: GATE WIDE OPEN

BOTH SIDES OF THE FENCE 2:
GATE WIDE OPEN

M.T. POPE

www.urbanbooks.net

Urban Books, LLC
78 East Industry Court
Deer Park, NY 11729

ISBN 13: 978-1-60162-230-3
ISBN 10: 1-60162-230-9

First Printing November 2010
Printed in the United States of America

10 9 8 7 6 5 4 3

Distributed by Kensington Publishing Corp.
Submit Wholesale Orders to:
Kensington Publishing Corp.
C/O Penguin Group (USA) Inc.
Attention: Order Processing
405 Murray Hill Parkway
East Rutherford, NJ 07073-2316
Phone: 1-800-526-0275
Fax: 1-800-227-9604

Dedication

This book is dedicated to the reader, for supporting me one more time. It is very *much* appreciated. Thank you for the love.

Acknowledgments

This is book number two for me. I owe it all to God for blessing me with a wonderful gift that He chose to spring forth at the appointed time. Thank you, God, for finishing another book for me. You poured out the words once again onto empty pages and made it flow so easily. You know Lord; I agonized over if this whole writing thing was for me and if you were approving of it. You answered by filling up the pages once again. I thank You for the grace and mercy that allowed me to get this far in life. I am . . . because You are, and I live . . . because You died. And I will die because You showed me how to live.

To my Mom, Lawanda Pope, a little woman with big strength. You make me smile every time I see you. You are the best mom in the world. I love you. My brothers and sisters: Shirley, William, Darnell, Darlene, Gaynell, Latricia, Nathon, and Yvette. I love you guys.

To my Pastor, Melvin T. Lee, and First Lady, Tanya Lee, for coming out and showing love at my first book signing and everything else I do in this life. I promise dad that the Christian fiction is coming. Lol. To all my Because He Lives church family members, I love you with only the love that God shines through me. We are . . . because He lives!

To Tracey Bowden and Arnisha Hooper, my two best friends in the world, I can't even begin to say how much you mean to me. I don't say it enough, and I don't show it enough, but I can't pay for friends like you two. You put up with my mess

Acknowledgments

and my mouth, and I am grateful for all the book signings you drove me to, all the books you sold for me, and all the bookmarkers you passed out. I appreciate it so much. There are just some things in life that you just know. I know that only God could have put us together, and you two were chosen just for me. I am honored to have you as my friends.

Carl Weber, once again, you had faith in what God has put in me to pour out of me. Thank you for this opportunity, and all that you do.

To all the Urban Knowledge Bookstore workers that pushed my book, it is appreciated. Will, Tracey, Renee, Daisy, Chris, Ruthanne, Tonya, Latonya, and any newcomers, thank you. May God bless you in all your endeavors.

To the Urban Books home office family: Carl, Karen, Natalie, George (Gee), Brenda, Shawn, A.D. (I still don't know what that stands for, but I will find out), you guys make this easier for me.

To Nichelle Washington (the first reader, again, lol), Darlene Washington, Renee Warner, Ruthanne Ryan, Latonya Towns, Aleesha Rock, Antonio Glover, Lakeyshia Dorsey, Latricia Baker, Martina Doss, Karen Williams, thank you for reading the first draft of this book.

To Kenneth Goffney, I am totally blown away by God and how He used you to bless me. You came out of nowhere and lent a helping hand when I needed it the most. I thank God for you and the time you've put into this project. Thank you, friend.

To all the book clubs that hosted me, thank you for the love and support as well. Especially my hometown book clubs: The B'more Readers with W.I.S.D.O.M. Kudos to Tasha and Pat. ShayRod Bookclub, my first book club meeting. Y'all are the bomb.

DC Book Diva (Tiah)—Thank you for having me as my first away signing. You are the best.

Acknowledgments

Davida Baldwin, Oddballdesigns (www.oddballdsgns.com), Thank you for another slamming cover.

I want to give a special thanks to a couple of people who really supported me from a distance:

Martina Doss, for giving me my first official review and selling my books down there in Atlanta. Also, thank you for calling me and letting me know how my book moved you. You have to finish your book now. Lol.

Leona Romich, my Facebook friend, thank you for being honest and supportive and passing my book on to the appropriate people. You were such a great person from the first time we chatted. Thanks to Toka Waters as well.

My literary best friend, J'son M. Lee (Just Tryin' to be Loved). Man, you are the best. We clicked from day one, and we have so much in common. Thank you for answering the phone every time I call. I'm waiting on that second book, sir. Chop, chop. Lol.

To Ashley & JaQuavis, you guys are the best at what you do, and you always are humble when I see you or talk to you. Thank you for the encouragement and the support.

My author friends that supported me. Karen Williams, Anna J., Dwayne S. Joseph, Ashley Antoinette, Jaquavis Coleman, Wahida Clark, Michel Moore, Kiki Swinson, Anya Ellis, Tina Brooks McKinney, Tra Verdajo, Kashamba Williams, Danette Majette, Tiffany Wright, Deborah Cardona (Sexy), La Jill Hunt, Kwan, Zoe Woods, Nanette Buchanan, Treasure E. Blue, Marlene, Dwayne Vernon, Mike Warren, Azarel, J'son M. Lee, and so many others.

To the people that encouraged me along the way. Kenneth Goffney, your words are so inspiring. I am glad to call you a friend. Marcel Emerson, boy, you are the coolest. Keep pumping out them hot books. To Dullivan Chavis for pushing my book like you wrote it . . . LOL!

A special shout-out to Deborah Richardson for helping a brotha out (wink, wink). You were a lifesaver. Thank you.

Acknowledgments

My Wal-Mart family: Shernae, Tamara, Renee, Wanda, Gary, Ms. Val, Danuiella, Keisha, Wayne, Sharon. Thank you guys for your love and support. I miss you guys, but not the work. Lol.

My Baltimore customers that I can count on: Ms, Cheetah, Ms. Janet, Ms. Connie, Charlene, Ebonee, Tanesha, Keyonne, Shavonni (Vonnie). If I left you out, put your name here: _____, because you are important to me too.

I can be reached at www.myspace.com/mtpope, www.facebook.com/mtpope
www.twitter.com/mtpope
or email me at chosen_97@hotmail.com.
Thank you for the love.

Letter to the Reader:

First, I want to thank you for picking up book number two. If you haven't read part one, please put this one down and go find part one first. Now!

Secondly, I hope that I have grown as a writer and that my messages will come across loud and clear to you. This book was a little harder for me, because I really didn't plan on doing a sequel, but you guys asked for it. So here it is.

I have to say that I love the characters and that they did whatever they wanted to do in this book. I mean it. I had no control over them. They are just off the hook, every single one of them. LOL. And, yes, just like the first book, I pushed the envelope to get my point across. So take your time and pay attention to everything. The gate is wide open in this one, so once again buckle up, enjoy the ride and turn the page.

Enjoy,

M.T. Pope

Be Encouraged.

Prologue

James

Payback

"Shut the fuck up!" I yelled out as I had my head in between my legs. Just leave me alone! I can't do this anymore!"

I rocked back and forth in the corner of the room, the only light illuminating from a small window just above my head. I banged my head against the wall several times, trying to get the voices to go away. I just wanted to knock myself unconscious so I could rest in peace.

"Ah!" I yelled again, this time clutching the sides of my head.

"Shut the fuck up!" I heard someone yell.

Or maybe it was one of the voices in my head. At this point, I was truly unaware.

Click! Click!

I heard what sounded like the door being unlocked and opened. Then a strange man in a white uniform walked in and headed toward me. I tried to focus my eyes, trying my best to get reacquainted with them again.

It seemed like I was in this room for years. My hair was matted to my head, my facial hair had grown to an unbelievable length, and my mouth tasted like I hadn't brushed my teeth in weeks.

As he walked toward me, I tried to get up in a defensive stance, but my legs wouldn't budge.

He put his hands underneath my underarms and helped me to my feet. "How are you feeling?"

"Uh," I moaned as my weak legs fought to straighten up.

He put one of my arms around his shoulders and his arm around my back and helped me take a few steps. "There you go," he said as I started to get the hang of using my legs again.

We walked down a long hall that seemed to lead to nowhere. After several minutes of walking, we finally made it to a dimly lit room. There was one table in the middle of a room with two chairs that sat across from each other.

"Here you go," he said as he sat me in one of the chairs. He then chained both my hands behind me, and my legs were shackled to the chair with handcuffs.

"What's going on? Why the fuck is my arms and legs cuffed?" I asked, puzzled by my now being held hostage.

He just ignored me. "Somebody's here to see you," he said with a smile.

I smiled as well because I needed to see a familiar face. As the unknown man made his exit, I sat there wondering who had come to pay me a visit. Just then I heard the doorknob turning and the hinges creaking as my visitor made his entrance. It seemed like an eternity as he made his way around the table.

My heart racing, I braced myself. I knew whoever came to see me must have loved me, because this was the only visit I'd had in my ten years trapped in this hellhole. I felt very special at this moment. I was overjoyed.

When my visitor finally came around, my mouth hit the floor when I saw the large jagged knife and the look of hate and revenge. Tears flooded my eyes, as I knew this wasn't a friendly visit.

My visitor scowled as he inched closer to me. "You thought you could just ruin my family and walk the fuck away?"

I yelled, but the words never escaped my throat. I thrashed in my chair, trying to break free, but I couldn't budge.

He began to call me all manner of obscenities, his face inches from mine. "I'm here to get my family back!" he yelled, the hot air that he breathed invading my nostrils. "The only way I can do that is to get rid of you."

I thrashed about even harder this time, knocking over the chair I was sitting in over and landing on my side.

"Please, God! Please! I'm sorry for what I've done to you!" I begged, my head on the ground, and tears and snot running down my face.

"You shoulda prayed before you ruined my family. *Bitch!*" He picked me up by my collar and sat me upright. Then he made his way behind me. "Jesus is waiting to see you," he whispered in my ear. He placed the knife to my neck, getting ready to take my life.

I pleaded one more time. "Please don't hurt me. I'm sorry. Please, just listen to me. I—"

Before I could get out my last plea, I felt a sharp pain around my neck as the knife cut my flesh, scraping my Adam's apple. I tried to grab my neck with my hands to hold the blood and life in, but my hands were tied behind me. Blood poured out of my throat like a running faucet. I gargled in my own blood, as more cries of distress tried to escape my throat.

The man turned and walked out of the room, and I felt myself slipping away into eternity.

"Ah!" I quickly sat up in my bed, drenched in sweat, breathing uncontrollably. I had been having this dream every night for the last couple of weeks and just couldn't shake it. "This shit is ridiculous."

I walked to the faucet in my cell and washed my face. I looked over at my cellmate and noticed his ass was out like a light. I'd polished him off with my signature blowjob that had him sleeping like a baby.

I prepared uneasily to make my way to the shower, to wash away the anguish of my nightmare. As usual, one of my loyal conquests, who I named Officer Buck, because his ass loved to buck and ride my dick like a soldier trying to ride a bull, came and opened my cell to let me use the shower before anyone else. On many occasions, we would sneak off together so I could fuck his ass in an office or a janitor's closet.

After my shower, I made my way to the phone to make a call to ensure my ride back to Baltimore would be ready to pick me up at the appointed time.

Back at my cell, I decided to read a book by Carl Weber called *So You Call Yourself a Man*. One of my accomplices on the outside had sent me this book and assured me it would be a good read. I finished the book in about six hours and was bored once again.

I lay back on my bed and reminisced on how I got where I was.

Well, let me start by re-introducing myself. My name is James Parks, and I have been spending the last ten years behind bars for embezzlement. Yeah, ten years ago, I was running around town on a revenge tip. I was caught up in some mess that ended with me spending time behind bars.

I am being released in a couple of days, and I plan on going after what is rightfully mine, my children, and I don't plan on getting caught up this time. Well, I don't really want them per se. I just want compensation for not being told about them.

About a year into my sentence, a friend of mine had sent me some info that I needed. I found out that Mona, one of the only bitches I'd actually fucked, was the mother of three kids that were mine.

When I get out, I am going after my kids and the family I'm supposed to have. I also have to pay a few other people from my past a visit, to impose some revenge.

Chapter 1

Shawn

Off the Wagon
October 28ᵗʰ, 2018, 10:15 P.M.

Boom!

I had hit the ground with a thud, but I didn't feel it. I was numb from the alcohol I was drinking. I had been sneaking off to this bar called Naughty's on Reisterstown Road. I had been cheating on my wife again, but this time with liquor. I had beaten the demon that was my homosexual desires, only to fall prey to the bottle.

Ever since I found out that the kids I have been raising are not mine, I just sunk deeper into depression.

I still love Mona, but sometimes I just can't seem to look at her. Ashley and Alex are sixteen now and are shining stars in high school. They are sure to go on to some prestigious college of their choice. Little Diana is ten and blossoming, growing more intelligent as the days go by. James still haunts me every time I look at Alex because he is becoming his spitting image.

"Yo, you all right?" a thuggish-looking guy said as he helped me back on my stool.

"Yeah, man, just a little too much to dringg," I said, slurring my words. "Thanks for the help, partner." I got back on my seat and proceeded to order another drink.

I felt my bladder about to explode, so I got up and stumbled to the bathroom to take a piss. I had been in the bar for over an hour and I already had five drinks. I stumbled my way to the urinal and whipped my dick out from behind my zipper.

I put one hand on the wall to hold myself up while I held my dick in the other hand and I relieved myself into the urinal. "Ahh!"

"Nice piece you got there."

I looked to the left of me, still a little unfocused, and noticed the thuggish guy standing next to me, his tongue wagging like a dog in need of water.

"Yeah, man, whatever," I said, brushing him off, and zipped my pants up.

"Man, you know you want this mouth on your dick. I'll give you a blowjob your grandfather could feel." He moved closer toward me, the look of lust in his eyes.

I glanced around to see if we were alone. I looked him up and down and noticed this dude was seriously flirting with me in a bathroom at a straight bar. Built like a pro wrestler, this dude was a straight-up thug type dude that you see on the block hustling rocks. And I knew he was strong, because I could see his pecks through his loose-fitting shirt.

When I pushed past him, trying to make my exit, he grabbed my arm and threw me against a wall and kissed me with a deep, passionate kiss, forcing his tongue in my mouth. As his tongue explored my mouth, I continued to struggle for control of the situation.

He finally let up and looked me in the eyes. "Yo, come on, man. Let me help you with that." He grabbed my dick and massaged it through my pants. "You know you want it," he said as he again squeezed my now throbbing dick.

I looked around again, hoping no one would come in and see this dude grabbing my dick. *This muthafucka is serious.* I struggled even more now, because I was getting weaker by the moment. The demon I thought I had beaten was fighting to take over once again.

He then pushed me into an empty stall and forcefully yanked my pants down.

I was in shock and awe. This dude was manhandling me, and I couldn't do anything to stop him. He was stronger than me, and the alcohol had me discombobulated to the point where I was staggering a little.

He turned me around, bent me over, and proceeded to eat me out right there in the bathroom. "Yeah, man. This ass looks good," he said as he parted my ass cheeks and played with my ass with his finger.

As he took his time and slowly eased his tongue in and out of me, my hormones took over and went into full throttle. I pushed my ass toward his face as he dove deeper into my ass.

After about ten minutes of him devouring my ass for a midnight snack, he turned me back around facing him and stroked my dick slowly until I was hard as steel. He then eased my dick in his warm mouth and slowly worked my whole length down his throat.

"Ahhhhh," I moaned as he swallowed me faster and faster. I continued to moan uncontrollably, holding on to the wall, trying to stabilize myself.

With one quick motion, he took my dick in his mouth until his mouth reached my balls. I put my hands around his now inflated throat and fucked his face like a wet pussy, watching his throat expand and deflate. I finally reached my climax as I jammed my dick down his throat one last time.

"Oh! Damn!" I yelled as he swallowed all my seed without

leaving a drop. I pulled out and let my dick hang as I tried to catch my breath. He wiped his mouth and burped, letting me know he enjoyed his protein shake.

"Thanks, yo," he said as he got up and left the stall, leaving me with my pants around my ankles.

After a few minutes, I slowly pulled my pants up and made my way out of the bathroom. I stumbled through the bar that was now almost empty and noticed a few people staring. The music was now off, but I didn't know how long it had been off. *Oh, shit! I hope they didn't hear us.*

I avoided eye contact as much as possible, hoping nobody had heard all the commotion going on in the bathroom. I quickly grabbed my coat off the bar stool I'd been sitting on and made my exit in shame.

I pulled up in the driveway to my house at about ten to eleven and turned the ignition to the car off. I noticed the lights in the house were on, but I wasn't ready to face my family yet. I reclined the car seat as far as it could go back and laid there for a minute to get myself together. I was tipsy on alcohol and overcome with emotion, and couldn't control either.

Here it is, 2018, and it seemed like I was still back in 2008. Technology had progressed some, but shit, cars weren't flying, and I was still attracted to men. You would have thought I was over this shit by now.

All the episodes of my past started to pop in my head. Meeting James in the parking garage, finding out he was fucking my wife; me fucking my father for screwing me up as a child and as an adult; him returning the favor at the fuck-fest James threw for me; finding out my mother knew about my father molesting me all the time, and the worst was finding out my kids weren't mine and that they were fathered by my fuck buddy, James Parks.

It was all coming back to me now. *My ass should be in a padded room with a straight jacket on dreaming about bunny rabbits or some shit.*

After all that, I should be leaving this faggot mess alone, but it just wasn't that easy. It seemed like the more I tried to remove myself, the more dick and ass were being thrown at me. On my lunch breaks, in meetings, my clients were throwing themselves at me. I had to take my secretary, Renee, with me almost everywhere, lunch breaks and even the bathroom, just to keep myself grounded. She was like a bulldog, so I knew I could trust her to have my back.

But she refused to go with me to the bar, and tonight of all nights was the night I needed her to be with me.

"Um-um-um." I shook my head in disgust with myself. "It is what it is." I pushed the button next to the seat to raise myself back up to an upright position and made my way out of my brand-new all-black BMW. It was fall, and the driveway and walkway toward my house were littered with fallen leaves, which I made a mental note to get Alex to rake and bag.

I looked up at my house and thanked God for letting me arrive home safely once again. I was blessed beyond measure, but I wasn't acting like it. I was a very successful lawyer and needed to start acting like one.

I sluggishly walked into a totally quiet house. Everybody must have been asleep, so I parked myself on the living room sofa, cut the television on, and just stared at it.

Chapter 2

James

On the Loose
*October 28*th*, 2018, 7:34* A.M.

"Parks, let's go," I heard the guard yell as I packed up all my belongings. My ass was finally getting out of this hellhole, the FCI in Cumberland, Maryland.

I was sent to this medium-security prison because, according to the judge, "I wasn't a real threat, but I had a potential to be one." I laughed to myself when he said that shit, because he really didn't know me well. I had some more tricks up my sleeve, and was still as wild as Oprah's hair at five in the morning.

The sound of my cell doors clanking open meant that I was now a free black man again after enduring ten long years behind bars.

The sentence turned out to be a breeze. At first when I got here, I thought I was going to have to fight my way through the time, but these punk niggas didn't see me coming. I had all of them eating out of my hands and my ass. I even had some of the guards on my "turned-out" sheet.

I pretty much did anything I wanted to. I showered when I wanted to because half these bitches in here liked it when

I sucked their dicks off as good as I did. I was so good, they asses could see their ancestors when I finished with them.

I even worked the warden off a couple of times. His ass was weirder than most. He wanted me to fuck his ass with a nightstick while he sucked his own dick. That muthafucka was flexible as shit though. He even taught my ass some tricks.

I walked down the tier with my prison gear in my arms, waving my good-byes and giving daps to guys who I fucked on the down-low. I even saw a couple of hard-ass niggas with tears in their eyes as I made my way to checkout. I slipped a couple of guards the number where I could be reached, just in case they needed to hook up on the outside.

This is it! I breathed a small sigh of relief as I walked out the final gate into the parking lot for new releases. It was really breezy and cold.

I looked around and saw all of the other guys being picked up by their girls and families. Kids were running and jumping into their arms. You could see the tears and hear the joy in their voices as they hugged and kissed their freshly released family members. I almost kinda felt like I was missing out, but that was short-lived when I spotted my ride home.

I made my way to my ride as he patiently waited for me to make my exit. I quickly hopped in the passenger seat, and we pulled off headed toward my destination.

"So how ya been?" I said, glancing at the now seventy-three-year-old Carl Black as he drove down the highway headed to his home.

"I've been waiting for you, baby," he said, patting my leg.

Carl Black was a nasty-ass bastard that blamed his son for his wife putting him out. His old ass was now totally fagged out, and he was so gross to look at, with his skin all wrinkled and blotchy. His Cadillac smelled of alcohol and Ben-Gay, which I could hardly tolerate in the behemoth of a car. And the heat in the car was on, making it quite warm and dry.

This isn't going to be easy. "Me, too," I mustered up the courage to say back. Just looking at him made my skin crawl. I so badly contemplated jumping from the moving car to end my misery.

When his ass mailed me the letter telling me about my children, I knew I had to use him to get my plans in order. He was so old, nobody really wanted his ass, so he clung to me by writing and calling me to say how much he wanted us to be together when I got out of jail. He also put me on his cell phone plan a month before I was to get out, and I gave my mama the number as soon as I got it, so we could keep in contact.

He said he lived in a retirement community ever since his wife had put him out and was receiving social security benefits every month. I almost laughed when he told me I could live with him and we could share his eight-hundred-dollars a month check. I knew that shit was only enough to pay my car note and insurance. I proclaimed my love for him over the phone a couple of times to get him where I wanted him, and his Depends-needing ass fell for it hook, line, and sinker. I'd only played along and agreed to live with him, because he said he would help me get my children from Mona, and his son, Shawn. I really didn't want to raise them. I just wanted Shawn to pay for cheating on me with his wife and my bitch of a cousin, Sherry.

"Hey, Carl, I've been wondering about something." I turned and looked at his senile, decrepit ass.

"What is that, baby boy?" he asked, keeping his eyes on the road.

"How did you find out I was the father of Mona's children?"

He cleared his throat as if he had to think about it. "Well, after the party you had with my son, I was leaving out of the hotel and I ran into an old buddy of mine from college. He was one of the guys I messed around with in my experimenting days in college. We decided to have a drink at the bar, and one thing led to another, and we started to fool around as well. His name was Henry Grant and he was a very successful gynecologist."

I nodded my head in approval of what I was hearing and signaled him to keep going. "And?"

"Well, after everything went down at my anniversary cookout and you were sent to jail, I started seeing him more. I wasn't in love with him. He was just someone to pass the time with. On one of his visits over to my place, we were in my bedroom, and he saw a picture of Shawn and Mona on my dresser. He told me that he was her doctor and that she had just come into his office for a paternity test on all her children. Since it was made public knowledge at the party that she had slept with you, I put two and two together and figured it out.

"He also confided in me that none of the children were Shawn's. He said he only told me because Shawn was my son and he thought I should know. So that is how I got the info to mail you. I knew you would need it to get back at that ho my son married. My son, on the other hand, should have left her cheating ass after he found out about it, but he didn't. I can't help what happened to him after he decided to stay with her. He got what his hand called for." He shook his head like he felt sorry for his son.

Again, I was in awe of how delusional this old-ass fart really was. I didn't know he was this sick. I was speechless. For one of only a few times in my life, I had nothing to say, so I just rode in silence, contemplating my next move.

"I'ma need you to stop by the bank before we go back to your place," I said, smiling at him while squeezing his leg. I almost threw up because his shit felt all clammy and mushy.

I had stored away over fifty thousand dollars for a rainy day. I knew putting that money away in that safety security box under my birth name would help me out in the long run. I had two birth certificates, one with James Parks, the other with Jerry Parks. I'd decided to change my name to James when I moved to Baltimore. I even had my crazy-ass cousin Sherry calling me James.

I walked to the teller and showed her my ID. "I would like to make a withdrawal from a security box," I said with my "just-got-out-of-jail" smile.

She made a couple of entries into her computer. "I'm sorry, sir, but we can't find a box with that name on it."

I immediately went into pissed mode. "Look, ya Cindy Brady lookalike, you better find my money because I know I put my shit in this bank."

"Look, nigga," she said with a little bit of sass, as if her ass had a little ghetto in her. She probably had a black boyfriend or some shit. "I'm sorry but—"

"Bitch, don't mess with my money," I almost yelled, cutting her off, my finger pressed into the middle of her forehead.

She had a look of fear on her face. She looked like I was trying to jack her for her car or something.

"You know what they say, bitch—Mess with my money and you mess with my emotions. And my emotions is about to beat that ass, ya hear me? Make it happen." I pulled back a little.

"I'm sorry, but I-I don't have a James Parks in m-my sys-system." She stuttered as she looked to see if anyone was coming to her rescue.

Shit! I gave her the wrong ID. "Oh, my bad. I'm so sorry, ma'am," I said now, embarrassed. "I gave you my twin brother's ID who's out in the car. He's handicapped, so I carry his info around with me just in case he has a seizure or something." I quickly snatched the ID up and handed her my other ID.

She punched away at her computer and handed me back my ID. Then she instructed me to follow her.

I trailed behind as we made our way to the room set aside for box-holders. As I walked a couple of people gave some dirty looks.

I had put on a little muscle in jail and decided to flaunt it. "What the fuck are you looking at?" I said to one of the patrons, who had the look of a person smelling something foul. I was bluffing, because my ass was on parole. "Don't make me beat your ass in this muthafucka!"

When the coward turned back around to mind his business, I continued on my way.

"You have a nice day," the teller said as she sat my box on the table and walked away, leaving me to handle my business.

I hurriedly placed my money in my empty book bag and swiftly made my exit, looking back several times to make sure I wasn't being followed. I know I wasn't, but ever since Kenny busted my ass after having me followed around, I constantly looked over my shoulders.

I hopped in the car, and we made our way back to Carl's house. I was back on the loose, and I was loving it.

Chapter 3

Ashley

My Life
October 28th, 2018, 10:03 P.M.

I slowly eased my key into the door and waved my ride off. It was about ten o'clock at night. I didn't see my father's car, and I was sure my mom was asleep by this time. I had been out on a date with Tony again tonight. We had made a trip to Inner Harbor just to sit and chill again this week. It was so cool just hanging out, just the two of us. We walked hand in hand, and sometimes we would stop and kiss. People would stop and stare at us like we were crazy or something was wrong. But we didn't care about what people thought about us.

Yes, Tony was much older than me, but was it a crime to date someone older? Well, maybe it was, because I was sixteen and Tony was forty. I just acted older when we went to different places, so I wouldn't seem so out of place, but people still stared at us like we were aliens.

My parents had no clue we were dating, or that I was "getting mine." My mom and dad pretty much had no friends, so I knew I didn't have to worry about running into anyone they knew. My mother, Mona Black, was a homemaker type, and my father, Shawn Black, was this big-shot lawyer. He was in court all the time and slept most of the time when he was off. My mother was busy all the time with my little sister Diana and my socially weird brother Alex, with his football practices and all that.

Alex and I were twins, but we were so different. He was older by ten minutes. He was a hermit and never got into any trouble, while I was more outgoing and popular.

We attended the same school, Randallstown High School, but I didn't see him that much, since we had totally different class schedules. I saw him enough at home anyway. Don't get me wrong, I loved him, but sometimes he could be such a boy—goofy, always on his computer, and never got tired of football.

I was talking to a girl from my economics class the other day, another pretty girl Alex had turned down, and she was asking about him. "Hey, yo, Ash. Why yo brotha be actin' so different than you? Is he gay or something?"

I looked at her for a sec. She was so ghetto-acting. We were standing at the lockers in the hallway getting books out of our lockers for the next class.

Alex was a good-looking guy from a sister/brother point of view, but I wasn't really paying attention to his dating habits, or if he even liked girls. I had my own social life to secure.

"I don't know, Jasmine."

"Gurl, what you mean, you don't know?" Her face frowned up. "He's your brotha. Your twin at that. If anybody should know, it should be you."

Okay, this chick is about to pluck my last nerve. "Ummm, Jasmine, why you so curious about my brother? I mean, what, you trying to get at him or something?" I had a hint of attitude in my voice.

"Well, maybe. He is a football player, and he is chocolaty-cute."

She smiled hard. She had a crush on him, I could tell.

"I was just wondering, why he got to be playing hard to get? He turned a sister down like I was one of them dirty chicks or something."

"Again, I don't know why he acts the way he does."

I really didn't know why he was the way he was. I mean, we did have lunch period at the same time, but he always sat across the room with some butch-looking chicks. To me, they didn't look interested, in that way, in each other at all. They just looked like they would converse while eating and go their separate ways afterwards. Besides, I spent most of the lunch period texting Tony on my phone anyway.

"Look, Jasmine, he is focused on his schoolwork and the football season. I don't think he has time for girls right now."

"Yeah, whateva, gurl." She sucked her teeth. "Just put a word in for a sister, okay."

"Sure thing."

That was a promise I wasn't going to keep. She was so out of luck.

Truth was, I thought Alex was gay myself. I had no solid proof, but frankly, it was his life, not mine. Regardless, I loved him. He was my brother.

Chapter 4

Mona

Bumpy Night
October 28th, 2018, 11:13 P.M.

I tossed and turned in the bed all night, trying to get me some rest, but it just wasn't happening. I heard Shawn come in at about eleven o'clock, but he had not come to bed yet. His behavior had become more and more erratic lately, and I was becoming suspicious. In fact, we were just getting back to being intimate again. It took us both a while to get comfortable with each other after all that went down in our lives about ten years ago.

The children were clueless that the one they were calling Dad wasn't really their father. There were days when I just wanted to sit them down and tell them the truth, but I chickened out every time with excuses that only appeased me. How could I tell my children that their father was a bisexual maniac that I cheated on their "father" with?

Shawn was of no help; he was still having nightmares about his molestation that he still didn't want to talk about. I didn't push him, out of love, but sometimes I wanted to shake him out of the funk that he got into that made him cut everybody off emotionally.

I sat up in bed and contemplated the task before me. I got up and walked sluggishly to the bathroom to sprinkle my face with some water to help wake me up fully. I looked in the mirror and surveyed the worry lines around my eyes. I had small, puffy bags under my eyes that also showed my restlessness.

The past couple of years had been rocky, but we survived. The cheating, lies, and homosexuality had taken their toll on Shawn and me, but we survived. The hours and hours of counseling both together and separately had helped us pull the bootstraps up, as they say, in our lives.

I pulled out some of that L'Oréal eye cream from off my vanity and smoothed it on my face, like I had been doing more and more lately. They say black don't crack, but I was an exception to the rule. I attributed it all to stress, though. Shawn was on track to recovery and healing, but I kept worrying about some of our secrets coming back to haunt us.

I walked downstairs and saw Shawn sitting in the living room with the television on the Golf Channel. Shawn wasn't particularly into sports, so I knew he wasn't watching it. He was in one of his moods again. His shit was almost as annoying as my PMS was. I didn't know what to expect.

I walked around the sofa and I noticed he was crying. I sat down and started rubbing his back, trying to comfort him.

"Baby, why is this shit happening to me? All I want is a normal life with my wife and kids." He laid his head on my shoulders as I wiped the tears that flowed from his eyes.

I knew and didn't know what he was getting at. I tried my best to sympathize with my husband, but sometimes I just didn't get him. To top it off, my shit was constantly staring me in my face as well. Literally.

I refocused my attention back toward Shawn and his issues.

He was in therapy for the last nine years for this molestation drama. It seemed like he was making headway, or so I thought.

"I am fucked up," he said, exhaling his frustration.

I continued to console him, knowing he needed my full attention.

"Baby, I'm sorry. I messed up tonight."

"Huh?" I moved away from him slightly with a look of fear. I wasn't ready for him to tell me what I already feared and knew.

"I got drunk tonight." Shawn hung his head low.

I breathed a small sigh of relief. I just knew he was going to say he slept with a man tonight. "It's all right, baby." I cradled him in my arms, like he needed at this moment.

Don't get me wrong. I was upset about the drinking. It just wasn't extreme enough for me to blow up over.

Besides, my ass should be on somebody's park bench with a forty-ounce and some weed, because I had my own demons to wrestle with. Each time I looked at my children and saw that monster James in every one of them, I wanted to sedate myself.

"Come on upstairs," I said as I helped him up and escorted him to our bathroom to get him in the shower.

I ran him some bathwater and bathed him like he used to do the kids when they were young. He continued to be apologetic as I helped him out of the tub and dried him off. I helped him to the bedroom and dressed him in his pajamas.

He slept like a baby as soon as his head hit the pillow. I looked at him as he slept, and wondered what he was dreaming about at that moment.

I got up again and went to check on the kids. I first went to check on the baby of the family, Diana. I peeped in on her. She was a sound sleeper, so I walked in and kissed her on her cheek. I looked at her as she was entangled in her sheets. She was a wild sleeper.

"Just like your fath"—I couldn't even say it, and it hurt even worse to think about it.

A single tear slid down my face as I made my exit to visit Ashley in the next room. I pulled myself together and just peeked in her room, because I know how teens like their privacy. She was sound asleep with earphones in her ears. She was probably listening to her iPod. She was becoming very musically inclined and sang in the choir at the church we now attended on a regular basis.

I then made my way downstairs to the basement where Alex slept. He was becoming such a little man. He'd begged Shawn and I to move him into the basement so that he could "get his world together," as he said.

I crept down the stairs and noticed him sitting at his computer. "What are you still doing up?" I rubbed his wavy hair.

He gently pushed my hands away. "Mom, you messin' up my waves," he said with a smile on his face.

I had to admit, he was easy on the eyes. "It's time to go to bed," I said in a stern voice. He was on that Facebook all the time, chatting with his friends.

"All right, Ma, as soon as I check this last message," he said as he gave me a kiss on the cheek.

I turned around and made my way to the kitchen to fix some warm milk to help me get some sleep. My grandma used to give me this remedy every time I was having a restless night. For some odd reason, I had a feeling that something was about to happen. I just didn't know what.

Chapter 5

Shawn

Keeping Tabs
October 29th, 2018, 9:33 A.M.

I woke up the next morning tired and depressed like never before. I didn't have the energy to even get out of bed. I just lay there and stared at the ceiling for a couple of minutes.

Finally, I dragged myself to the bathroom and relieved my bowels. I sat on the toilet bowl and wondered how I was going to tell Mona that both my drinking and homosexual demons were calling me again. *She may be able to take another round of my drinking binges, but definitely not the sleeping with men. I don't think I could make it through another round of either myself.*

After all that James put us through, I just couldn't fathom the outcome this go-around. I often still thought about my sexual sessions with him. I couldn't seem to get him off my mind, now that I knew his sentence in jail was about to be over.

Being in the legal field wields its benefits, so I had checked on James' jail status every so often, just to keep tabs on him, I think. Or maybe I wanted to see him as soon as he got out.

"Fuck!" I slapped myself upside my head, trying to jar the memories from my mind.

I walked down to the kitchen and I saw Mona sitting at the table. "Hey, babe," I said as I walked over to give her a kiss.

She got up and hugged me and squeezed me tightly. I could feel the love that now was rekindled between us.

"How are you feeling this morning?" she said as she slightly released me, looking into my eyes.

I looked at her intently and mustered up a, "Great." It was partially true. I was feeling great. Great *stress*, that is. But I couldn't let her know. She had her own shit to deal with.

"I have decided to do something that my therapist has been pushing me to do."

"What is that?"

"I've decided to go visit my father and get some closure. I've been putting this off for a long time. I need to man up and do this." Just hearing it coming from my own mouth made it feel so real. I just didn't know if I could go through with it.

Mona hugged me again. "Baby, you want me to go with you?" she said, love and concern in her voice. She looked like she was back in love with me again.

"Nah, babe. I have to do this on my own. My therapist said that it's best." I lied about the last part. I didn't want Mona there just in case I broke down, or broke him down, for that matter. I knew that this visit could go smooth, or it could go south for the winter. I couldn't get Mona caught up in any of my shit again.

I got dressed, made my way to my car and headed toward my destination.

I had finally mended my relationship with my mom about five years back. I was so relieved because I needed her in my life regardless of what happened in the past, in both my life and her life.

Anyways, Mom had said my father had been sending her letters, apologizing for hurting her so. She gave me a letter, which she said was for me. I took the letter with no intentions of reading it, but I did. His sorry ass tried to say his father did the same thing to him, so that's why he did what he did to me.

That shit didn't sit right with me, so I talked to my therapist, and she told me that it was true indeed. She said that a lot of things parents are exposed to and go unresolved with can be passed down to their offspring. Generational curses, she called it. She went on to say that these curses can be broken if the person seeks help with a therapist, a counselor, or a spiritual leader.

To say I was shocked was an understatement. That shit meant one of my grandparents was dealing with this shit too. It didn't take a rocket scientist to tell me that one of "my children" might have to deal with this. I prayed to God that it wouldn't, because I didn't think I could handle my son going through the same things.

My father gave me his address and said, if I could ever forgive him, that we could reconcile in person. At first I was like, *The hell with that shit.* That was five years ago, and it took me all this time to get up the courage to seal the deal.

I pulled up to the address he had given me and prepared myself mentally to make amends with him.

Chapter 6

James

Home, Sweet Home
October 28th, 2018, 2:12 P.M.

We pulled up after about an hour of driving and made our way into the retirement building. I was totally disgusted by my temporary home. *Ah, hell, nah! This shit ain't even gon' work.*

Most of the old heads in this place looked like they were well past their expiration dates. Somebody needed to nuke this muthafucka and put these wrinkled-ass people outta their misery.

I damn near rushed to the elevator, almost forgetting that Carl's black ass was trailing after me. "Hurry up, man. Damn." I wanted to scream, but I was afraid I might kill one of these senile bags of skin and bones by raising my voice. I pushed the elevator button several times, trying to hurry it, but it too was taking its time, just like its tenants. I was starting to get light-headed from the fumes of Bengay, alcohol (non-medicinal) and just plain old funk mixed together from these rusty-ass people.

When the elevator came, Carl scurried his way in with me. His ass had some nerve to stop and converse with his friends.

I knew my stay here wouldn't be long. My ass is outta here as soon as I find me a new spot. ASAP.

Carl opened the door to his bachelor pad and my mouth hit the floor. This bastard was a fucking slob. Shit was everywhere—beer bottles, TV dinner boxes, and just plain filth. It looked like his ass hadn't cleaned up since he been here. His dishes were piled up so high, you couldn't see the sink. And the carpet was filthy as well with stains that had grown fungus.

I stepped over beer cans and bottles of alcohol as I looked for a clean spot to set my stuff down. Man, that shit seemed almost impossible to do because just about everything was filthy.

"Make yourself at home, baby." He smiled like his ass had Martha Stewart decorate his shitty-ass house.

A mouse—no, make that a rat—scurried across the top of the sofa, dodging shit like it was in a maze. The muthafucka paused and looked at me like, "This shit don't make no sense. Even I don't live like this."

My sympathy was with his ass because I was breaking camp with the quickness as soon as I could.

"Ah, okay, baby." I walked past Carl toward what looked like a bedroom. Before I made it to the bedroom, I peeked into the bathroom to see its present state. "Maybe he just let the living room go," I said to myself.

No such luck. I held my hand over my mouth and nose as I noticed the stain around the tub and the toilet. Both looked deplorable. The tub was almost completely brown, and the toilet had shit floating in it, literally, with a stench that almost made me wanna go back to prison and throw away the keys.

I knew my ass wasn't squatting on anything in there. I didn't want no shit crawling up my ass, except what was invited. I closed the door to the bathroom. Someone should tape this dump off with some crime scene tape, because his ass should be locked up for living like this.

To my surprise, the bedroom was in good shape, almost the complete opposite from the other parts of the house. Carl had a nice queen-sized bed with a comforter set that looked like it was from Ikea or someplace like that. It wasn't top of the line, but it was good enough for the time being. He had a pretty decent bedroom suite as well with cherry wood dressers and nightstands, and a forty-two-inch plasma television attached to the wall.

I hesitantly sat my stuff on the floor and made myself as comfortable as possible. I didn't want any "tag-alongs" like mice or roaches trying to set up camp in my shit when I made my exit.

I looked around and noticed he still had pictures of his wife, Shawn, Mona, and even some of his "grandkids." I picked up the one of Shawn and noticed how distinguished he looked in his tailored suit posted up against one of his cars with the children gathered around him. I gazed at the photo and noticed that the children did resemble me in some of their facial features and eye color, among other things.

I wondered what it would be like to have a family like that one, and come home to a wife that made a home for me.

Fuck that shit! I didn't need no family, and especially some bitch dictating to me my whereabouts.

Carl came in the room and startled me, so I placed the picture back on the dresser and pretended to care about his needs. I gave him his usual spanking, and he nutted and passed the hell out. Typical male.

Chapter 7

Shawn

I walked toward the retirement home my father was staying at in the west side of Baltimore City, formally called Lexington Terrace Projects, but now it was a homeowner's haven. It was an okay neighborhood with some crime here and there. I walked into the building with butterflies in my stomach and sweaty palms. I was hoping it wouldn't take too long. I just wanted to get in, forgive and forget, and get out before I lost my cool.

I checked in at the front desk and made my way up to the apartment, walking up the stairs to the sixth floor. I was prolonging this as long as I could. I paused in front of his door and gave myself one last pep talk before I knocked. *Shawn, you can do this. Just let him know how you feel and get this shit off your chest. If things get rough and he comes off at you wrong, just walk out. Don't do anything to him. He's not worth it. Remember the three R's—Relax, relate, release.*

I knocked on the door and waited patiently for it to be answered. The door opened, and before me stood the man who wreaked havoc in my life, James Parks. He tried to ruin my family, and brought out the worst in me. I couldn't believe this muthafucka was standing here before my eyes.

"Hey, boo," he said with a smug smile. "Long time no see, Shawn."

My mind instantly flashed back to the cookout and all the shit he took me through ten years ago. My flesh wanted to kill him right there on the spot, but I couldn't move. I stood there like a deer caught in some headlights as my blood boiled rage and my heart fought back with lust and passion. How could the two exist at such a moment as this heartless monster stood before me? How could I still be attracted to this . . . this . . . beautiful man that had aged, but yet was still handsome and toned just so right?

I was shaken back to my present state by my father coming to the door.

"Hey, son," he said with a smile as he put his hands around James' waist.

The sight of it threw me. "What the fuck is he doing here?"

"He's here because you weren't."

What? Was he really saying it was my fault that my mom put him out? *He molested me, and now he is shacking up with the homewrecker, and it's my fault.* I couldn't believe my ears. He was blaming me. I was the victim here, not him. Me.

I turned and walked away, just like I'd promised myself if anything popped off.

Fuck that shit! I turned around and went for blood. I ran and tackled my father and sucker-punched him, knocking him to the floor. "You grimy bastard! How could you do this to your family? The only ones who really cared for you." I spat on him and walked away.

Then I turned around and charged him one last time and kicked him in his ribs and walked away, shaking my head in disgust. "I wish you were dead!" It seemed like the word *dead* bounced off the wall and repeated itself a couple of times.

"Shawn, I'm coming to see my kids soon," I heard James yell as I stood at the elevator.

"Over my dead body, muthafucka!" I yelled back, pushing the elevator button constantly. "This muthafuckin' elevator needs to hurry up before I catch a case," I mumbled to myself.

"I can arrange that, you know!" he yelled back.

"Yeah, man, whateva," I said, knowing his ass had lost his mind with that threat. This bitch was testing me, and he knew it. He disappeared back into the apartment as I continued to wait on the elevator.

The elevator finally arrived, and I hopped on and pushed the button for the ground floor. I stepped out and noticed police walking toward me.

"Excuse me, sir. Can we have a word with you?"

I pointed to myself, not sure who they were talking to.

"Yeah, you."

"We were called because someone reported a disturbance."

My first thought was to run, but I opted against that because that would show guilt. Being a lawyer, I knew that wasn't in my best interest. I stood there as the police placed me against a wall, placed my hands behind my back, and proceeded to frisk me.

"Do you have any weapons on your person?" One officer patted me down, getting too damn close to my dick.

"What?" I turned my head around in disgust. "Does it look like I am carrying any weapons? I'm not a thug."

I had on jeans, a Morgan State University sweatshirt, and some Timb boots, but my pants weren't sagging or anything like that.

"Shouldn't you guys be out getting those degenerates off

the street corners selling our people drugs?" I was steaming, to say the least. How in the hell could they think that an upstanding citizen like myself would be causing a disturbance? A nigga can't even beat his father's ass in peace.

A large buffed officer that looked awfully familiar instructed me, "Sir, please keep still, and this will be over in a minute."

I calmed down, knowing these officers were looking for someone to take out their stress on, and it wasn't going to be me. Being a lawyer, I had seen some pictures of Black and Latino males that were accosted by police before they made it to the local precincts.

"I was just here visiting my father. You can ask the receptionist at the front desk if you don't believe me."

They removed my wallet and checked my identification. They also told me that they were going to run my arrest record and check to see if I was wanted in any other states. I just remained still against the wall as the once-quiet lobby was now swarming with residents who wanted to see what was going on.

I looked at the faces of the men and women shaking their heads in disapproval. *Another black man in cuffs.* My head hung low in shame.

Out of nowhere I heard snickering, and I looked into the crowd of people and saw James with a wicked smile on his face as he watched me.

"I'ma get you, muthafucka," I mouthed before the police escorted me outside and into a waiting police cruiser.

They pulled off and went around the corner and parked in a dark alley.

"Look, man," one of the cops said, "we going to let you off with a warning if you do us both a favor."

"Yeah, man, we heard about your excellent services."

They both snickered.

I was clueless, until one of the officers got out of the car and got in the back seat with me. "What the hell is going on?" I asked in fury and confusion.

"You know what the deal is, bitch!" The burly cop unzipped his pants and exposed his dick.

My eyes got big as silver dollars.

"You one of them bastards that raped me at the party that James had for me."

"Yeah, man. I was there too," the other cop chimed in.

The burly officer smiled as he stroked his dick to full length.

I slowly edged my way toward the end of the car, trying to unlock the door with my cuffed hands. *Shit. No luck.* I was stuck.

"Come here, man. I ain't going to hurt you this time. I just want you to blow my dick real good," he said, shaking it in my face. "Not unless you want us to punish that ass again like we did at the party."

I shook my head as I remembered the beating they put on me the last time. "Please, man, don't make me do this," I pleaded with the horny officer.

Before I knew it, he shoved his dirty dick in my mouth, causing me to gag.

"Suck this dick, bitch!" He pushed my head down toward his lap. His strength overpowered my neck muscle as I tried to pull away, but I was fighting a losing battle. I had no choice but to do his bidding.

I sucked his dick the best I could. I must have been doing a good job, because his ass was moaning like a wolf at a full moon.

In the middle of the blowjob, the other officer got into the backseat with us and proceeded to pull down my pants, exposing my bare ass. I prayed to God that he wasn't going to violate me again, but to my surprise, all he did was eat me out as I sucked off his partner. I couldn't believe this shit was happening to me. I was being treated like a common whore in the back of a police car.

And to make matters worse, the beast inside of me was enjoying every moment. It took over, and before I knew it, I was a willing participant in this *ménage à trois*. They took turns eating me out while I blew each of them off.

When they were finished with me, they forcefully threw me from the car. "Tell James thanks. That muthafucka always knows how to show a brother a good time." They laughed and pulled off.

I made my way back to my car and cleaned myself up with some Wet Ones I had in the car. I sat in my car as tears streamed down my face. I realized I wasn't finished battling this beast inside of me.

I didn't want to go home, and I didn't want to stay out and cause Mona any worry. I would usually go get a drink to suppress my homosexual urges. How could I tell her I was still attracted to men? I just didn't think she would understand again.

I was planning on asking her to renew our vows in a couple of weeks, but I didn't know if I could just act like I wasn't bisexual. How could I do this to my family? I was a fool for thinking that all I had to do was stay away from other guys altogether, and a couple of sessions with a shrink would cure me. Truth was, I only went to about ten of the fifty or so sessions before I decided that they were a waste of time. I didn't need anybody trying to get into my head and mess me up any further.

I got myself together and decided to keep this shit to myself and handle it on my own. I pulled up to my house, parked, and went to my door about to enter my home. I fixed my clothes and adjusted my facial expression to put on the act of a loving husband returning home to a loving family and a warm, inviting home.

"Honey, I'm home," I yelled as I walked through the door and made my way to living room, where the kids were gathered around the television watching the classic, *A Few Good Men*.

I walked in just as my favorite line in the movie was coming up, when Jack Nicholson said, "You can't handle the truth!"

That statement was so true in the movie, and even in my life. I knew that I couldn't handle the truth. I had no clue what that truth was, but I was hoping that it would reveal itself very soon.

I sat down and joined my family as they replayed that part over and over again, amazed at Kevin Bacon's face as the truth came forth from his mouth. I just sat there and pretended to be focused on the film and not on the façade that I was presently putting on.

Chapter 8

Mona

Last Straw
October 29th, 2018, 6:32 P.M.

"I am tired of your shit, Shawn!" I yelled at him as I ran from our bedroom. My voice was so loud, it echoed throughout the house.

I wasn't going to forgive him this time around. His ass was going to pay for what he did to me. I had only been gone out of the house for about an hour or so. I went over to my mom's house to check on her and the children, and I didn't give him a specific time that I would be back. He said he had some work that he needed to catch up on, and that he would see me when I returned home.

Alex and Ashley were teenagers now, but they still loved to go over to my mom's house for her famous cooking. I had brought home some plates of food for Shawn and me to eat because he loved her food as well. We were just getting things in our life back in order, and I was falling in love with him all over again.

I stormed back into the room again with a bat in hand ready to break bones. The two cheaters scrambled around the room looking for shelter to cover their vulnerable bodies.

"Baby, I'm sorry. You gotta believe me. He tricked me. You know I would never hurt you like this again."

I wasn't trying to hear it. "Tricked you?" I swung the bat at his head, barely missing him, and putting a large dent in the wall. "What the fuck you take me for, Shawn? A fuckin' crackhead or a gotdamn dummy?" This time, I swung and cracked him in his back as he leaped across the bed, trying to dodge me.

"Baby, just calm down and let me explain." Shawn held his arms out, trying to grab the bat from me.

I had him and James hemmed up in the corner of our bedroom. They both had a look of fear as they knew that I was planning on doing bodily harm. I was going to numb the pain in my heart with their screams of pain and agony. I planned to make every swing count. I was going for a new record in RBI's (Real Bad Injuries).

"You faggot-ass muthafuckas have played me for the last time," I said, cocking my bat getting ready to swing.

"Come on, Mona, baby. Think about the kids. What would you say to the kids?"

"Fuck the kids! Right now all I'm worried about is breaking this muthafuckin' bat over y'all's faggot-ass heads."

Both still naked, they covered their prized jewels with their hands.

Pow!

I swung the bat, and it connected with Shawn's head, sending him careening to the ground as blood and teeth flew everywhere. He hit the ground unconscious and bloody.

Next, I set my sights on the bastard who was trying to take my family away again.

He looked at me with terror in his eyes. He musta knew that he was about to meet his Maker.

"Your turn, you home-wrecking bitch!" I swung the bat at him.

Just as I was about to hit bone, he leaped and tried to make it across my bed. He slipped on the satin sheets that I had bought from Pier 1. I smiled with an evil grin, knowing he was now at my mercy. He looked up at me with fear, but he didn't beg one bit, probably because he wasn't sorry for what he had done to me and my family.

"You gonna pay! I'ma make sure they take your ass outta here in a body bag, muthafucka!" I swung the bat with all my might, breaking his ankle.

He yelled in agony as I took my time and broke his knees. *Crack!* His ass bone.

Crack! Crack! Both his arms.

He was stretched out on my bed, beaten, bloody, and moaning in pain. I flipped him on his back, making sure he saw the last hit coming. I aimed for his head and went for it. *Pow!*

He wasn't dead, and I was glad. I decided to let the muthafucka live the rest of his life in a fucking wheelchair.

To my surprise, Shawn jumped up and bolted for the door. Like a jackrabbit, I pounced after him with the bat in hand. Just as he reached the steps, I threw the bat at his feet and watched it clip him. He lost his balance and hurled down the uncarpeted steps like a ball.

As he fell, I could hear him breaking numerous bones in the process. He lay at the bottom of the steps in a mangled mess moaning for help.

"Ain't nobody here but me and you, Shawn," I said, bending down and whispering in his ear, "so your bitch ass can cut out the crying. I left yo boyfriend upstairs barely breathing, and your ass is next."

"Mona, please!" he moaned in a low but audible cry.

I picked up the bat that followed him on his trip down the steps. "What am I going to do with you?" I questioned him. "All you had to do was stay on this side of the fence, but oh no, you wanted to play on both sides again. All I ever did was love you, Shawn. I forgave you for your infidelity, and vice versa. This is the last straw, and your time here is up." I swung the bat one last time and hit him in the head. I watched as his eyes rolled in the back of his head and his breath faded away.

I knelt down and placed my ear to his mouth, to make sure he was gone for good. After I was sure, I threw the bat down and walked out of my house.

I got into my car and drove until I couldn't drive anymore. I sat in my car on the side of the road and cried my eyes out because of the chaos of my life. I banged on the steering wheel with my hands and my head, trying to get the visions of my madness out of my head. I couldn't, because they were forever burned into my memory.

I just wanted all the pain to go away. It was too much for me to bear. I just couldn't live this life any longer, and I wanted it to end now. I prayed to God and asked for forgiveness for what I was about to do. I asked Him to take care of my children and my mom.

"Please, Lord, let them know that I loved them the best I could."

I unbuckled my seat belt and stepped from my car and ran into traffic just as an eighteen wheeler came bustling down the road.

"Noooo!" I screamed out loud as I sat up in my chair with a look of fright. I looked around the room and noticed I was alone. I had fallen asleep at the kitchen table. Luckily, the kids had a movie playing that was louder than it was supposed to be, so they didn't hear me scream.

"It was only a dream," I said, calming myself down. "Oh, shit! It seemed so real."

I had been having dreams of this nature on and off lately. I was hoping and praying that Shawn was done with sleeping with men, particularly James. Shit, I was hoping I was done sleeping with him.

I got up and walked to the kitchen sink and splashed my face with some cold water. I sat down at the table again and calmed my self down mentally and physically. My breath was still erratic, and my thoughts were everywhere.

"What in the hell is going on?" I whispered to myself. "All these dreams and shit is bugging the hell out of me."

I couldn't help but wonder if Shawn was being honest about his homosexual desires. *Were they all gone? Could a man just stop being attracted to men? I mean, he has had psychological evaluation by a licensed psychologist. I checked this woman's credentials, and she came back with a perfect record. I don't know if I could take another blow, while trying to keep this family alive and together.*

I bowed my head and said a short prayer. "Lord, please fix this family. I can't take this anymore. You have to do something now. Lord, I need You. Please, God, fix this. Amen."

As I lifted my head up, I heard Shawn open the front door to the house and come in. I heard a little exchange with the kids, and then his footsteps headed toward the kitchen. I gathered myself emotionally and prepared for his news, good or bad.

Chapter 9

Shawn

Keep It Tight
October 29th, 2018, 6:48 P.M.

I walked into the kitchen totally baffled and at a loss for words. *This nigga is playing me. Again!* I can't believe the hold he has on people. It's like he has some kind of power that keeps people spellbound with him. I can't let this nigga do this to my family again.

I knew the children were his, biologically, but I was their father in every sense of the word. I was paying the bills in the house they lived in. I was the one who fed and clothed them, and I wasn't letting any psycho take them from me. Never. If he wanted a fight, then a fight was what he was going to get. I was going to beat him at his own game.

"Hey, baby," Mona said as I walked in the kitchen. "How did everything go with your dad?"

I put on a fake smile. "Everything went great." I couldn't possible tell her that my father was sleeping with the enemy. Again.

I didn't think Mona could relive the memories of the past again. She still tossed and turned in the bed at night. In fact, many nights I had to hold her tight, just so she and I could get some sleep.

I couldn't let her know that James wasn't out of my system, like I'd said. I wanted him to pay for the things he did to her and me, but at the same time, I wanted him sexually too. I was torn, and there were days I just wanted to end it all. But I couldn't just take the easy way out. I had to deal with this beast head-on.

"Yeah. Well, he apologized for the things that he did, and we made up right then and there. I told him that it would still take me some time to get used to him again and to be able to call him Dad. He said he understood, and we left it at that."

"Oh, that is sooo good, Shawn," she said, embracing me tightly. "I am so glad that things are getting back in order."

"Me too," I said as I hugged her back. "I know things have been rough for us, but I think it's time for us to move on with our lives."

A tear slid down her face. "You know what, baby? I was thinking the same thing earlier today. I was thinking that we should renew our vows again to rekindle the love in our relationship. We can invite the whole family and your dad even can walk me down the aisle, since my father is deceased."

"Sure, Mona, baby. I was thinking about the same thing earlier," I said with a little less enthusiasm. "We can start planning it this week coming up."

Chapter 10

James

Plans in Order
October 30th, 2018, 1:40 P.M.

I marveled at the fact that I could still toy with Shawn and manipulate him the way I wanted to. A couple of down-low cops are always a necessity on your team. They are always looking for a good time. They called me after they turned Shawn out again and said they were up for some more fun, and that any time I needed them, give them a call, on duty or off. I knew I was definitely going to use them again real soon.

Shawn still hadn't learned that he was up against the best, I guess. I was going to have to take him to school again. If my guess was right, and it usually was, Mona and Shawn still hadn't told the children about their biological father.

They were making this shit way too easy. I was in need of some more entertainment, and these two fools were in line again begging to be a part of my show. *Man, this shit making me horny.*

The only thing was, this old fucker I was staying with was bugging the hell out of me. He wanted me to hold him at night and tell him I love him and all that shit. I was so close to telling him to fuck off. His ass was making me sick as a muthafucka.

I woke his old ass up early this morning, so I could go and get me a ride. I had to run some interference in some people's lives that shitted on me and thought they were getting away with it. I had sat in jail for ten years planning out my revenge on those that placed me there, and I was going to make sure that they got what was coming to them. They may have forgotten about me, but I sure hadn't forgotten about them. I was sparing no one this time around. Their asses didn't know I was coming, but when I was finished with their asses, they would be passing down stories about me to the grandkids.

We pulled up to the dealership, and I got out and told gramps to stay still until I was finished. His ass was as obedient as a dog, and loyal as one too. He was begging for a piece of dick, and if I got my way today, he just might get a treat, if I could stomach looking at his wrinkly, mashed-up ass cheeks.

I walked into a rinky-dink car dealership and asked to speak to the man in charge. I walked to the counter, and a weave-wearing receptionist bitch with red and yellow hair looked me up and down and returned to the conversation she was having on the phone. Ghetto bitch was acting like she didn't want to help me, but she didn't know she was fucking with a crazy muthafucka that was messed up in the head. I was all the more pleased to show her my ghetto side as well.

"Excuse me," I said with a smile. "Don't you see me standing here waiting to be serviced?"

"Yeah," she said, rolling her eyes. "And? I got you when I get up off my call. Damn!"

"Damn?" I said to myself, shocked at her boldness. "Oh, I know this bitch is asking for it."

She continued to have her conversation on the phone, ignoring my presence once again. "Yeah, girl, do you know that muthafucka had the nerve to want me to work and come home and fix his dinner? He must've lost—"

I let this bitch ride too long, so I grabbed the phone and hung it up. I then grabbed her "phony tail" and flung it across the room. She watched as the weave hit the ground.

I grabbed her by what little hair she had left and pulled her ear close to my mouth. "Look, bitch, if you want the rest of this shitty mess you call hair, then you better skip your can't-keep-a-man ass to the back and get the man that own this shithole."

Her ass finally got up and went into a back office and out pops this dude that look like he was straight out of prison himself. He was tall and muscular and from the bulge in his slacks, I could only hope that he was packing a big dick. I always sized up a man's dick before I even looked them in the face.

I put on my around-the-way swagger and walked up to him. We shook hands, and he showed me the way to his office.

I went straight for the kill and put my cards on the table. I looked him dead in the eye. "Main man, I need a favor."

"What kind of favor you talkin' about?" he asked, adjusting himself in his seat.

"I just got out the joint, and I need me some wheels, and all I have is cash money." I knew from my sources around the hood that car dealerships have to report to the IRS anyone that buys a car with cash outright.

"Well, homeboy, you came to the wrong dealership because I don't deal with that shit no more," he said, giving me a wink.

His ass musta thought I was wired, or somebody was listening in on our conversation or something. I just played along and handed him fifteen grand for my choice of a car off the lot.

He walked me to the lot, and I picked out the car that I wanted. Then we went back to his office to fill out some paperwork.

And, boy, he had all of the paperwork I could handle. His ass fucked me so good, I thought his dick was going to come out of my mouth.

I walked out his office with a new ride and a good piece of dick. He gave me his number and told me anytime I need anything, just give him a call. Trade. Gotta love them.

When I left his office, the ghetto-ass receptionist waved good-bye to me as she was trying to put her makeshift ponytail back on her head. Her ass just got a lesson in customer service that you couldn't get at your local Wal-Mart. *I betcha her ass will act right for the next customer that comes in.*

I walked up to Carl's car and instructed him to go home. I told him that I would be home in a couple of hours. I didn't need his ass with me when I went to purchase the supplies I needed to exact my revenge. I needed the least amount of witnesses possible.

I had plans to get back at my old boss for snitching on me. I had a special plan for him. His ass was retired, and I knew exactly where he was staying. He and his wife had a ranch out in Upper Marlboro. Her dumb ass didn't even know her husband liked black dick. Sorry bitch was gonna have to be punished with him. Her flat ass was going to be an innocent bystander to my fury and wrath.

Then I was going to go after the "lick-'em girl," Keisha, Kenny's baby mama. While I was getting arrested, her lesbian ass had the nerve to go through my pockets and take the keys to the car Kenny bought me. And the bitch stole the money I was going to steal for myself. *She and her dyke girlfriend gonna wish they had left town.* But, first things first, I was going to get me a decent place to stay.

I pulled off the car lot in a black Ford Expedition that had tinted windows and chrome rims. I could tell that this shit was almost new because it still had that fresh leather smell. It must have belonged to a drug dealer or something like that.

I went out to a spot out on Liberty Road called Dunhill Village Apartments. One of my old acquaintances had lived here for a short while, and I liked the area.

I went in, filled out an application, and I was given a full tour of the grounds. I knew this was the spot for me. The place was quiet and spacious. Despite my raunchy sex life, I loved to spend quiet evenings at home in my soft, plush bed.

The rent was $950, which was no problem at all. They ran my credit while I toured the place, so by the time we made it back to the leasing office, I was approved with no security deposit and given a date to move in. It was close to the end of the month, so I only had a couple of more days to stay in Carl's rat trap of an apartment.

I was so happy, I went to The Room Store and purchased all the furniture for my new home. I went shopping crazy as I normally do. I went to Anna's Linens for all my linens and Pier 1 for all my accents, like vases and candles. Then I went to Best Buy for my two flat-screen televisions, computer, and various surveillance equipment that I needed. I finally made a trip to the Wal-Mart Supercenter on Route 1, and finished up with pots, pans, and other household essentials.

I ended up spending close to $8,000 to fix up my new crib. Exhausted, I finally made my trip back to my temporary home for some much-needed rest.

Chapter 11

Ashley

The Good Girl
October 30th, 2018, 11:25 A.M.

"Hey, Tony, baby," I cooed into the phone.

Every time I spoke Tony's name, it just sent chills down my spine. Tony knew what I liked sexually and did it well. We would sneak off and we'd go to some secluded place and make out. Tony knew all the right spots to lick and nibble on to send me to heaven. Again, you see, Tony was much older than I, and knew how to treat me like a lady. Tony took me on dates to the movies and dinner, and sometimes we drove to New Jersey to go shopping.

My parents didn't know I was out with Tony, because they were so wrapped up in their shit. I didn't give a fuck anyway. It was my life, and if I wanted to give my body to Tony, then that was my business. I would tell them I was going over to so-and-so's house, and they would believe me, because I was a good girl who never lied to them, or so they thought.

Some of my friends thought we were the perfect family. Yeah, right. If they only knew about my alcoholic father and my pillow-smothering-me-to-death mother, they would know what our family was really like. I got four words for you—*dys-func-tion-al.*

Anyways, I can remember the first time we made out, we almost went all the way. It was so sweet and toe-curling.

"You ready, baby?" Tony whispered in my ear as I pulled my sundress up to my waist and over my head. Tony squeezed my perky breasts and licked on them like they were two chocolate-covered strawberries.

I moaned in pleasure as my teenage pussy oozed between my legs. I reached down between my legs and felt my warm juices flowing. I eased my hand back up seductively and placed it in Tony's mouth. Tony licked my hand clean and made the trip down to my throbbing clit to get a better taste.

"Ah," I moaned. I squeezed my legs around Tony's head as what I came to know as an orgasm rocked my world. My legs shook violently as Tony's tongue took off again, trying to give me a heart attack and an orgasm at the same time.

"Tony! Um ... Stop! Umm ... Please ... Stop!" I yelled, all the while pushing Tony's head closer to my womb. I climaxed once again and collapsed out of exhaustion.

"That's what I am talking about," Tony said, coming up for air.

I breathed heavily as Tony too collapsed beside me.

"Ashley," I heard my name being yelled, breaking me out of my reflective state.

"Oh, I'm sorry, baby. I was thinking about something."

"I hope it was me."

"You know it was. You the only thing that's important to me right now."

"Meet me at our spot in an hour," Tony said seductively into the phone. "I need some of that lovin'."

"Sure, baby. I'ma leave out now."

I hung up the phone and speed-dressed. I put on my easy-access dress and made my way downstairs. I grabbed my back-pack, for perpetrating purposes. My parents didn't know their sweet little girl had an inner ho. In fact, I had a sexual appetite that rivaled most men's. If they knew I was seeing someone much older, I knew they would've flipped a lid. But, again, I didn't give a fuck. I was out to get mine.

"Hey, Ashe, baby," my mom said as I entered the kitchen.

I put on my good-girl routine. "Mom, I'm going over Katie's house to do some studying. I'll be back about ten."

"Sure, baby," she said as she kissed me on the cheek. "And don't forget you have to help me with the ceremony that me and your father are having to renew our vows"

"Oh, okay. Sure, Mom, whatever." I turned and headed for the door. I could care less what they renewed.

Diana, my little sister, squealed as she ran up to me and hugged me. "Hey, Ashley. Where you goin'?"

"Out," I said, a little annoyed. I was just trying to get to Tony so we could spend as much time as possible together.

"Can I go with you? Please?" she said, clasping her hands in front of her like she was praying. "I promise I'll be good."

"Sorry, Diana. You can't come this time, but I promise that this weekend we'll go out shopping, just you and me."

"Really?" she said with a just-got-a-happy-meal smile.

"Yep, but I gotta go, okay." I kissed her on the forehead and made my way out the door, headed for my destination.

Alex was raking leaves in the front yard. "Hey, Ash. Where are you headed in such a hurry?"

"Out!" I kept my answer short and sweet.

"I know that, Ash. And technically we're both out, since we're standing outside." He stood within hands reach of me with the rake in his hand and a goofy Joker smile.

I wanted to punch him in his face for being such a smart ass. "Is that all?" I asked, my hand on my hip.

"No, I just want you to be careful." He walked up to me and hugged me real tight. "You're my little sister, and I get worried about you when you come in so late at night."

"You be spyin' on me?"

"Well, not really. I just think we, as brother and sister, need to make sure each other is safe." He had a sincere look on his face that melted me. "Feel me?"

"Yeah, I feel you. I promise I'll be careful." And, with that, I walked off toward the bus stop to meet Tony.

I got in the house at about seven o'clock at night. There were no cars in the driveway, so I knew my parents were out. I walked to the kitchen to get a few things to entertain myself with in my room. I put my ear to the basement door and listened to see if Alex was home. I didn't hear anything, so I continued on my way to my room.

I walked into my room and went into my closet for my secret "Sinner Girl" stash, which consisted of R. Kelly's *12 Play* CD, a vibrating rabbit, and a nude picture of Tony. I was all set to go as I stripped down to my birthday suit. I had shaven my pubic hair just like Tony liked it. I put the CD in the CD player and turned it up so that any neighbors that happened to pass by wouldn't hear my moans of ecstasy. My parents had a reputation as the "quiet family," and I didn't want to ruin it with what I was about to do.

I lay back on my pink silk sheets and spread my legs apart, ready to pleasure myself, my eyes focused on Tony's picture. I flipped the switch to my Rabbit vibrator to full speed and gently applied it to my clit. I closed my eyes and moaned.

The sensation was making my hips lift off the bed. I threw my head back as an orgasm caused me to explode all over my pillow, making my hands sticky.

But orgasms were like Pringles. I couldn't have just one. I was going for the put-my-ass-to-sleep orgasm. The stronger, the better.

I put the vibrator back on my clit and went at it again. My ass was off the bed now, and I felt the explosive energy of another orgasm in my stomach. Twitching and moaning, my eyes were going far back in my head. I was in heaven. "Ah! Ah! Ah!" I was exploding like never before.

"Ashley!"

It took me a minute to get my eyes focused. When I did, I wanted to disappear. Alex was standing in my doorway, his mouth open as wide as my legs. I was mortified. I wanted to know, how long was he standing there?

"Oh, shit!" I belted out.

I still don't know if it was the orgasm, or seeing the look on Alex's face. He raced out of the room like a bat out of hell. I didn't know what to do.

I knew I had to do something, so I went to get out of bed and ended up falling on my face. The last orgasm must have taken all my strength in my legs, because I could barely get up to my bed again. I managed to pull my housecoat off the end of my bed to cover myself.

"His ass must've been down there 'sleep," I mumbled.

I was more mad at myself than at him. I should have put a chair under the doorknob to block the entrance into my room. My parents, well, mainly my mother, took off all the locks to our bedrooms, saying, "People who pay bills get locks on their doors." I didn't have a job, so my door was without a lock.

After about twenty minutes of waiting for my legs to get back to normal, I went downstairs to talk to Alex. I made my way to the living room, where he was watching television.

I had no idea what to say to him. I shook my head in disgrace. "Hey, um, Alex, er, can w-we talk?" I was nervous as shit.

"Yeah, Ashley." He never looked at me.

Shit, I wouldn't have wanted to either. Getting a bird's-eye view of his sister's private area probably devastated him for sure. He probably had never seen a woman's privates before.

"I—I—I'm sorry about what you saw upstairs." I couldn't believe I was apologizing for pleasuring myself in my own room. "You know you should have knocked, though."

"I did knock." He huffed. "Your music was up too loud for you to hear me knocking. I just thought you were talking on the phone and listening to music like you usually do when we're home alone."

"Oh, okay."

"You know it's a sin to do that stuff, right?" Alex looked me square in the eyes.

"Yeah, Alex, we go to the same church, remember?" I was a little angry. I didn't need him to remind me of my wrongdoing. I knew I had an addiction to sex. "Look, I know I have a small problem. I just need you to keep this between us."

"Okay." He put the television on mute. "Besides, we all have secrets."

I looked at him, a puzzled look on my face. "What secrets do you have? You're a Goody Two-shoes, and you always stay in the house. Football, school, church and home. That's your routine, and everybody knows it." I slightly laughed at him.

"Yeah, okay." Alex had a smug look on his face. "You keep on believing that. I gets mine. Believe that."

We quieted down for a second as I wondered what he could possibly be doing to get his.

"Alex, are you gay?" I blurted out.

He started laughing uncontrollably, as if I had made the biggest joke possible. He never answered my question. When we were kids, Alex would always get caught in a lie because he would laugh or smile, giving away his guilt.

"Stop laughing." I pushed him hard.

He kept on laughing.

"Tell me. I won't tell anybody." I was dead serious. I could keep a secret like it was nobody's business. All my friends knew that.

He stopped laughing and looked at me with a smirk on his face. "I can't believe you asked me that." He was avoiding answering the question like a squirrel avoiding cars while trying to cross a street.

"Well, are you?" I posed the question again.

Before he could answer, my parents and Diana came through the door and interrupted us.

"Hey, you guys." My dad took off his coat and sat down next to us. "So what were you guys doing while we were gone?"

"Oh, nothing," we both chimed, like twins usually do.

"We were just sitting here watching cable and talking." I gave Alex a menacing stare and then got up and headed to my room.

I wasn't through with him yet. The next time we were alone, I was going to find out what I wanted to know.

Chapter 12

Mona

The Curse
October 30th, 2018, 12:09 P.M.

"Ashley is such a good girl," I said to myself as I prepared to go down to the basement and get the last little load of clothes out of the dryer. My job as a wife and a mother never paid well and had absolutely no sick days. Some days, I just wanted to walk away from it all, but the love of my family kept me onboard this ship that sometimes seemed to be headed to nowhere.

I had to walk through Alex's room to get to the laundry room. When it came to neatness and organization, he was just like his father. Everything had its place, and his bed never went unmade. I marveled at the décor and color scheme that he put together so well. Even as a woman, I couldn't get the rest of the house coordinated as well as he had his little habitat in the basement.

I proceeded on to the back of the basement and removed the clothes from the dryer so I could fold them and put them away. "Let me hurry up and get this done," I said to myself. "I need to get dinner started."

Since I was already down in Alex's room, I decided to put his clothes away for him. I went to his dresser, which was labeled for shirts, underwear, pants, etc., and began placing the items in the appropriate drawers. As I got to the last drawer to place his underwear away, I got the shock of my life.

I placed my hands over my mouth to muffle my whimpers of shock. "What in the hell!" I mouthed as tears flooded my eyes and ran down my face. I picked up the thick, veined dildo and slowly sat down on his bed. Thoughts of Shawn's demons and his past that involved him sleeping with men flooded my mind.

I balled up on Alex's bed and sobbed. "Not my baby, Lord! No! Not Alex!" I cried uncontrollably as I clutched the plastic toy. I couldn't take the thought of my only son being gay. It couldn't be true. It just couldn't.

I heard the noise of footsteps above me and assumed it was Alex coming home from football practice. I scrambled to get myself together and quickly placed the dildo back where I'd found it. Then I removed the clothes I had previously placed in his drawers and made my way back to the laundry room to pretend like I was there the whole time.

As he came down the basement steps, I dried my tears and made my way through his room. I don't know what most parents would've done in this situation, but I didn't plan on forcing him to come out to me. If I'd done that, he might have rejected me and even run away. I couldn't have my baby running the streets, so I decided to just keep this to myself. I wasn't even going to tell Shawn. That would've definitely sent him back to counseling.

"Hey, Ma." Alex greeted me with a kiss on the cheek as he walked into the laundry room.

I fumbled with the clothes a little longer, just to distract him and myself from my nervousness. "Your clothes are over there." I pointed away from myself, trying not to make eye contact with him. "I didn't want to invade your privacy, so I just folded them. All you have to do is put them away." I brushed past him and made my way toward the steps in a faster pace than normal.

"Hey, Ma," he slightly yelled.

"Yeah, baby?" I turned around to see what he wanted.

"You thought I wouldn't notice, didn't you?" He had a serious look on his face.

"Ah. Notice what?" I said, afraid that he'd noticed that someone had been through his things. My palms began to sweat as he walked toward me. I wanted to run and leave him standing there.

My eyes quickly darted around the room, making sure I had placed everything back as I'd found it. In my haste, I could have left a drawer open or something. To my relief, I left no evidence of my previous invasion. *Whew!* I sighed mentally.

"You thought I was just going to let you walk away from me without giving me a hug?"

"Oh. Ha-ha." I laughed nervously and placed the laundry basket on the floor, preparing to be hugged.

He hugged and squeezed me really hard, like he normally did. I had forgotten that Alex was a very affectionate person. Even as a child he hugged everyone that he greeted like they were family.

"Alex, baby, you know you can talk to me and your dad about anything, right?"

"Yeah, Ma. Why you getting all mushy?" he said, a smile on his face.

"Alex, I just want you to know that, okay," I said in a serious tone.

"I know, Ma, I know."

I turned around, picked up the laundry, and headed upstairs with a load in my hand, and on my mind.

Chapter 13

Shawn

Gate Wide Open
November 2nd, 2018, 10:13 A.M.

I was contemplating killing James as I sat in my chair at work. I couldn't believe that muthafucka was out of prison and living with my pedophile of a father. I checked my database for any info on him and found out that he'd just got out of jail. What I didn't understand was how he and my father hooked up again. That shit was mind-boggling. As soon as I thought I was back on the right side of the fence, here his ass go opening the gate again and dragging me back through.

Bzzz!

My thoughts were interrupted by the sound of my secretary buzzing into my office.

"Mr. Black, you have someone here to see you. He has no appointment, but he says he isn't leaving until he sees you."

"Okay. Tell him to hold on, and I will be with him in a minute."

Before I could get up and make my way to see who had shown up unexpectedly, in waltzes James, of all people. This bastard had the nerve to show up at my office.

"How are you doing, Shawn?" he said, a cynical smile on

his face. He immediately made himself comfortable, like we were old college buddies or something.

"Fine." A one-word answer was all I could muster. My emotions on the inside were a bit volatile, and I knew I could blow at any moment.

My next thought was to buzz my secretary and get her to call security, but I opted otherwise. I had to see what this lunatic wanted now.

"How can I help you, Mr. Parks?" I wasn't gonna let him make me act a fool again.

"Shawn, why you actin' all professional and shit? You know, any other time your ass would be calling me by my first name, especially when we made love." He smiled even harder after that.

"James, we *never* made love. I was just fucking you. You know that. Like the whore you were." I was smiling now.

James had the look of defeat on his face. He just sat there like he had something to say. I had taken a seat after my last comment and started fumbling through some papers on my desk, trying to distract myself.

"Look, Shawn, this don't have to get ugly, if you just cooperate," he said, breaking the silence.

"What in the hell are you talking about?"

"You know what I am talking about. Stop playing dumb, Shawn. You know good and well I said I was coming to get my kids."

"Your kids?" I said, bristling. "You don't have any kids. They are my kids, not yours. You got that, shit-chaser?" I stood up, ready to kick his ass.

"So what you are telling me is that you want to go to court for custody of my children?"

James stood up as well. He actually thought he could come

up in here in my office and demand to take the children I raised and nurtured? He was dead wrong. Dead wrong.

"Shawn, I know for a fact that you and Mona have not told my children about me. They don't even know I exist, do they?"

"Why should they know about a home-wrecking faggot?" I said as I walked around the desk. I knew I couldn't even begin to explain to Alex, Ashley, and Diana about James Parks. What was I going to tell them? That their dad and mom had sex with the same guy and he was their father? I still couldn't bear the thought of it myself, never mind speak about it.

"Shawn, if you don't tell them, then I will, and I know for a fact that you would love to keep the 'happy Huxtables' together forever. You and Mona think that you were going to keep secrets and never tell me about my offspring. You two are crackheads if you thought I was just going to walk away and let this be. You know I can't do that shit."

I had to admit that he had me by the balls. I did want to keep my family together, at any cost possible.

"Look, this is what I propose. I'ma need a little dick every now and then, so when I call, be ready." He grabbed my dick through my pants. "You know I used to love riding this donkey dick of yours." He started walking away but suddenly turned back around. "Oh, and just in case you think about fucking me over, I took the liberty of finding out the schools that Ashley, Alex, and little Diana attend. I can have their asses scooped up and thrown in the back of a truck at the drop of a dime. Then I would disappear, and you would never see me or them again. Think about it, my love, and I will see you soon." Then he made his exit in the same fashion as he came in.

I just stood there in the middle of my office absorbing all that he'd said. I was flabbergasted and short on words.

Even angry, I was still turned on by the thought of the heated sex sessions we had over ten years ago; waking up to him tossing my salad, to sex on his table, and then the shower sex that changed showers for me for the rest of my life. It sent me over, standing right there in my office.

"Was this muthafucka serious?" I pondered to myself as I made my way back toward my desk.

My secretary came in a couple of minutes later. "Is everything okay, Mr. Black?" she said, a concerned look on her face.

"Yeah, I'm okay, Renee." I sighed. I truly wasn't. I wasn't being the man I was supposed to be by letting this mofo run me like this. This is getting old, fast. When am I going to stand up to my lies and put this situation in check? Or am I just fooling myself into thinking James would give up this charade that easy?

"You don't look too good. You want me to get you something?"

Renee was so nurturing, there were times I would forget she was my secretary.

"Yeah, that would be great," I said as I went in one of the desk drawers and pulled out a personal-size mirror. I was a little flushed in the face, but that would go away in a couple of minutes.

Renee quickly exited and returned with a hot tea that she said calmed you down after you drank it. I wasn't the home-remedy type of guy, but to my surprise, twenty minutes after I drank the tea, I began to feel at ease.

"Mr. B," she said, standing with her hands on her hips, "you need to fuck somebody up? 'Cause I got four brothers that don't mind breaking their foot off in a nigga's ass."

I was a little shocked. At work, she was always professional. I'd never seen her like this.

I contemplated it a little but let it pass. I knew I could handle this alone. "No, thanks, Renee. It was just an old friend that was heated about something I couldn't help him with."

"Oh, okay. 'Cause you fam, and I would do anything for you."

I stayed in my office a little later than usual trying to figure a way out of the mess I was in. Coming up with no immediate solution, I left my office and headed to the local corner store to get me some liquor. I needed to inebriate myself to deal with this situation.

Chapter 14

James

Down on the Farm
November 2nd, 2018, 10:35 P.M.

I left Shawn's job amazed at my cunning and conniving ways. I was confident that I had him shook again. What most people don't know is that gay men have the best of both worlds. They can be sharp as a woman, and at the flip of a switch, subtle as a man.

I was now headed out to Upper Marlboro, Maryland to surprise an old friend, who I know wasn't expecting me.

As I drove down the long, winding roads that seemed to lead to nowhere, I wondered how my old boss was doing. I wasn't concerned with his health or some shit like that. I was just wondering if his ass was still being dicked down by men and coming home to his wife, like he was with me.

A sucker for scenery, I was enjoying my ride down the country roads. With the act I was about to commit, you might wonder how I was so calm. See, I felt like I was exacting revenge on a deserving party. All my life it seemed like people used me, abused me, then tossed me in the trash, like a used condom.

While I was in jail, I thoroughly thought about my past and my future. I was sure I was going to end up happy after I settled down with the right man.

I'd even thought about having a relationship with the children that knew nothing about me, but that was only a thought. With my lifestyle, I wouldn't be in it wholeheartedly. I just wanted Mona and Shawn to think I was interested, to get more money out of them, and to just plain torture them some more.

I slowed down and looked at my map to make sure I wouldn't miss the house. I pulled up to the entrance to the address and turned my lights off, slowly driving down the road that led to a nice house surrounded by a field. It was late, and starting to look like a scene out of "Children of the Corn," because the grass and weeds were taller than my car.

"This muthafucka out here in the boondocks and shit," I said to myself. I saw a scarecrow out in the middle of a big field and got an eerie feeling, but I shook that shit off. I had to stay focused.

I stopped my car and picked up the binoculars that sat on my passenger seat and surveyed the house. It looked as if everybody was asleep because all the lights in the house were off.

I got out the car in my all-black fatigue with matching lace-up boots. You would have thought I was the black 007. My adrenaline pumping, I crept up the driveway and noticed two cars parked outside, telling me, his wife had to be home as well. I didn't give a fuck. It was now or never, and her ass was going pay for just being a dumb-ass, naïve white bitch.

I eased up the creaking steps and tried to open their screen door. *Their dumb white asses still think it's safe to keep their doors unlocked. In this day and age, your ass could end up on the midday news because somebody split your shit or something like that, for being so careless.*

I slowly opened the door, making sure not to make any noise. I had my flashlight in hand, knowing full well I couldn't cut any lights on. I moved my flashlight around as I walked around the house and surveyed the horrible taste in décor. Their house was decorated with pink-and-purple paisley furniture, which they had the gall to wrap in plastic. That shit needed to be torched. "Fucking tacky," I mumbled to myself.

I continued to look around at the pictures of the family, and boy, it was hard to contain my queasy stomach. His wife was a beast. Her mug looked like a damn pit bull's, and their kids' looked even worse. I could see why he messed around with men. I took out a Magic Marker and drew mustaches on all the girls' faces, because they truly looked like men.

After getting a few chuckles, I headed up the stairs and made my way toward what looked like the master bedroom. The door was wide open, and I walked in with my gun in hand.

I looked at the happy couple as they lay on their backs, snoring with their mouths open. I decided to wake him up with a surprise. I pulled out my dick and massaged it, making it semi-hard, and eased it in his gaping mouth, as his head hung off the bed. He woke up gagging.

"Honey, I'm home," I said, grinning from ear to ear.

He looked as if he saw a ghost. He shifted in his bed, waking his wife in the process, and she let out a scream.

"Bitch, shut the fuck up!" I said, pointing my gun in her direction.

She immediately silenced herself.

"Get up, you dog-faced whore!"

She slowly rose from the bed with a look of fear and anguish.

"Sit over there."

She moved to a chair that was placed at what I assumed was

her makeup table. I was tempted to tie her up and beat that ugly mug myself, but as bad as she looked, it would've taken me days to fix her shit.

I tied her hands behind her back. I noticed her eyes peeking at my dick as it hung out of my pants. *I should fuck her ass to show her that the stereotype about black men was true.* But, again, I couldn't get past her ugly-ass mug.

I put tape over her mouth, making sure she didn't say a peep, and focused my attention back on my old fuck buddy, who was balled up on the bed with his back toward the headboard.

I walked over to him and waved my now limp dick in his face. "You remember this?"

His ass played dumb and looked the other way, like he didn't want it, so I smacked him with my gun, letting him know it wasn't a request.

As he hesitantly scooted over to me, his wife was watching the whole time, her eyes bugging out of their sockets.

"There you go," I said as I eased my meat in his mouth.

He latched on to my dick, like a newborn to its mother's supple breast, and started going crazy sucking my dick.

I glanced over at his wife to see what she was doing. Her ugly ass was crying as she watched her husband pleasure me. "Yeah, bitch, this is what we did all the time at the office. Betcha didn't know he was a faggot when you married him, did you?"

I pushed his head closer to me, so he could swallow me whole. My eyes rolled back into my head, showing how pleased I was with his work. I could hear muffled cries from his wife, but continued to ride his face.

Then I roughly pushed him away, making him fall back on the bed again. "Get on all fours! I'ma tear that ass up!"

He did as instructed.

I strapped on a raincoat and forcefully pushed my dick in his waiting ass. He pushed back like a pro and started riding me like a bull at a rodeo.

His wife, by this time, had passed out cold. I guess she couldn't handle me fucking her man.

I fucked him for a good twenty minutes. She woke up sometime during the show, but this time she watched her husband devour dick like a homeless man who hadn't eaten in days in a soup line.

"You like what you see?" I said, directing my attention to her.

She just stared like she was in a trance of some sort.

I turned back to her husband and began smacking his ass and grinding my dick in him harder.

"Oh, yeaah," he moaned, throwing discretion to the wind.

His ass was enjoying it, and it seemed like he didn't care that his wife was there.

I was nearing my climax, so I pulled out my man meat and let his mouth do the rest of the work. I came in his mouth, and he swallowed it like it was a protein shake.

"All right, my turn," I said as he stood up and started massaging his own meat.

I went to work on his dick, and he was loving it. He leaned his head back, and his mouth flung open as he let out pleasured moans.

As he moaned, I reached down in one of my pants pocket and pulled out my serrated Rambo knife.

His wife now thrashed about as if she knew she was about to witness her husband's demise.

"Ah!" he screamed as my knife cut through his dick like I was cutting fresh bread.

Blood splattered the walls and bed, and there was a big gaping hole where his dick used to be. Lorena Bobbit would be proud of me. It was a clean cut. He thrashed around like a headless chicken.

"You thought I was coming back just to get me some ass, muthafucka? Didn't you? You thought you could snitch on me and have my ass sent up river for ten years and get away with it? This payback for all the years I rotted in that jailhouse, you fuckin' asshole! I treated your ass good. And I know you loved this dick I have." I still had his dick in my hand, waving it in the air, as I ranted and raved around the room.

I walked over to his wife and pulled the tape off her mouth.

"Please don't hurt me! Please! I promise I won't say a thing. Please, sir! Please! Do what you want with him, but please let me be! I didn't love him anyway. Please just let me be."

Her begging was making me madder. I needed this ugly bitch to shut her mouth, and fast.

I jammed her husband's bleeding dick in her mouth just to get some time to think. "Look, horse face, you ain't seen shit! You hear me? Your ass better play dumb, deaf, and blind like Helen Keller, if anybody ask you anything. Okay, bitch!"

She nodded in approval.

I looked around the room and noticed her pocketbook and his wallet. I retrieved both of them for "insurance purposes," just in case they changed their minds. I untied her and then hustled my way down the stairs. I quickly detoured to the kitchen for a drink.

Out of nowhere, a cat jumped on my arm as I snatched a can of Mountain Dew out of the refrigerator. I tussled with the cat, trying to shake him off, but the more I shook, the more he dug his claws in my arm.

I quickly dropped my soda and pulled my knife out again and jabbed him one good time in the face, and he went down fast, taking all of his nine lives with him.

I retrieved my soda and scurried my way toward my car and made a speedy exit. "Muthafuckin' fur ball," I grumbled as I rummaged through my glove compartment for some pain medicine.

I decided to go to Northwest Hospital instead. I couldn't risk the chance of having rabies or some shit like that. I made sure I changed my bloody clothes in the back of my truck before I went into the hospital.

After I got out of the hospital, I went back to my apartment to really clean myself up. When I got home, my two new cats greeted me at the door with meows that spoke of hunger. I temporarily ignored them and did the three S's—shit, shower, and shave. After that, I fed them and got in my bed for some much-needed rest. I still hadn't decided how I was going to torture Mona, but I knew when I awoke in the morning, I would have the perfect plan.

Chapter 15

Carl (Shawn's Father)

Lights Out
November 2nd, 2018, 10:25 P.M.

I bobbed and weaved back to my apartment after taking a trip around the corner to the Windy Spirits Liquor Store. I was already intoxicated from early in the morning. It was breezy outside, but I sweated the whole way back to my door. Being an alcoholic does that to you. Drowning my shame and pain with vodka and gin seemed to be working up until a couple of weeks ago. The agony of the way I had been treating my family these last few years was taking a toll that liquor couldn't hide.

I was a seventy-three-year-old fuckup that didn't grow up. I fucked up my son from when he was a child on up. I didn't deserve him. I knew it. I didn't deserve my wife, when I had her, either. It was too late to make amends, but I still wanted to. Yeah, I was sorry. But, how does one apologize for solely screwing up their family? I was too far gone, I figured. All of these things flooded my old mind as I made my way in the building and rode the elevator up to my apartment.

I leaned up against my apartment door, my head pressed hard against it, and cried like a baby. It was long overdue. Too late, you might say. The opportunity to do right had sailed years ago.

I managed to fumble in my pockets for my keys and hold on to my only true friend wrapped up in a brown paper bag. Even James had kicked me to the curb. I knew he was using me, but he was being used by me as well. He was a warm body at night. A convenience. And now he was gone too. No son, no wife, no James.

"Just me and you." I looked at my bottle of vodka as if it could talk. In a couple of minutes it would, to my liver, that is.

Turns out, my door was already unlocked. I must left it unlocked when I rushed out in a hurry to get to the store. My door swung open with force as I used it as leverage to hold me up. I almost hit the floor, but I gathered myself just in time. I managed to close it and staggered to my kitchen, which was only a few feet away, to grab me a cup.

The lights were out, but I could navigate like I was Ray Charles, especially to get my "taste" in a cup, and down my throat as quickly as possible. I reached the kitchen and opened the cabinet. Not a clean cup in sight. I went through the dishes in the sink and grabbed the cleanest one I could find. I poured me a quick shot, to add to my already lingering buzz, and quickly threw it back.

That's when I felt a blow to the side of my head.

Pow! Then another blow. *Pow!*

I fell against my stove, and another blow came, sending me downward. I tried to grab hold of something to stop my fall, but it was useless. It was a no-win situation, though I still managed to have my vodka firmly in hand.

"Where is James?" the intruder barked.

"Who?" I muttered. The blows had shaken up my mind. I wasn't sure who I was at the moment.

"You know who, muthafucka!" He towered over me with what looked like a bat in hand.

I lifted my hand to my head and felt the blood flowing freely. I started to panic. "I—I—I don't know where he—"

He kicked me in the ribs.

"Ugh!"

"Stop lying, muthafucka! I know he was here." The intruder knelt down beside me.

I couldn't make out his face, because I hadn't managed to cut the light on in the kitchen when I'd come in. Only a little light from the small window over the stove gave light to the room. And that was little. He was a rather large dude, and his hot breath showed that he wasn't playing with me. He was breathing fast and erratic.

"I'm giving you one mo' chance to get this right, pops!"

"I swear, he left me a couple of hours ago, and I haven't seen him since." My heart was racing. I was a healthy old man, but a heart attack felt like it was coming.

"Ummm-hmm."

I couldn't tell if he believed me, but the knife he plunged in my stomach gave me the answer.

"I hate liars!" he breathed out. He picked up my body and dragged me to my bedroom.

It was dark in there as well. I was in excruciating pain, but I felt him tying me up to the bed. I didn't know what he was doing or going to do, but I knew it wasn't going to end good for me.

He flicked on the light in the room, causing me to shudder and try to adjust my eyes to the light. He had on a mask, but I could see the hate in his eyes.

Whatever he was angry about had nothing to do with me, but he was going to take it out on me for sure. He pulled out several knives and a gun. He made his way to the bed, yanked down my pants, and smiled before jamming a long, jagged knife into my groin. That was the last thing I felt.

Chapter 16

Mona

I woke up this morning in a very chipper, upbeat mood. The sun was shining, and the birds were singing their songs. Shawn was still sleeping in, and I had a very busy day ahead of me. Shawn opted to stay out of the planning of this event, saying it was women's work.

But I knew different. He didn't want to upstage me again. See, what most people didn't know was that Shawn had arranged our wedding. He refused to let people know that it was him, because he had to protect his precious manhood. He said if his boys found out that he was "décor inclined" they wouldn't let a day go by without teasing him.

I was ready to start planning the anniversary/renewal party, and nothing could stop me. I enlisted the help of two shining stars, Ashley and Diana, to help me go out and shop for the decorations, caterer, and for various other tasks.

Diana was all go, but I could see that Ashley was in her own world, like her brother. She was always over one of her girlfriends' houses studying, so I knew I'd have to drag her to the car. *If she wasn't an A student, I would suspect foul play.*

It was about nine thirty in the morning, and I wanted to get going. I peeked in Diana's room, and she wasn't in there. I was so glad that she was such an independent little girl at the age of ten. I knew she was probably already downstairs eating a bowl of cereal and watching the Disney Channel until I was ready to leave the house.

I peeked into Ashley's room, and sure enough, she was knocked out. I walked up to her bed and gently shook her until she was awake.

"What, Ma?" she said with an attitude. She rolled back over and pulled the covers over her unkempt hair.

"Excuse me?" I said with a little more attitude. She must have forgotten I was an adult. I snatched the covers off. "Let's make it!" I said with a tone that meant business. My mom used that statement with me when she absolutely wasn't accepting any rebuttals. "We have to leave the house in forty-five minutes, so get dressed and let's go."

I left her room, headed back to mine. I needed to shower and get dressed as well. She must have forgotten that she was supposed to help me with all the arrangements today. Shawn had given me a good budget to spend, and I was going to do it up my way the second time around.

I showered and dressed in thirty minutes flat and made my way down the stairs for a light breakfast. I bypassed Diana in the living room, and she was entertaining herself as usual, like I assumed she'd be.

I walked in the kitchen and noticed Ashley on her cell phone talking in a hushed tone. She didn't even hear me when I came in because she was so engrossed with her conversation. I stood in the doorway and eavesdropped.

"Sure, baby. I want to see you too, Tony, baby," she whispered in the phone. "As soon as I take care of some stuff wit' my moms,

I'ma hit you up, okay. I'll try and ditch her by one o'clock . . . All right, boo. Love you, too."

I made my way to the refrigerator, startling her in the process.

"Oh! Hey, Ma," she said as she swiftly put her phone in her pocket. "How long were you standing there?"

"Long enough to want to know who Tony is." I looked her dead in the eyes, one hand resting on my waist.

"Oh. Ah, Tony is just a friend, Ma."

I knew she was lying. As a child I could tell when she was being dishonest because she would get this silly smirk on her face that always told on her.

"So do you say, 'I love you,' to all your friends, Ashley?"

She looked at me sideways because whenever I said one of my children's names in a statement, they knew I was on to them. After going though all that I had gone through with Shawn over the last couple of years, I couldn't stand being lied to by anyone, especially my family.

"No, Ma," she said, her head hanging down.

"Look, Ashley, I really don't have a problem with you having a boyfriend. It's when you lie to me about things like this that really makes me mad. You kids know you can come to us about anything. Your father and I always told you that we would always have an open mind when it came to our children."

I gathered my purse and my list of things to do.

"So when will we meet this boyfriend of yours?"

"Ma, Tony is kinda shy."

"Okay, Ashley, whenever you are ready to introduce him, just let me know, so we can do it as a family."

"Okay," she said, getting up and following me as I made my way out to the car.

We traveled to Marley Station Mall, Columbia Mall, and made

a special trip to Security Square Mall that day. I slowly took my time just to see how Ashley was going to react. She pouted and groaned as I made my way down each aisle. I could care less. I was in charge, and if she thought for a second she could ditch me, she was dead wrong.

I purposely asked her input on each arrangement and color scheme, knowing she really didn't want to be with me and Diana. I was a little shocked at her sassy little attitude. I was starting to see a totally different side, a side she got from me, I have to say. She was a strong-willed, yet naïve adolescent.

I finally let her go on her merry way about five o' clock. I dropped her off at Owings Mills subway station, and she scurried into the station and disappeared. I drove off with a smile on my face because I loved spending time with my girls all alone, even if they didn't fully cooperate with it.

I wanted to teach them the value of family and bonding, schooling them on the birds and the bees and things of that nature while riding in the car when it was just us girls. Ashley would squirm and moan as I gave her lessons in feminine hygiene, but I knew she was better off getting it from me than some girl in her class who was still learning things herself.

As we pulled up to the house, I called the house phone to get Alex out to the car to help me with the bags. Like a good son, he came and scooped up the bags, and I made my way into the house along with Diana in tow, who hurried to her room to play with some new Bratz dolls I had bought her, leaving me and Alex to ourselves.

"Dag, Ma, you guys sure went crazy wit' all this shopping and stuff." Alex laughed as he carried the loaded bags toward our living room. "Y'all sure the malls got enough stuff left for their other customers?"

Pop! I playfully smacked him upside the head. "Boy, mind yo business."

I was cut short by the phone ringing.

"Hey, Momma Black," I said with a smile. I was always so happy to hear from my mother-in-law. I was as close to her as I was to my mom.

"Is Shawn home, Mona?"

She sounded like she was crying. I'd never heard Shawn's mom crying, so I knew something was wrong. "Is everything okay, Ma?" I said, concern in my voice. "He's not here right now. He's at work, but I can click over and call him on three-way."

I did so. When she spilled the beans, I was in complete shock. This news was so unexpected, I had to take a seat on the chair. Tears flowed from my eyes, and my mouth hung open in disbelief as I sat on the living room chair.

All I could think about was how Shawn was handling this news, because his response was just, "Okay," and he hung up the phone.

Chapter 17

James

Sponsorship
November 6th, 2018, 11:53 A.M.

I decided to give the Black family and myself a break. Like a television show needed commercials to pay for their airtime, I needed me a new sponsor to fund my life. My money was halfway gone, and I quickly needed to find me somebody with some deep pockets. I decided to cruise around Kenny's old stomping ground. After only about five minutes of driving, I spotted my new trick-and-treat, which was what I called them, because after I tricked them out, they would treat me to anything I wanted. Most people would say I was selling my body, but the way I saw it, it was simply a case of supply and demand. I was supplying what the community damn sure demanded.

I pulled up to the side of the curb and heard somebody yell, "Got that Ray Charles."

I couldn't believe they was giving crack cocaine names now. I laughed to myself because the thought of a crackhead chasing something that could make him high and blind blew my mind.

I ignored the drug calls and focused my attention on a dude

posted up on his porch like he was just an average homeowner. I honked my horn and yelled, "Aye, yo!" as manly as I could.

It worked because he slowly rose up and made his way to the car. He was about the same height as I was. He had that hung-like-a-muthafucka walk, caramel-colored skin, and a couple of tattoos that flowed down his small but muscular arms. His dreads were neatly placed in a ponytail, and his face was shaped up, with a goatee to match.

His eyes said, "Fuck wit' me if you want," as he walked up to my car.

My kind of nigga. Trying my best to keep my eyes above his waist, I eyed him up and down like he was a hot, tempting treat.

Looking at another brotha's crotch is a sure way to get yo ass sent to Bon Secours Hospital intensive care unit with a busted rib cage and some more shit. Not that it's ever happened to me, but I'd heard stories of guys getting beat down for approaching a dude that was legitimately straight.

"What's up, main man?" I said, putting on a superb around-the-way-gangsta act. "I'm tryin'-a get work. How can I be down?"

"Depends," he said, looking me up and down.

I couldn't figure out if he liked what he saw, or if he took me for a cop or something. "Depends on what?" I asked, partially knowing the drug game.

See, I did have the privilege of listening in on some of Kenny's conversations while he was making drug transactions over the phone a couple of times. He'd even answered a couple of my questions after some of our sexual exploits. I'd learned a long time ago that asking a question is free and the knowledge that you get from asking could be very valuable in the future.

"Depends on who you know!" His face was still as stern as

it was when he'd walked up to my car. This brotha was about his business. If he was trying to holla at me, I couldn't tell, and I was an expert.

"I'm a friend of Kenny. I was in the joint wit' him. He told me to get at you if I needed any work when I got out." I marveled at myself because even I was impressed with what I was spitting.

"Man, that's all I needed to hear," he said, his hard exterior softening. "Let's take a ride around the block, so we can talk"

I unlocked the passenger door, he hopped in, and I pulled off.

Wallace hadn't the slightest clue I was playing his ass. When I was locked up, word got back to me that he'd helped Kenny's baby mama, Keisha, set him up for some extra dough. I was going to use him to get Keisha back and get me some more dough in the process. From the looks of him, he was dressed like an average joe, you know. Nothing flashy, but just enough to keep the girls hollering at him.

"Yo, what they call you?" he asked me.

"James." I decided to give him my real name. I was getting tired of being two different people. That shit was exhausting.

"So how did you know Kenny?"

"Oh, we just served some time together." I lied.

He said, "Oh, okay," like he didn't believe me. "So what you get locked up for?"

His ass sure was nosy. I shrugged it off because I would be too if I was in the position he was in. "Attempted murder."

"Oh, okay," he said again, like he wasn't believing me one bit.

After a few seconds of silence, he burst out in laughter. "Man, you's a straight-up liar," he said, a big smile plastered on his face.

He caught me off guard. I was totally dumbfounded now.

"Look, man, let me be straight wit' you. I know all about you and Kenny."

"Excuse me!" I said, faking a serious look on my face. I was shocked, to say the least.

"Yeah, I know you and Kenny was fuckin'. We was fuckin' too."

"What!" I pulled over to the side of the road to get myself together. "Y'all was what?"

"Man, stop actin' all surprised and shit . . . like you was the only one. Who you think he was goin' to Club Bunz wit'?"

My mouth continued to hang open as he dropped another bomb on me.

"Yeah. And I was the one who helped his baby mama set Kenny up too. She didn't know we was fuckin' either. And the only reason I helped her set him up was to get him out the way so I could get at you."

"Really?" I said now, a smile on my face. A nigga always liked to feel wanted. My ass was really cheesing now.

"Yeah, man. I been trying to get wit' you the first time I saw you pick him up off the block a couple of times. A fine-ass nigga like you is a hot commodity on the streets." His hand now made its way over to my lap, and he was squeezing my thigh.

I instantly became aroused, and from the looks of things, he was as well. And just like I thought, he was well hung. Shit, his dick was halfway down his thigh.

"Hold up," he said. "We need to go back to my place and finish this."

"Look, before we go anywhere, I got one question for you," I said with a serious expression on my face. "You got any baby mamas chasing you or some shit?"

"Nah, man." He laughed. "I'm strictly dickly."

With that said, he gave me the directions to his place, and I pulled off in hopes of some mind-blowing sex.

About twenty minutes later, we arrived at his condominium-style apartment, The Avalon, located in Pikesville. It was a gated community, so I knew he had to be loaded with money. He gave me the code to punch in the keypad. I made a mental note to remember the number, just in case I needed it later.

As we pulled up to his apartment building, he told me to park next to an all-black Bentley. We both got out, and he took his keys out and pressed the button, popping the trunk to the extravagant piece of machinery. He removed what looked like a duffel bag full of laundry. But I knew it had to be something like cash or dope.

"That's a nice whip you got." I could imagine me flexing in it someday just to go to the market.

"Yeah, man, I just bought it last month. I drive me a Honda or Toyota around the hood just to fool the young'uns that might wanna try me or something."

I just nodded my head. I could have cared less about that shit. My mind was clouded by dollar signs. I was gonna have to step my game up because this nigga was ballin' better than Kenny ever was.

We made our way up to his apartment, and my mind went crazy as we entered. He had a short marble vestibule that had swirls of cream and chocolate. He dropped his keys on an ivory and tan table with gold trimming.

Just as I was about to step on the plush carpet, he instructed me to take off my shoes, because he didn't want to track anything on it. He did the same then told me to take a seat while he went into his kitchen to get us something to drink.

I admired his wall-to-wall chocolate-carpeted living room as I sat in the chocolate and tan, suede-and-leather sectional, which was soft to the touch, and felt good on my skin as I made myself comfortable. He had a fireplace that had a traditional mantle, with various pictures of family members spread across.

I got up and walked around the room, my feet feeling like they were on clouds, to look at his CD collection and other things on his entertainment center. He had a nice collection. gospel, jazz, R&B, neo-soul, rock.

I made my way back around to his mantle and looked at some of his family members. My eyes bugged out my socket as one of the pictures had a guy in it that looked a lot like one of my exes. *This shit must run in his family.*

"You ready?" Wallace came up behind me and surprised me. He pressed his dick against my ass as he licked the back of my neck like an ice cream sundae, sending shivers down my spine and causing the blood to flow to my third leg.

"Ummm."

He handed me a glass of red wine, which I threw back in one swoop, gulping it down, because I was long overdue for some good, old-fashioned fucking.

He moved his coffee table out of the way and made room on the floor in front of the fireplace. He had a remote control that controlled everything in his living room, so before long, there was a fire going and the sweet sounds of Mario's "Let Me Love You" filled the air, setting the mood.

He slowly and methodically removed my clothes piece by piece as well as his own. I marveled at the toned yet aged masculine Adonis that sat across from me, and my dick instantly swelled in throbbing pleasure. We immediately started kissing, letting our tongues do the talking for us.

After about ten minutes of kissing, we both made our way down to each other's manhood and devoured it whole. The sound of slurping and moaning was now in rhythmic competition with the music in the background.

He then laid me on my back and made his way down to my puckering asshole that awaited his attention. He dove in like he was eating watermelon at a summer family feast. He was licking the crack of my ass from my back all the way to the tip of my dick.

I lifted my ass off the floor and thrust it toward him. "Oh, yeah!" I moaned. "That's the spot right thereeeeeee."

I needed my ass pounded like never before. "Fuck me now!" I commanded. I watched as he placed a Magnum XL condom on his pulsating muscle. I turned over, because doggy-style would let me get every inch of his dick in me.

He slowly pushed himself in me. But taking one's time wasn't my method, so I forcefully pushed back, letting his dick fill me up. He immediately got the hint and took over, pounding my ass like a jackhammer hitting concrete.

I was loving every minute, whimpering and moaning, "Ahh! Yeah, daddy! Take this ass. It's all yours."

He pulled up and placed me against the wall, placing my arms and legs over his shoulders, pressing me against the wall hard. It was a painful position, but it was soon replaced with pleasure.

He fucked me like he was trying to go through the wall. With every pump, I yelped in pleasure. This too was going down in the record books as one of my best sexual positions.

He punished me for another good ten minutes before he erupted, and we collapsed on his floor, panting for air. I didn't even realize I nutted on myself, because he was fucking me so hard.

He nibbled on my ear as he whispered other ways and places

he wanted to fuck me. Then he scooped me up and carried me to the shower. Mind you, he was the same size I was.

It was still unbelievable how tender he was. I'd learned that men on the down low are some of the most giving people you could ever meet. Yet, on any given day, you probably would see a dude like him beating a crackhead down for shorting him or trying to con him. It was like dealing with Dr. Jekyll and Mr. Hyde.

We both washed up, and afterward, he showed me to his master suite.

Once again, I was shocked at how his taste was exquisitely on point. Everything in his apartment was earth-toned with combinations of brown, cream, tan, and black. I was truly fascinated by his sense of style, and sexual prowess as a thug lover.

He'd told me to make myself comfortable. He just didn't know how much so. I was going to milk him dry.

I walked around his large sleeping chamber, taking in all of the beautiful art work strategically mounted along his walls. He had naked men entangled in all types of positions. Some just nude, others racy. He even had a wide selection of gay porn. I knew his boys didn't know he had a side like this to him. Then again, who knows how many of his boys probably participated in this lifestyle?

He was still naked when he came back in the room with wine flutes and fruit on a platter, his dick swinging from side to side like an elephant's trunk. I was again aroused just by the sight, as I lay spread out in his king-size bed on the softest sheets I had ever laid on.

He eased his way on to the bed, smiling from ear to ear. He picked up his remote control from the nightstand beside the bed and chimed on his wall-mounted digital music player, which was next to his plasma television.

Aaliyah's "One in a Million" serenaded us as he slowly fed me. The song was one of my favorites, and I truly knew I was one in a million. Nobody could tell me different.

After we finished off the fruit tray, our refreshed bodies once again became inseparable magnets. I then pleasured him like only I could.

I should have gotten the "Nobel Piece Prize," because I knew how to milk a nigga's piece dry. After I made him cum on my face. He then bent over, pushing his ass as high in the air as it could go.

That's what the fuck I'm talking about. I love a brotha who could give it good and take it even better. My dick wasn't as big as his, but I could tell he was enjoying himself, from the way he moaned and groaned, telling me not to stop.

We again collapsed on the bed and snuggled as he held me from behind. As we both drifted off to sleep, I could smell the sweet faint fragrance of sandalwood on his pillows. He had every base covered. I loved it.

I woke up to an empty bed. I looked around the room for a clock and noticed it was going on eight o clock in the evening. Wallace was gone, and there was a note on the pillow where his head once was.

Yo, James.

I went to take care of some business. Holla at you later. I left you your own key and the password to the gate to get in when you want. I enjoyed your presence today and hope to have many more experiences with you. Oh, and I left you some spending money just in case you want to buy yourself something. Here's my cell phone number if I don't make it back before you leave.

443-228-7965.
One.
Wallace.

"Got me another one," I said to myself. *Once again, this shit is too easy.* I made my way to the bathroom and showered.

I got dressed and made my way to my car. I couldn't believe he would trust me this fast—money, keys, passwords, all of it in record time. I was like fine wine. Getting better with age.

Wallace had left me four grand on the nightstand. I almost felt like a whore. *Nah. Whores don't get paid this good. And they damn sure don't look this good.*

Before I left I noticed the duffle bag he'd brought in still in the same place where he'd left it when we came in. I was tempted to check its contents, but my better judgment told me to leave it be. I wasn't nobody's dummy. Wallace's ass could be recording my every movement. And this could be a test to see if I was trustworthy or not. *It would behoove me to be content with what I have for now. I'm sure there would be other times when I could get more money out of him.*

I made my way toward my home in a hurry because I knew my cats needed to be fed. I also needed to call Carl and check in with him, just to keep him happy. My job was never done.

Chapter 18

Shawn

A Pleasant Surprise
November 8th, 2018, 12:34 P.M.

I guess I was supposed to be sad and distraught right about now but I just couldn't get to that place yet. I embraced my mom tightly in the middle of my dad's grotesque apartment. The news of his death had hit her hard. I, on the other hand, was in another place. I was kind of glad he was gone. I felt like a burden had been lifted off of me.

"It's gonna be okay, Mom," I said, looking at her in the face. Tears continued to stream down her face. She shook with unrecognized emotion as I held her as tightly as I could. My mom had forgiven my father a lot faster than I did. If I did. I still didn't know. I didn't know how or why she forgave him after all he put us through.

I had called in a favor to the police chief of Baltimore City, and he granted me permission, but under police surveillance only. The police didn't allow us to touch anything, but from the looks of the place, I can say that my father was a total slob. He must have totally fell off after my mom put him out.

When we first came in, we went into the bedroom, which was the scene of the crime. My mom altogether lost it as she saw blood splattered on the walls. She immediately ran out of the room crying and hollering. The only reason we were in the apartment was because my mom and I both wanted to see the condition my father was living in. She really hadn't seen him in the ten years they had been separated.

I told my mom to go stand in the hallway and wait until I got there. I stayed around just to get a better look at the crime scene. Being a criminal lawyer, I knew a little about what to look for in a crime scene.

I was interrupted by the phone ringing. *Ring, ring, ring!*

"Hello," I said, wondering who was calling for my father.

"Hey, Shawn," James said with glee in his voice "What a pleasant surprise. I didn't expect to hear from you. Especially at your father's house."

"Muthafucka, you ain't gonna get away with this shit, you hear me!"

"Shawn, baby, what are you talking about?" he said, confusion in his voice.

James was playing dumb, and I knew it.

"Look, bastard, stop calling me baby. And you know what the fuck I'm talking about, bitch."

"Shawn, I'm not going to be too many more of your bitches, okay," he said, losing his cool as well. "What the fuck are you talking about?"

"My father is dead, muthafucka, and I know you had something to do with it." I was heated, but not about my father's death. It seemed like whenever this bastard popped up, he brought some drama with him, and I was simply tired of his shit.

"What?" he said, like this was the first he had heard of this news. "Your father ain't dead. I was just with him the other day. And, besides, I would have heard about it because . . ."

"James, why would I be lying about some serious shit like

this?" I was now pacing the living room floor with one of my hands on my hip. "So you saying you didn't have anything to do with my father's death?"

"Shawn, you ain't talking to no damn dummy. I would have to be one stupid ass to be calling the house of a man that I murdered. Give me some kind of credit. Damn!"

"All I am saying is, you better have a solid-ass alibi for last night, because I will be sure to mention your name to the police." I was now smiling because I knew I had him where I wanted him, for a change. He wasn't talking, but I was sure he was searching his mind for one that I knew he didn't have.

"Oh, believe me, I do," he said with confidence. "And the next time we talk, please be ready to apologize."

"Whatever, man."

"Whatever too, Shawn!" he snapped back. "Do whatever! Just spell my name right, bitch!" *Click!*

I was steaming mad, but nevertheless, I exited my father's apartment, consoled my mom once again, and then we made our way down to the car so I could drive her home.

"You okay, baby?" she asked as I got in and buckled my seatbelt.

I'd coached myself on not letting my emotions show when I got to the car, but she was my mom. And mothers could tell when something was wrong with their children even when we try our hardest to hide it and keep our heads held high.

"Yes, ma'am," I said, placing the car in drive and pulling off. "I'm just fine."

"Shawn, baby," she patted me on the leg as we were stopped at a light. "You know it's all right to cry, son."

"I know, Ma." I wouldn't even turn my head to look at her in the face, for I knew if I did, I surely would break down in the car. She'd always had that effect on me. "I'll be all right."

"Yes, you will, son," she said as she reached for the volume button on the radio and turned it up.

"Goin' up Yonder" by Tramaine Hawkins was playing, and she hummed and rocked as we drove up Route 40, headed toward her house.

After I dropped my mom back off home, I made my way back downtown to the Baltimore City Central District Police Precinct to look at the pictures of the crime scene. I checked in my credentials at the front desk, where the detective on the case met me. He escorted me to his office to begin filling me in on my father's murder.

We entered his office, and I sat down across from this burly, black man that had to be around the same age as me. He leaned back in his chair, his hands behind his head, and began to speak.

"Well, Mr. Black, I first want to convey my condolences for the death of your father. I know this won't be easy to talk about, but I need any information you can give me on the people or person that may have wanted to harm your father."

"Well," I said, hesitating a little, "my father did have a lover that was living with him. I don't think he killed him, but he may know who did." Even after all that James put me through, I still felt a little sorry for him.

"Oh, really," the detective said, now sitting in straight posture, giving me his full attention.

"His name is James Park. I don't know where he lives now, but I know he does still live here in Baltimore," I said, now smiling a little. "Oh, and he does have a record, so that should make it easier too."

"Yes, indeed. That would greatly help."

"Is there any way I could see the pictures of the crime scene?"

"Look, it's against procedure to let anyone this close to the victim see these pictures, but I will in this case. He handed me the case folder that held the pictures and other evidence pertaining to the case.

I then leaned back in my chair and proceeded to review the snapshots of my father's gruesome murder. The first picture almost knocked me out of my chair. To say that my father's body had been totally mutilated would be an understatement. The murderer had carved the word *faggot* into his chest.

The second picture showed the disfigurement of his face. His lips and eye lids looked like they were cut off with a scissors of some sort. The next picture showed a bat pushed far up his anal cavity.

I turned away slightly as my stomach churned with nausea from the next photo, which showed his genital area had been cut clean from his body and was hanging from the ceiling like a mistletoe ornament. This was definitely going to be a closed-casket funeral.

I returned the folder to the detective and made my way out of the precinct and disturbingly wandered home, pulling over a few times mid-trip to throw up.

The pictures flashed in and out of my head as I made the trip home. As bad as my father was, he still didn't deserve to die in such a manner. I didn't know if James had anything to do with it, but it was all going to come out in the end.

Chapter 19

Ashley

All-About-Me Syndrome
November 11ᵗʰ, 2018, 5:30 P.M.

The news of my grandfather being murdered didn't bother me one bit. I was in my own world and could care less about his wrinkled, old ass. I was sixteen, and I had my own life to live. He lived his shit, and I was definitely going to live mine.

The funeral was going to be in two days, and I was wracking my brain, trying to find an excuse to get out of going to it. Tony and I had plans for that day, so I wasn't trying to hear no shit about no old dude's life. People crying and carrying on made me sick. I was like, *Man up, and stop all that crying shit.*

Tony planned on taking me on a trip to New York, to get away from dry-ass Maryland. I was pretty sure Tony was going to have a lot of money to spend on me. I needed all the new outfits and shoes I was going to get, so I couldn't turn that shit down for no funeral.

Plus, we planned on getting a hotel room in one of the expensive hotels like the Waldorf or some shit like that, so we could fuck till we fainted. Ever since Tony had given me that bomb-ass orgasm in the back of the car, I was like an addict chasing that first high. I had to get out of this shit somehow. I just had to figure it out.

I walked out of my room and down the steps toward the dining room, where my mother and grandmother were sitting at the table, putting the finishing touches on my grandfather's funeral. I walked through the room and put on the best about-to-get-sick act I possibly could. I was going to get an Oscar for the scene I was about to put on.

Cough! Cough! I tried my best to sound convincing without overdoing it. "Hey, Ma." I kissed her on the cheek. *Cough!* "Hey, Gran," I said as I slowly hugged and kissed her on the cheek as well.

"Hey, baby," she said with a bright smile.

I loved my grandmother. She was a mean cook and always so attentive to her grandchildren. I hated to pull this fast one on her, but I gotta do me.

"You okay, baby? It sounds like you coming down with something."

Cough! "Oh, nah, Gran. It's nothing but a little cough. It will probably go away in a couple of days." I wanted to scream, "Yes" but I held it in. My plan was now in full effect, and I was going to milk this one for all it was worth.

It was Saturday morning, and everybody was getting dressed for the funeral. I was still in the bed, putting on the best "deathbed" act I could muster. I hacked so loud that even I thought I was sick.

"Ashley, what's going on in here? It sounds like you about to cough up a lung in here." My mom walked over to me and began to check me for a high fever. "You don't have a fever."

"Really?" I said, a look of distress covering my face. I quickly grabbed my mouth and darted for the bathroom and closed the door. I stuck my finger down my throat and vomited up my dinner from the night before. I wiped my mouth and headed back toward my room.

"Are you okay?"

My mom trailed behind me with the look of worry on her face. She was making this easy.

I leaned up against the wall halfway back to my room, pretending to be too weak to finish the short journey back, and she assisted me as I slowly crept in my bed.

"Mom, I—I don't think I can make it to Granddaddy's funeral," I said with the most pitiful face I could muster.

"I wasn't going to let you go even if you tried, with the condition you're in." She tucked me into bed as if I was a toddler again.

"Mom, please tell Dad I'm sorry I missed Granddaddy's funeral." Everything in me was screaming, "Suckers!" I sealed the deal with a trivial request. "Can you bring me back a flower and obituary, since I can't make it?"

"Sure, baby, whatever you want." Mom turned and made her way toward my door. Then she turned around, ruining my plans with this one last statement. "We will be gone for most of the day, but I will be calling the house to check up on you."

Shit. Shit. Shit. Shit. "Okay, Mom." I was truly pissed. I wasn't expecting this shit. I guess I was going to have to change my and Tony's plans.

Everybody was gone, and I had the house to myself. I called Tony with the change of plans. I decided, since my family was going to be gone most of the day, that I would invite Tony over, so we could enjoy ourselves in privacy.

What I didn't expect was my father to come back earlier than expected. Luckily Tony and I were in the living room watching movies before we decided to have sex, because that shit would have been hard to explain to my father. His image of his chaste, loving daughter would've been shattered if he'd caught me having sex in his house.

"Hey, Dad." I quickly jumped to the other chair in the room as I heard his keys opening the door.

"Hey, pumpkin," he said, looking at Tony.

I assumed he was waiting on me to explain the unknown visitor.

"I thought you weren't feeling well."

"Oh, Dad, this is Tony."

Tony got up and shook my dad's hand.

"Tony had called to check up on me and came over to bring me some ginger ale and saltine crackers for my stomach."

"Oh, okay," he said with a look of tiredness on his face. "Nice to finally meet you."

When Tony first started calling the house for me, I had told my father that Tony was my mentor for the mentorship my school was sponsoring. He had no idea we were being intimate.

My dad exited the room, and I assumed he was heading to his room to be alone. I quickly ushered Tony out of my house, just in case my father wanted to have a more in-depth conversation with us.

Knock! Knock! Knock!

"Come in," my dad called out.

"Hey, Dad." I walked in and noticed he was sprawled out on his back across the bed facing me. His face was wet with what probably was tears. "You okay, Dad?"

"I'll be okay, baby girl," he said, sounding exhausted and worn. "Just going through some stuff."

I walked over and sat down on the bed next to him. He looked up at me with a faint smile. He wasn't fooling me. I knew he was hurt that Grandpa was dead.

"I know you hurting, Dad." I rubbed his hair, hoping it would relieve some of the hurt. "I'ma miss Grandpa, too."

I scooted over some more and placed his head on my lap and brushed his hair some more. His tears flowed freely. Seeing him this way made me tear up as well.

"All you have to do is remember the good times you and Grandpa had, and it won't hurt as much."

I was feeling bad now for not going to the funeral. I was nothing like my father. He was caring, and he loved to share whatever he had. I, on the other hand, was selfish and sneaky. I was crying harder now.

"Sorry, baby girl," my dad said in a voice a little higher than a whisper. "I got you in here crying like a baby."

He wiped my tears with the back of his hand as he sat up next to me. He put his arm around my shoulder, and I laid my head on his shoulder. I was a daddy's girl indeed.

"You feeling better, I see." He smiled harder this time.

"Dad, you always make feel good." I smiled. "You're my favorite daddy."

He looked at me like he had seen a ghost.

"Why you look at me like that, Daddy?" I was confused.

"Oh, ah, sorry, pumpkin," he said, shaking his head and rubbing his temples. "You saying that reminded me of something I forgot to do at work."

"Oh, okay, Dad." I smiled. "I thought you was seeing dead people or something." I playfully hit him on his leg, and we both chuckled a little.

"Hey, pumpkin, how about you and I go downstairs and fix us something to eat? Daddy's gonna make you some of his favorite banana pancakes."

"Really?"

"Yep. So go down and get the kitchen ready. I'll be down after I wash my face."

I zoomed down the steps and was in the kitchen in seconds. I loved spending time with Dad, and he always made time for just us.

Chapter 20

Mona

I sat in the front row of the funeral parlor with Alex, Diana, and Mrs. Black. I was a little worried about Ashley being home sick and alone. Shawn had made his exit before the service even started. I knew he was going home, and he and Ashley would be home together, which put my worries to rest.

I knew this would be too hard for Shawn to bear, even with him reconciling with his father only weeks earlier. I could understand, and I didn't even try and stop him from leaving.

I held on to Mother Black, who softly sobbed as the mourners passed the closed casket, touching it and whispering sweet prayers. Despite their tumultuous marriage, she still held her head up proud and free. I was so proud of her.

The parlor was almost filled to capacity, and I was a little shocked at the turnout. I guess people really didn't care about Carl's faults. There were a couple of old faggots in the bunch, which wasn't a surprise to me, but seeing my gynecologist, Dr. Grant, sitting in the pews definitely was. I wondered how he knew Shawn's father, and made a mental note to check in on that later on.

After a couple of sorrowful solos and hymns, a string of people got up and spoke about Carl Black's life.

Just then, public enemy number one, James Parks, waltzed down the aisle in all black like he owned it. All eyes were on him as he made his way to the coffin.

What in the hell? When the fuck did he get out? And does Shawn know he is out? He probably didn't because, if he did, then he would have told me. Or would he? Shit. I just can't shake this muthufucka. All I know is, his ass better stay away from me if he knows what's good for him.

I can't believe I fucked his crazy ass. Twice. In California when I was burying my uncle and then again on my living room floor. I still can't believe that shit, with my whoring ass.

I was broken out of my trance when James's whimpers of sorrow escalated to loud moans. He went all the way Hollywood. He even had the nerve to open the casket. He moaned and sobbed loudly as he leaned in and kissed Carl's corpse.

People gasped all over when he kissed Carl's cold, dead body. I was pissed that they didn't superglue that shit closed. I was going to talk to Momma Black about this mess after service.

James then walked toward the podium to let us know what Carl meant to him. Though noticeably older, he was still handsome in the face.

My mouth gaped opened during his entire spiel. He ranted and raved on and on about how Carl was his all and all, that he couldn't live without him. Momma Black too was shocked and appalled with his over-the-top display of grief.

Finally, James came over to me and Carl's wife with his condolences and made his exit as quickly as he had come in. I breathed a sigh of relief, hoping this was the last time we would be seeing him again. But I knew his ass would pop up again sooner or later.

After the service concluded, everyone headed to Lou-don Cemetery for the interment. Thankfully, James didn't show his face.

On the way back to Mother Black's house for the repast, the car was completely silent. Mother Black was in the passenger seat as I drove toward her house.

"Hey, Ma," Alex yelled from the back of the car. "That dude was straight crazy." He chuckled. "You woulda thought him and Grandpa was dating or something." He laughed again. "He was a straight faggot."

"Alex, don't talk about your"—I caught myself before I said something I didn't want to deal with yet.

Mother Black stepped in, saving me from disaster. "Alex, baby, that man was just a close friend of your grandfather. That's all. Some people get really emotional when they lose someone close to them."

I don't know about that emotional shit. James is a pain in the ass, and as far as I am concerned, he has no emotions. That bastard was just there to torture our family again. It's like he feeds off drama. I wish his ass would leave us the fuck alone.

I also wondered how Alex acted like he hated gay men when he too had that same demon riding him as well? It's amazing how men can cover that shit up and dress it up to look like it's not what it really is.

I prayed every day that Alex wouldn't take the same road that his "two fathers" took, and I lay on the altar every Sunday praying that the men in my family would be spared from their homosexual demons.

Please, God, help them!

Chapter 21

James

Getting Cranky
November 13th, 2018, 2:03 P.M.

I just left the Betts Funeral Parlor and was walking to my car, giddy as shit. I had everybody in that muthafuckin' joint eyes on me. I knew they'd be talking about that shit for weeks. I got in my car and was getting ready to pull off when my phone began to ring.

"Hello? Hello? Hello?"

No response.

"Stop calling me, bitch, if you not going to say anything. Coward-ass muthafucka!"

I was fuming hot. I had been getting crank calls for the past couple of days, and the shit was getting on my nerves. Whoever it was blocked out their number so they couldn't be traced.

Ring, ring, ring!

I answered the phone with an attitude. "Hello."

"Bitch, you're next," a muffled voice yelled into the phone. *Click!*

I stared at the phone in disbelief. I just shrugged it off. Somebody was sure mad at me, but I could have given a fuck. It was probably some bitch pissed off that I had fucked her man or some shit like that. There was always a hater in the bunch. Cunts be hating me because their man be hanging round me like a cat to a can of tuna. Like I always say, "You fucked after I fuck him, because he ain't coming home after he had a taste of my lovin'."

Ring, ring, ring!

I looked at the phone and smiled. It was my first love. My momma. "Hey, Ma."

"Hey, baby," she said, her voice a little on the weak side. "*Cough, cough, cough!* How's mama's baby? Is my Jerry being good? When was you going to call your old mama?"

"Mama, you're not old." I sighed. Hearing her say that just melted me. My biggest fear was losing her. She was my everything. "I have been meaning to call you, Mama. I was just trying to get myself situated and all. I'm sorry, Mama."

"No need to apologize, baby. *Cough, cough, cough!* Mama knows you be busy."

"Mama, is everything okay? You sound like you are sick, Mama."

Mama was up there in age, and she was a smoker too. Having to take on so much with being a single mom and working two jobs all the time contributed to a lot of stress.

"Well, Jerry, baby." She hacked a couple of times and started to wheeze a bit. "Them doctors at the Mercy Liberty Hospital says I gots me that lung cancer going on. I got a few months to live, at the most, six."

I sank down in my seat and slumped over. I couldn't grasp what she was telling me. I couldn't be hearing this. I put the phone down for a second and let the tears flow. I was like a baby in need of tender care.

"Mama, *sniff, sniff,* Mama, *sniff,* Mama, are you sure? I mean, what did they say?"

"Well, baby, I've been feeling out of breath the last couple of weeks, and I knew something just wasn't right. So I went to them white folk over at the hospital, and they ran some test and gave me the results about two weeks ago."

"Mama, you shoulda told me right away." I sobbed some more.

All the past years of foolishness came to my mind. I'd wasted so much time trying to get even and spending time in jail, I missed the time I was supposed to be spending with her. *What kind of son am I? I should've been home and taking care of my mother instead of fooling around.*

"Baby, you had your own problems and your own life. Jesus has it all in control, baby." Mama went into another coughing fit, which sounded as if it was getting worse by the minute.

The words *your own problems* echoed in my ear like I was in an enclosed room. I was selfish and angry—Those were my only problems—and I let them rule and ruin my life.

"Hold on one sec, Mama." I fell forward onto the steering wheel and cried some more. A heavy, uncontrollable cry. After a few seconds I got back on the phone with her.

"Jerry, I gots to take this medicine them doctors gave me." Mama went into another coughing fit. "I'll give you a call back later on. I need to take a nap too."

"All right, Mama. I'll call you later. I promise." I hung up the phone and started my car, whimpering the whole time.

First, a stalker, and now the news of Mama being sick. I needed to slow down. Things were starting to get to me.

I pulled off the parking lot and made my way toward Wallace's house. I had to admit, he was a good lover and a helluva fucker. I enjoyed spending time with him. I truly didn't deserve someone like him. I was just wondering how I fell for this nigga so fast. It'd only been a couple of days, and we were all over each other most of the time. It had always been this way with me. I fell in love easily. I got attached to people too easily, and then they always ended up handing my heart back to me cut into pieces.

I decided to give him a call and see if we could set up a play date or something.

"Hey, baby," Wallace said, his voice sending chills all over my body.

I could picture his hot sweating body as he spoke through the phone. "I was wondering if we could hang out at your spot today." Yeah, I was falling for this nigga, and my ass knew better than to trust a no-good man. They all dogs, whether they gay or not.

"I'ma be out here on the block for a minute, so you go ahead and let yourself in the apartment. I'll be home, and we can play house when I get there."

"Oh, okay," I said a little disappointed. "I can't wait, baby."

"Muthafucka, I said wait!" he yelled into the phone.

"Excuse me?" I said, a little thrown off.

"No, not you, baby," he said to me now in a calm tone. "These muthafuckin' crackheads is pushy as shit. I'ma holla at you later."

"All right, baby," I cooed into the phone.

I still couldn't believe he was so tender and calm when we were alone. I placed my phone on the passenger seat and proceeded to make my way toward Wallace's house.

As I was driving, I was listening to one of my favorite singers, Jennifer Hudson, rock her classic song, "Spotlight." It was old, but I was loving it.

I felt so free and happy, knowing I was finally getting a good man. My ass should've known better, from the first bastard that screwed me over, but I was going to take a chance on

Wallace. Still, I was going to keep my eyes open, just in case this nigga tried to flip the script on me. You know what they say, Believe half of what you hear, and none of what you see.

I hopped on I-695, cruising to the sweet melodies playing in the car, thoughts of affection and adoration playing in my mind.

Wham! Wham!

"What the fuck?" I yelled, turning around as a truck behind me slammed in the back of my SUV with tremendous force. The truck behind me was tinted, and I couldn't see who was driving.

Wham! Wham!

The driver slammed into the back of my car again, causing my car to swerve.

I gripped the steering wheel and tried to maneuver myself back into a good position. My temperature raised. Whoever was behind me was surely trying to harm me. Cars passed me by ignoring the fact that a crazy muthafucka was purposely trying to take me out. That's Baltimore for you. These nosy-ass people were watching this bastard try to kill me, and they did nothing. I tried to speed up to get away, but my assailant sped up right along with me.

Wham! Wham!

This time my car went careening across two lanes, and I barely missed a semi-truck by inches.

I tried to reach my phone, which was on the floor of the passenger seat, and not crash into anything. Luckily, just as I reached for my phone and positioned myself upright, the SUV pulled off at an exit, leaving me distraught and fearful.

I pulled over to the side of the road in the emergency lane to get myself together. I just couldn't believe this was happening to me. Well, it wasn't like I didn't deserve it. My ass was definitely not in denial. I just didn't need this shit right now. I rested my head on the steering wheel and breathed a sigh of relief for escaping with my life intact.

My mind flashed to Shawn and his promise to get me for murdering his father. The truth was, I didn't murder his father and didn't know who did. How did they know my number? Were they following me? I didn't have answers to none of my questions. I know I had fucked over a lot of people in my past, and all of them had a reason to want to hurt me, but I just couldn't figure out who.

I got out of my car and walked around to the bumper to see the damage inflicted on my car. "Muthafuckin' coward-ass bastard!"

My shit was royally fucked up, and it was going to cost a grip to get it fixed. I stormed back to the front of my car and got in. I reclined my chair back and closed my eyes as a single tear slid down my cheek. I was more angry at myself for letting this shit get to me than at the damage to my car.

After about another ten minutes of resting, I cautiously got back on the road and proceeded toward Wallace's house. I almost didn't go because I wasn't sure if the person was still following me. I wasn't a punk bitch, so I pressed my way and decided that whoever was trying to take me out was going to have to bring it and bring it hard.

I pulled up to Wallace's place about fifteen minutes later and hurried my ass indoors. A little apprehensive about this stalker shit, I wished the coward would have just come to me and meet me face to face.

Anyway, I walked straight to the kitchen and pulled me out a bottle of champagne, the name of which I couldn't even pronounce. I downed about three glasses as I lounged in the huge spa-type tub with candles flickering all around me. I had Anita Baker playing on the entertainment center.

My mind drifted off to my checkered past and the next person on my shit list. Keisha must've been thinking her ass got away with what she did to me, but I was gonna pounce when she least expected it. Her ass probably knew I was out of jail, but was too wrapped up in her life to give a rat's ass about my whereabouts. *Her ass won't forget me when I come at her. I'm gonna leave a lasting impression, for sure.*

I got out of the tub after finalizing my plans of revenge and went to the bedroom to watch me a flick and wait for Wallace to come home. I ended up falling asleep totally nude.

I was awakened by Wallace licking my inner thigh. "Ahh," I cooed as he made his way up my chest and then to my neck and lips. *Folgers coffee ain't got nothing on this.* I liked to be awakened by a man suckling on my various body parts. I moaned and panted as he licked the outer rim of my ear, making me tingle and twitch with pleasure.

He was naked, and his dick was rubbing up against me as he continued to lick me down. Then he started deep-throating my meat like a pudding pop.

"Right there, baby. Shit! Gotdamn!"

I grabbed his head and pushed it down, jamming my meat down his throat, lifting my hips off the bed to make sure he took it all in. He was moaning. I was moaning. And I could see him tugging at his own meat at the same time.

He pulled off and walked over to the dresser and pulled out a condom. He seductively walked back over to me, got down on his knees, as I was now sitting on the edge of the bed. He unwrapped the condom and slowly placed it on my dick with his mouth.

"Ahh, yeah," I moaned.

He pushed me back on the bed aggressively. "You ready?" he said, looking me in the eyes, placing my dick at his awaiting asshole. Then he slowly eased down, taking me in all the way.

His dick was now hard and slapping against my stomach with every thrust. He quickened his pace as I jerked his dick. He was a pro, and he was putting his ass on me better than I'd ever had it.

The bed shook and squeaked as I flipped him over and fucked him with his legs on my shoulder, pounding him with all of my might. Both drenched in sweat, we climaxed at the same time. Collapsing side by side, we struggled to get our breaths once again.

We woke up about an hour or so later to replenish our famished bodies. Wallace could burn in the kitchen, which was no surprise to me, because he was so good at everything else.

I still couldn't find any flaws in him, though I knew he had some. I just didn't know what they were. He was a loud snorer, but that wasn't what I considered a character flaw.

I sat at the table with a plate of shrimp and fettuccini and a side of steamed vegetables, totally trying to figure this dude out. He was so good to me. Almost too good.

"Hey, baby." He looked at me from across the table. He had a napkin in his collar, to protect his designer sleepwear. He was so adorable, I almost couldn't stand it.

"I saw your bumper was smashed in when I pulled in. What happened?"

"Some crazy muthafucka wasn't paying attention when I was driving here, and crashed into the back of my car." I lied, not too sure how he would handle me telling him about somebody being after me for some shit I did in my past. I also felt, the less he knew about my past, the better. He didn't need to know about all that. So I screwed over a couple of people. Who didn't?

"Whoever it was hit my shit and sped off like a bat in hell. I didn't bother calling the police because I knew it would be a waste of time, because whoever it was probably didn't have any insurance."

"Oh, okay," he said, a smile on his face.

"Why you smiling?" I wasn't sure if he was smiling at my misfortune, or if he could tell I was lying.

"Well, I'm not happy this happened to you. It's just that I was going to surprise you and give you my new car and buy me another one." He was now up and cleaning off our empty dishes, loading them up into the dishwasher.

I peeked at his nice ass as he bent over.

"How would you like that?" He came over to me as I was getting up out of the chair, embraced me from the front, and passionately kissed me with his butter-soft lips. "I can't have my baby riding around in a beat-up ride."

My baby! I thought. This shit was moving too fast, but I had to say it just felt right here with him.

"Well, I guess—"

He placed his finger to my lips. "I won't accept no for an answer."

I thought Wallace was a bit possessive. Usually I normally didn't let any niggas dictate to me, but he did sound sincere. And his baby-soft lips pressed against mine made me melt.

"Oh, and one more thing." He pulled away from me.

I had an instant flashback of when Kenny had threatened me. I was hoping he wasn't another nutcase as well.

"I don't think it's best for you to be living across town when you can be living here. So I was hoping you would move in with me . . . if that's okay with you."

Before I could blink, I had said yes, and asked him if my cats could come as well. He agreed, as long as they were de-clawed and neutered.

I drove home happy and elated that I was moving on up as The Jeffersons said it. I decided to keep my apartment as a precaution. I still had my plans that included the Black family and my children. I was just going to have to modify my revenge agenda a little.

When I got home, I checked my mail and saw that I'd received a letter requesting my presence at some kind of hearing for Carl Black's estate.

Chapter 22

Shawn

Thy Will Be Done
November 30th, 2018, 12:35 P.M.

It was the Thanksgiving holiday, and Mona, my mom, and I made our entrance into the office where my father's will was being read. I didn't have turkey on the brain either. I was wondering how all of this was going to affect me.

We walked into the mediation room and gathered into our seats. Mona and my mom had looks of sorrow on their faces. I, on the other hand, had a look of "Let's get this over with." I really could care less what my father left me. He had passed this homosexual demon to me. Now I was sitting here, my mind clouded with anger and resentment. I wanted the shit to be over and now.

"Hey, all," I heard out of nowhere.

I was broken out of my trance by none other than James Parks. I sat up straight and looked at Mona, and we both had the look of, "Not today" on our faces.

"I said, 'Hey, all,'" he repeated with a little more force.

Sometimes he seemed to be so gay, other times you just couldn't tell. There was united silence in the room as we all pretended he wasn't there.

"Well, fuck y'all too," he said with a happy-go-lucky look as he sat back in his chair and crossed his legs.

I was wondering why the mediator hadn't entered the room yet. I wanted out of here fast.

I had to admit, knowing his ass was under investigation for my father's murder, James was holding up well. He looked good in his navy blue Gucci velour sweat suit though.

The bastard was sitting across from us glowing, not a hint of remorse on his face. He musta thought he was going to get away scot-free.

"So, Mona, baby, how are my kids?" he said, looking at her.

She just stared at him as if he wasn't there.

"I know they missed their father." He paused. "Oh that's right. They still think my old lover over here is their father."

I was fuming and ready to explode.

"Hey, Aunt Jemima." He snickered. "How you doing over there?"

I assumed he was talking to my mother. I wasn't going to let him sit here and degrade her right in front of me. "Look mutha—"

My mom put a finger over her mouth, cutting me off. "Don't pay him any mind, baby," she said, rubbing my back. "He's not worth it."

I hated that she could be so calm with this homewrecker sitting across from us. I wanted to . . . to . . . jump across the counter and kiss him square in the lips. His ass was turning me on, and I wanted him badly.

How in the hell can I hate someone and want to sex them at the same time?

It was official. I was crazy for even thinking about his ass in that way again. *After all that he put us through, I should be putting a hit out on his ass.*

The mediator walked in. "How is everybody this morning?" he said, all seriousness on his face.

My mother, Mona, and I just solemnly nodded, but James just had to be James.

"I'm doing fine, Mr. White-man, sir." He smiled and rocked in his chair. "And they should be too, because I brought sunshine to their dull little lives once again."

All of our mouths dropped open, except for the mediator's, who didn't look happy with the Mr. *White*-man comment at all.

"My name is Mr. Whitman."

"Whitman, *Whiteman*, potato, *patata*—That shit is all the same to me," he snickered.

Again the mediator didn't looked pleased.

"Can we get this show on the road? I got places to be, and people to do." He glared over at me and smiled.

Oh, man! His ass was pushing his luck!

After a couple seconds of shuffling his papers, Mr. Whitman got down to business. "First, I would like to convey my condolences to your family for your loss. Mr. Black was a great asset to his community and a well-loved man."

What the fuck? Asset to his community? Yeah. Fuckin' right! This muthafucka must be reading from some kind of script or something.

"Well, let's get right down to business. I'm going to be reading Carl Black's last will and testament: I, Carl Black, of sound mind and body, hereby leave my wife, Brenda Black, the property at 2356 Wilshire Lane. I leave to my only son, Shawn Black, my car note, mortuary cost, and other unpaid debts.

"What the fuck!" I yelled out loud banging my hands against the table and standing up in an outrage. My nose flared, I felt like I was going to breathe fire at any moment.

"Shawn, baby, let him finish," my mother said, standing with me.

Mona got up as well, trying to console me, but I was as done as a turkey on Thanksgiving Day.

I glanced over at James with disdain and pure hatred. "This is your muthafuckin' fault, bitch!" I yelled, pointing at him. I could care less that my mother was there at all. I couldn't believe this shit.

James just shook his head from side to side.

"Excuse me, Mr. Black, but I need to finish the will before I can close this case."

I looked over at the wrinkled-ass white man staring back at me. "Fuck you!"

He immediately lowered his head back down toward the will, waiting for me to finish.

"Baby, please." Mona wiped away a tear that slid down my face as I took my seat, my head lowered in defeat.

"Can I continue?" the mediator asked, a look of fear on his face.

My mom and Mona nodded in approval.

"Finally, I leave the love of my life, James Parks, my insurance policy cash valued at one hundred thousand dollars."

Before I knew it, I had jumped out of my chair and clear across the table on top of James, knocking him out of the chair and on to the floor. Amazingly, my mom and Mona stayed seated as I tried my best to strangle him. It was like they wanted me to beat his ass.

Two security guards rushed in and started pulling me off James.

"That's a good idea, Shawn. Give the white man something else to talk about us for," he said, getting up off the floor, and straightening up his appearance.

The guards ushered me outside, with Mona and my mom

trailing me. I was fuming. The rational me was gone. I wanted to kill my father again and bury James with him.

I walked to my car with a quick pace, not caring if my mom or wife caught up to me. I sat in my car as they got in and buckled themselves in.

I sped off and quickly dropped my mom off at her home. She kissed me on the cheek and told me to go home and rest. She said that God had it all under control and to leave it in His hands. I didn't disagree with her. I just didn't want to hear that at that moment. I wanted revenge now.

I pulled off and headed home to crawl into bed, hoping this all was a bad dream.

I was awakened in the middle of the night, groggy and hungover from the stress of my life. I lifted my head up to see Mona feverishly at work giving me a blowjob, bobbing up and down.

"Hey, baby," she said, lifting her head up as she noticed I was awake. "I was hoping this would make you feel better." She continued to work her mouth on my dick.

I sat up and lifted her up as well. I was fully awake now, ready to finish what she started. I unrobed, and so did she.

As we fondled each other, I immediately went to work on her breasts, trying to stuff both of them in my mouth at the same time.

She was laid out in the bed as I laid between her legs and sucked her breasts, making my way down to her womb. I was in need of this release, and I knew she was as well.

I let my tongue do the talking as I parted her pussy lips, and inserted my tongue, flickering at her clit. She moaned and panted as she arched her back as I pulled and tugged lightly on her clit in between my lips, licking it with my tongue at the same time.

Coming to an orgasm, her legs slammed against my head like they had lockjaw, causing me temporary dizziness.

I continued to work at her womb as she thrashed about, releasing her clit and inserting my tongue in her like I was trying to find gold.

She again clamped her legs around my head, coming in my mouth.

I swallowed and went back to work, flipping her over on all fours and proceeding to eat her out from behind. Her face was buried deep in a pillow as I pummeled her pussy, causing another violent orgasm to squirt me in the face.

I wiped off her juices and stroked my dick as I positioned myself behind her and slowly inserted myself.

We had been having sex regularly now, but tonight it felt different. Mona was moaning in ecstasy as if I had entered her for the first time.

I plunged harder and harder as I closed my eyes and moaned and howled her name. "Mona, umm, baby, you working this shit tonight," I yelled. "Oh, yeah, Mona. Oh, yeah. Oh, God! Yeah! That's it, Mona. That's it. Yeah, right there."

I was fucking her like crazy. She was yelling. I was yelling. It had to be the best sex we'd ever had.

"Oh, yeah! Oh, yeah! Fuck me, James!"

"What?" I paused, noticing she had yelled out that muthafucka's name. I jumped up ready to blow a fuse once again.

She just looked at me with fear and regret.

I slowly gathered my things and made my way down the stairs, headed for my office. I closed the door behind me and pushed my desk up against the door, blocking it from being opened.

Mona knocked on the door for at least an hour, but there

was no explaining calling out another man's name during sex. Especially James's.

I had no idea what to do, so I stayed away from everyone for as long as I possibly could. But I had to eat, bathe, and urinate, so that lasted all of six hours.

When I finally made an appearance, it was Saturday morning, and everyone was at the kitchen table eating break-fast.

"Hi, Daddy," Diana squealed as she ran up to me and hugged my waist.

I loved my kids, and even though I was going through a rough patch, I tried my best to keep the children out of it.

"Hey, Dad," Ashley and Alex both greeted me.

I retrieved some orange juice from the refrigerator and sat down at the table. I watched Mona as she busied herself around the kitchen. I knew she knew I was in the kitchen. I also knew she was afraid to look at me.

I couldn't help but wonder if she thought James was a better lover than I was, and how she would have reacted if I'd called out his name during sex.

"Mona, can I have a plate to eat?" I asked as she stood at the stove flipping pancakes.

She filled my plate and placed it in front of me, making sure not to look me in the eyes while doing so.

"Thanks, babe."

I decided to go ahead and forgive her. I couldn't let James continue to have a hold on my family any longer.

As soon as the kids cleared the kitchen, I made my way over to her and wrapped my arms around her waist. "Mona, forget about last night," I said as I sat my head on her shoulder. "I know it was a mistake. And I won't hold it against you."

Actually, I was feeling guilty as well. Me locking myself in my office for half the night was a front. I was mad at myself because I was thinking about James as I hit her off last night. I just wanted her to think it was all her, that I was totally over James. Which I wasn't.

She turned around with tears in her eyes and hugged me tightly as I held her back. I wasn't even sure whether I could really forgive her or was just pushing another issue under the rug.

Chapter 23

Mona

Sunday Service
December 2nd, 2018, 10:04 A.M.

It was another Sunday morning, and we were on our way to church. BHL (By His Love) Ministries was our home away from home. We had joined the church about five years ago and had been faithful members ever since. Many Sundays, I answered the altar call. Our family needed prayer, and I wasn't in denial about it. With secrets and lies still lurking about, it was truly going to take a miracle for us to survive.

We walked into the sanctuary and made a beeline to our favorite seats. Ashley had made her way to the choir loft, and Alex was a drummer with the band. Diana was too young to join anything as of yet, but I had a feeling she wanted to be on the choir with her big sister. She practically worshiped the ground Ashley walked on.

We had come in just as testimony service had begun. People shared their testimonies of faith and love, while others rejoiced at their victories.

I had to admit, I was a little jealous, because I wanted to share testimony. I was just too afraid of the people and their judging stares.

How could I share the scars of the fresh, painful wounds of my past? My husband was a recovering alcoholic and bisexual. And my children were fathered by the man my husband was sleeping with. Some Sundays I wanted to get up and tell it all and get it out of my system, but I was too ashamed and hurt. I just couldn't live with the looks on the face of my own family. I know there would be a day when I would have to, I just didn't want to believe the truth. It was too painful to bear.

Testimony time came and went as the praise and worship team and Pastor Jonathan Walker made their entrance into the sanctuary. This was a part of the service I loved and could always count on to get the pressures of life out of my mind. The praise team was headed by Malcolm Walker, the pastor's son, an anointed psalmist, I could see him being used by God in a greater magnitude one day.

As the singing began, I felt the spirit of God enter the room, and I was immediately enraptured by His presence. People began to move, and shouts of praise could be heard throughout the sanctuary. All of my pain and frustrations became tears that flooded my face. By the end of the singing and worship, I felt as if a weight had been lifted off me.

Offering time had past, and it was time for the choir to sing a selection. It was Ashley's turn at the mic. I was so elated to hear her sing. Their rendition of "Don't Take Your Joy Away" by Kirk Franklin brought the house into a high ruckus as praise turned into shouts, and those into speaking in tongues and running around the church.

I too couldn't contain my joy as I sprinted around the church a lap or two.

Diana and Shawn just looked in awe as I made my way back to my seat completely exhausted and spiritually filled.

The praise died down as the pastor made his way to the

altar and began to pray for the congregation. He went straight into the Word. His title for the sermon was, "The Truth Will Make You Free."

By the end of the service, I was convinced that, to get my family back in order, it had to be truth and honesty reigning in our household.

After the service ended, we socialized for about fifteen minutes or so and made our way back home.

Chapter 24

James

Moving on Up!
December 7ᵗʰ, 2018, 1:32 P.M.

I had moved most of my clothing out of my apartment and into Wallace's. Now I was on my way back to do some last-minute cleaning up, since I would still be leasing the place. I was looking into subleasing it, or just putting it on pause if me and Wallace didn't work out. Which I doubted, because he was, for lack of better words, perfect to me.

I pulled up to the parking lot and made my way to my building. I noticed someone sitting on the front steps, which was unusual. This was considered a good neighborhood, where people didn't congregate around the entrance of the building. As I walked up, I noticed the face but couldn't believe my eyes.

"Cousin!" she yelled out as she ran up to me and squeezed my neck.

My first thought was, *What the fuck is she doing here?* And the next was, *How in the hell did she find me?* I reluctantly hugged my cousin Sherry back and looked at the little boy who sat on the steps patiently waiting to be acknowledged.

"Hey, Sherry," I said dryly, backing up and taking a good look at her. She was older and looked a little worn for her age. She had to be at least forty, but she looked around forty-fiveish. "Long time no see."

"What in the he—I mean, what are you doing here?"

"Oh, I was in town, and I thought I would look you up to see how you are doing."

I looked at her like, *Bitch, please . . . your ass wants something.* I let her go on with this charade, just to see where she was going with this mess.

"Can I please use your bathroom? I really have to pee?"

"Um, excuse me, Sherry," I said, pointing to the young child sitting on the steps with their bags. "Are you going to explain to me who this is?"

"Oh, yeah, just as soon as I come out of the bathroom." She picked up the bags as I opened the door and walked up the stairs to my apartment.

The little boy just tagged along, extremely quiet and docile. As we entered my apartment, I told him to have a seat in the living room.

"You want something to drink?"

He nodded.

I walked in the kitchen to see what I had in the refrigerator. I didn't stay there much since meeting Wallace, so all I had was a couple cans of Pepsi left in a case I'd bought when I first moved in. I walked back into the living room just as Sherry was making her way out of the bathroom. She sat down on the sofa next to the boy, who I assumed was her son.

"So, Sherry, let's cut to the chase. What do you want?" I wasn't in the mood for her shit. I knew good and well that she didn't like me for sleeping with Shawn and messing up her chances with him. She didn't have a chance when I had my claws already in him, but what did she know? She was just another dumb cunt trying to hook somebody else's man.

"What do you mean, What do I want? I can't come by to see my cousin if I want to?" She smiled, showing her missing tooth.

Before I knew it, "Bitch, please!" had escaped my mouth, shutting her down instantly. "Sherry, I don't have time for this foolishness. Just get this shit over with so I can be about my business."

"Okay, okay," she said, looking down at the floor. "After I left town and went down to Atlanta, a couple of weeks passed and I became sick and I went and got tested. I was afraid that I had caught something from having sex with Shawn. We used a condom, but it broke during the time we had sex. It turns out that I didn't have anything, but I found out I was pregnant. I decided to keep the baby and raise him on my own. I was doing it at first, until I lost my job and had to move back to California with my mom. Up until now, I didn't want to bother with trying to get child support for Li'l Shawn. Times are rough now, so I decided I would come back to Baltimore to see if Shawn would help raise his son."

I looked at the little boy for a minute. He did have a strong resemblance to Shawn.

"I need a place to stay until I get in contact with Shawn so he can see his son and make arrangements for child support. Do you know if he still works at the same law firm?"

"Sherry, I have no idea where Shawn Black works. When I got out of jail, I decided not to look back and just to concentrate on my future." I lied intentionally. This broad didn't need to know all my business.

My mind started thinking of ways I could use her to help me get back at Shawn and Keisha. *Shit, I could kill two birds with one stone.*

"Sure, baby, you can stay here as long as you need to. All I ask is, whenever the time comes, to return the favor and be there for me."

"James, I have no problem with that. We're family, and I would do anything for you. All you have to do is ask."

I nodded my head. I had more evidence to manipulate Shawn with. Sherry didn't know it yet, but we were both about to get broke off. I was pretty sure that Shawn would pay handsomely to keep this shit hush-hush.

"Hey, Sherry, when you do find Shawn, let me know because I want to go down with you and make amends with him for the things I have done to him."

I left my extra set of keys and some money for them, so they could eat. I walked to my car giddy and as excited as I was when I'd first met Shawn in the parking garage.

When I got home Wallace was there. I was so turned-on and horny, I gave him back-to-back blowjobs.

Chapter 25

Sherry

Payback Is a Bitch
December 7th, 2018, 5:12 P.M.

"Hello," the distorted voice said over the phone. "Did you do what I told you to do?"

"Yeah, he fell for it! That lame-ass shit I was feeding him." I had a wicked smile on my face because my ass was gonna get some major payback for the shit Shawn and James took from me. Shawn was supposed to be my husband now ,and we were supposed to have a happy-ever-after life. "I'll call you back when I get all the details in order."

"Don't mess this shit up or try to mess me over. If you do, I will kill yo ass like I did the old man. Keep me posted." *Click.*

I hung up my phone and marveled at the plans I had before me. That faggot-ass James was going to get what was coming to him, and I was going to get broke off in the process.

Payback was a forty-year-old bitch, and I was taking no prisoners. I looked over at my son that was definitely Shawn's seed and smiled. He was my baby, and I loved him dearly. He was also my cash cow. Shawn was going to rue the day he fucked me over for James.

"Mama, I'm hungry," Li'l Shawn moaned as he sat down next to me on the couch.

"Okay, baby, let's go get something to eat." I had seen a 7-Eleven about a block away as the cab drive drove us down Liberty Road to the apartment complex.

As we walked up the street to the 7-Eleven, I looked at my little man and adored the miracle beside me. He was unplanned, but I never let him feel like he was a mistake.

I should have known going after a married man would have led me into trouble. Besides, I was the result of the same kind of relationship, but it wasn't my father who cheated. It was my mom. And I never really got to know my father. You see, he was a married man as well and already had a family, and I wasn't a part of it. I never knew the truth until I overheard my father (or who I thought was) and my mother arguing about money.

I heard him snarl through their bedroom door, "Go tell that nigga you fucked and cheated on me with to buy her some school clothes, since he's her real father!"

I heard my mother whimper and wail in pain. It was late, and I was supposed to be in bed sleeping and dreaming of sugarplums and stuff like that. Instead, I was a ten year old who just found out that my daddy wasn't really my daddy. He treated me with love and never said a word to my face about our true relationship.

I never mentioned that I knew the truth, until one day when my "daddy" had an operation to remove a brain tumor. It was just us three sitting in his hospital room days after his operation. I don't know why I picked a time such as that, but my emotions were getting the best of me, and I needed to hear it from both of them. I was seventeen and wanted to know the truth.

"Who's my real daddy?" I just blurted it out.

An immediate silence came over the room. They both looked at me with fear of this moment. I was sure they were trying to prolong it as long as possible. Shit, I was too.

"Sherry, baby, what are you talking about?" My mother looked at me with tears in both eyes threatening to fall. "This is your daddy lying right here."

"Candice! Candice!" my father called out. "It's time to tell the girl the truth. We can't hold on to this forever. You need to forgive yourself, because I already have forgiven you."

Tears streaked down my face as mother broke down the truth to me. With every detail she spoke, the more my heart crumbled into itty-bitty pieces. The truth is a painful thing, but I would've had it no other way, then or now.

That wasn't the best way to bring up a baby, because not having a relationship with both parents in your life can cause you to have an unbalanced life. I didn't want that for Li'l Shawn. I wasn't naïve in the least.

I knew I couldn't have Shawn for myself, and that I could no longer support our son on my own. I had put this off for long enough, and it was in Li'l Shawn's best interest to get to know his father. I was just benefiting in the process. I know it sounds like I was a scheming ho, but I had to look out for me as well as my son.

We walked in the 7-Eleven, and Li'l Shawn went berserk, grabbing packs of Doritos, Funyuns, Oreos, and other snacks. Plus, when we got to the counter, he ordered two big bites and a large Slurpee. He was a growing boy, and it showed.

I grabbed a couple of things to last us a couple of days and loaded them on to the counter. Our purchase came to about thirty dollars and I was not surprised. We both smiled as we walked out of the store and back toward the apartment to fill up and get some sleep.

I was awakened at about ten o'clock at night by a call from James. He was ready to cash in on his favor, and I wasn't happy at all with what he was asking me to do.

"Hello," I said, groggy as hell. Me and Li'l Shawn had eaten and laid down at about nine thirty.

"I need you to do something for me." James was vibrant, like he had just got some good loving.

"Already?" I was still half-asleep. I got up out of the bed and walked into the living room, so I wouldn't wake up Li'l Shawn.

"Yes, already, bit"—He stopped short of calling me out of my name. "So strap up yo bootstraps 'cuz you goin' in." He laughed.

"Okay." I huffed. "What you need me to?"

"I need you to get some info on someone of interest."

"For what?"

"Bitch, don't ask me about my business when you and your offspring are living up in my shit for free."

"Sorry."

"You sure is. I'm starting to wonder if we really family, with your dumb ass, getting pregnant by a nigga you ain't have no chance in getting. You didn't know what the hell you was doing, did you?"

"Uh—"

"Of course not. You ain't got nothing to show for it but a kid. No money, nothing. And you want me to help you get some money from Shawn to take care of his kid? You owe me big time, so listen up."

I didn't say anything, because he was right. I just listened to what he asked me to do.

"I need you to follow this chick around and see what she's up to. She's a lesbian, so you might have to do a little licking to get her close to you."

"Do what?" I belted out, but quickly covered my mouth.

"Bitch, you not deaf. You heard me."

"I—I—I don't know if I can do that." I wasn't a lesbian. I liked dick very much. I couldn't see me doing a chick. Even the thought sent shivers down my back.

"Oh, you will. Or your ass is on the street."

"What about Li'l Shawn? Who goin' to keep him while I'm doin' this . . . stuff?"

I was desperate. I needed help getting Shawn to pay child support illegally, because I wanted more than the state would give me if I went to court.

"I'll take him while you doing what you need to do for me and give him back when you're finished. And don't think you're going to try to get me by leaving out of town or some shit and sticking me with him, because you never know when my ass is going to be on your ass. I will drop his ass off at Child Protective Services in a heartbeat and think nothing of it."

"James, I would never do that."

"Yeah, okay."

He gave me the info I needed and hung up the phone.

The only reason I was doing it was because he'd promised me he could get me and him a nice piece of change from Shawn. His ass was crazy, and I knew it, but if anybody could do it, it was James.

I knew I was going to have to do some stuff that was completely out of character, even for me, but I was doing this for Li'l Shawn.

Chapter 26

Keisha

"Oh, excuse me." I'd accidentally bumped a lady as I pushed my cart down the cereal aisle in the crowded Shopper's Food Warehouse at Mondawmin Mall.

"Oh, no problem. This aisle is small as shit anyways," she said with a slight chuckle, showing her chipped tooth in her mouth. "It's always like this around the first of the month. Everybody gets their government checks around this time. And the Christmas holiday doesn't help either. I don't know why I can't remember to do my shopping in the middle of the month, like a normal person who works for a living."

"Girl, you ain't say nothing but a word," I said, pulling off in the direction of the deli. I wasn't that talkative. I had about thirty seconds of conversation in me before getting bored and walking away.

I had to hurry up anyway and get home and feed these kids. I was so glad they were old enough to fix their own food, I could dance.

***

Li'l Kenny and Jeremy were twelve and fourteen and were spitting images of their faggot-ass father. I still got pissed off every time I thought about Kenny's dick-lovin' ass. I was so glad he took the easy way out and took his life in prison. He was a waste of good dick anyway.

That's why I let his sister lick the pussy at night when he was on the town with his boys. Antoinette's ass sure could lick a pussy just right. She had my ass climbing the walls the very first time she fucked me. The best thing about Antoinette was that she wasn't one of those butch, man-lookalikes. She was as pretty and feminine as any other woman, but she was like a straight-up dude when it came to the bedroom skills. If her ass could have made me pregnant with her tongue, I swear I would have about fifty muthafuckin' kids right about now. That was just how good she was.

We didn't live together for the sake of my kids. I didn't tell them about their father, and I wasn't going to let them see their mother sleeping in the same bed hugged up with no woman. She had her own place, and I had mine, and when we wanted to do what we did, we made sure the kids were in school or spending the night over my parents' house.

I wasn't in love with her, but I did care for her greatly. We were supposed to be in a monogamous relationship, but I had this feeling that she was cheating on me. Her patterns were changing, and I noticed that she wasn't as attentive as she used to be. Her cell phone was switched to voice mail a lot more now, and whenever I did call her, she always had some lame excuse, like she had to baby-sit her sister's kids, or she wasn't feeling well and was just going to stay in the house and rest. I was hoping she wasn't, but all the signs were there. I wasn't going to have her deceive me like Kenny did.

***

I continued to walk around the corner as I went down my grocery list. I turned down the ice cream aisle and bumped into the same lady I'd collided with earlier.

"So we meet again," she said with a smile that went way past friendly. "It must be fate that we keep bumping into each other like this."

"Yeah. Mm-hmm," I said, an awkward smile on my face. I wasn't for this shit today. Nowadays I had women hitting on me just as much as men. I didn't mind, but today was just too much since I felt that Antoinette might be cheating on me.

I quickly maneuvered my cart around hers and made a beeline for the checkout lines. As I continued my route, I looked back and noticed the chick still eyeing me down like a Jell-O Pudding Pop. I quickly refocused my attention straight ahead and made my way through the maze of people, trying to find a short line and get the hell out of there.

I made my way out of the supermarket, trying to get to my car, and damn near ran an old lady over with my cart. I wasn't in the mood for another chick to be breathing down my neck. I had one I couldn't control. I definitely didn't need two.

I swiftly threw my bags in my car and got in, prepared to pull off and get home as quickly as possible. Just as I was about to pull out, the front of my car was blocked in by another vehicle. To my dismay, it was the lady that was getting fresh with me in the market. I sighed a breath of frustration. I looked at her as she got out of her car and walked over to mine.

Oh, shit! This bitch is crazy! was my first thought. I put my hands on my keys and grabbed my Mace that was attached to it, just in case this bitch was a mental patient escapee from Spring Grove.

"I was wondering if I could get your number, so I can call you sometime?"

I was in awe at the audacity this broad had. She hadn't

known me more than a couple of hot minutes, and she was already trying to get in my panties.

"Look, today ain't a good day for all that, so can you back your piece-a-shit of a car up so I can be gone?" I truly didn't care if I hurt her feelings at all.

"You's a fiesty one, ain't you?" she said with a smile.

I didn't see anything funny. I just wanted to get home and get in the bed.

"How about I give you mine, and you can decide to call me when you're ready to ride this ride?" She flickered her tongue.

I snatched the piece of paper with her number on it and watched as she jumped into her beat-up SUV and drove off. I unfolded the paper and looked at it—Sherry 589-4588. I didn't have any plans to call her, but I stuffed it in my pocketbook anyway, just in case. "You never know," I said, shrugging my shoulders and driving off.

Chapter 27

James

You Have a Right to Remain Silent
December 13th, 2018, 2:00 P.M.

I didn't think the bitch had it in her. She actually pulled that shit off. When I'd first asked her for the favor, she was like, "I don't lick no clit." I wanted to tell her tore-up ass, the way she looked, she should be accepting applications from anybody that would sleep with her, but I held back because she was family. I assured her that it would never get to that point, that I would make this payback as easy and as fast as possible. I needed her to string Keisha along until I had a definite solution of payback. I wanted Keisha to remember me for as long as she lived.

Right now, I was headed on my way down to the police department because I got a call from a detective saying he needed to talk to me about Carl Black's murder. I wasn't in the mood to be questioned. I didn't have anything to do with it, because I was somewhere else at the time.

I walked in the precinct. As usual, all eyes were on me as I made my way to the front desk and asked for the detective I was scheduled to see. I was told he would be out to get me shortly.

Just as I took a seat, my cell phone rang, and it was my baby on the phone. "Hey, Wallace, baby. How are you doing?" I said sweetly into the phone.

"Everything's good. I was calling to check on my shortie."

The bitch in me was like, *Awww*, but I kept that part of me inside. "I'm good. I'm out running some errands," I said, a huge smile on my face.

Again, I couldn't believe how attentive this dude was. I was still a little skeptical that his ass still didn't let any flaws show, but I was watching him closely to see if he had any.

"I can't wait to get home and show you how much I love you." Hearing those words come out of my mouth puzzled even me.

I noticed someone walking toward me, so I decided to cut our conversation short. I didn't need him in my business either. I liked my personal shit to be on lock. "Look, baby, I gotta call you back real quick. My momma's on the other line, and I need to talk to her about some things."

"Sure, boo. I'll see you in a li'l bit."

"James Parks?" The burly officer extended his hand out to shake mine.

I hesitantly shook his hand back because it looked like his fingers were sticky from eating donuts. At least that's what it looked like, but his ass could have been doing anything in his office, if you know what I mean.

We walked into his office, and to my surprise this dude had his shit together. He must have been a neat freak or something, because as soon as he entered his office, he began cleaning the doorknobs and chairs, like somebody had contaminated them.

I took a seat in front of his desk as he made his way to his file cabinet. I looked around the room and noticed a chalkboard with pictures of Carl's mangled flesh spread out across it. Whoever killed his ass did a number on him because from the look of the pictures, they had torn his lips off and other crazy-ass shit.

I immediately had flashbacks of the prank phone calls and the reckless driver that tried to take me out on 695. I cringed a little because this muthafucka was after me now, and I hadn't the foggiest idea who had that much hate toward me.

The only real person I could think of was Shawn, but could he have that much hate toward his father to do something so heinous to him? I mean, yeah, his father did abuse him as a child and turned on him to get my attention, but this was too far-gone. I just didn't know. Maybe he could have enough hate in his heart to want to kill his father and me. Nah!

"Mr. Parks?" the detective called out, waving his hand in front of my face, breaking me out of my trance. "Is everything okay?" he said, a concerned look on his face.

"Oh, ah, yeah. I'm fine. I was just thinking about some stuff, that's all."

"Do you know why I called you down here?" he said, looking me straight in the eyes.

He was looking all intense and shit, like he was accusing me of the crime right then and there. He was barking down the wrong tree, and I wasn't to be fucked with. If I had done that shit, they wouldn't have found Carl's old ass, because I would have done some Jeffrey Dahmer type shit and chopped his ass into little pieces.

"I have a couple of ideas, but I'ma let you tell me," I said, looking back at him just as intently. He was going to have to come harder than that to get my ass to talk.

He leaned back in his chair and massaged his chin like he was thinking about his next move. Again, he didn't know who he was fucking with.

"Do you know a Carl Black?"

"Well, he was a friend of mine, and we'd hang out from time to time. Why?"

"Well, he turned up dead a couple of weeks ago, and we found your fingerprints in his home." He sat up again like he had caught me red-handed.

"I have been over his residence from time to time, but it was only for the parties he was giving," I lied.

He again sat back in his chair, and this time he scratched his head, fishing for more things to ask.

"Look, Mr. Parks, let's stop bullshitting around. You and I both know that you and Carl Black were lovers. I have sufficient proof that includes phone records and other correspondences that back up my claims. You will need a rock-solid alibi to cover your whereabouts on the night of the murder. Otherwise, I'm going to order a warrant for your arrest in the murder of Carl Black."

"Fine." I looked at him and smiled because I had all the evidence I needed in my man-bag. Thank goodness I went to the hospital that night I'd mutilated my ex-boss, because my ass would've been up the river with no paddle. I reached into my bag and handed him a copy of my vaccinations for the bites I had on my arms from the cat that tried to take out a chunk of my arm. "Here you go."

He eyed down the piece of paper doing a couple of "huh hum's" and then looked up at me. "Well, this looks to be legit. I will still be calling the hospital to verify this."

I looked at him. *Whatever, man.* I reached down and got my things together to leave. I glanced down momentarily, making sure I didn't leave anything.

When I got up, the detective was already up and walking toward his door. I proceeded to do the same thing, but he quickly shut and locked his door.

"What the fuck is wrong now?" I said, looking at him with a mean mug.

"I'm going to need you to handle something for me."

I looked at him like he was crazy. "And what the fuck is that?"

He quickly unzipped his pants and exposed his rock-hard dick. I was a little shocked to say the least. The myth about fat men having little dicks was just that, a myth. This big muthafucka was packing.

"I heard about your services from some of the fellas that work here, and I was wondering if you could help a brotha out."

I looked at him as a smile crept across my face. I was like "what the hell" I got a little bit of time. I got down on my knees pulled a condom and did the damn thing.

After I sucked him off, I bent him over his desk and read him his rights.

"You have a right to remain silent." *Wham! Wham!*

"Anything you say can and will be used against you." *Wham! Wham!*

"You have a right to an attorney." *Wham! Wham!* "If you don't have one." *Wham!* "One will be appointed to you." *Wham! Wham!* "Do." *Wham!* "You." *Wham!* "Understand?" *Wham! Wham!*

He yelped out, "Yes!"

I finished punishing his ass and came on his back. Then I cleaned myself up and walked out of the precinct with yet another officer of the law under my belt.

I pulled up to Wallace's condo and quickly made my way to the shower. I had to wash the scent of sex off me before he got home. I knew for a fact that he would want to fuck when he got home, and I couldn't have another man's scent on me.

Just as I got in and out of the shower, Wallace was making his way in the front door. I breathed a sigh of relief, knowing I barely escaped an altercation. I jumped right into baby-I'm-glad-you-home mode. He didn't suspect a thing, or at least, he wasn't giving off any vibes like he knew something.

"Hey, Wallace, baby." I walked up to him as I walked out of the bathroom and down the hall to the foyer where he was placing his keys and another duffle bag. "My baby is tired?" I cooed slyly as he embraced me face to face. I pecked small kisses on his neatly groomed face.

"Umm, baby," he moaned. "That's what I like to come home to."

I sashayed away and let him get a good look at what he was missing all day. "Baby, if you get in the shower, by the time you get out, I'll have dinner ready for you, and then we can have some dessert by the fire."

"Sure, baby boy." Wallace slapped me on the ass as he walked by and went into the bathroom to start the shower.

I walked into the kitchen and grabbed two steaks out of the freezer, seasoned them, and threw them on our jumbo George Foreman Grill. I preheated the oven and then grabbed some pre-cut red potatoes out of the refrigerator and threw them in the oven, along with some green beans from a can. Wallace liked to take long showers, about twenty to twenty-five minutes, so I knew I had some time to make sure everything was hot for him, including me.

About fifteen minutes into preparing the meal, my cell phone began to ring. I looked at the caller ID, not prepared to talk to who was calling. I didn't not want to; I just wanted privacy when I did. I hesitantly pushed the talk button and answered the call.

"Hello," I said, adding a chipper, upbeat spark to my voice. Again, I didn't not want to talk to her. I was still shook from the news that she gave me about her sickness. I was ecstatic to hear her voice again, sick and all. I cleared my throat and spoke again. "Hey, Ma!"

"How's Mama's baby?" She coughed a couple of times.

Tears flowed from my eyes freely as the realization hit me again that she wasn't going to be around forever.

"Now, I thought you said you were going to call me back." She sounded a little heartbroken.

"Oh, ah, Ma, I've been meaning to call you," I said, cowering like a little boy.

I was fumbling with various things in the kitchen as I tried to keep my composure. I wasn't strong when it came to sickness and death.

"I'm sorry, Ma. I-I-I'm just trying to adjust to the news you gave me. I'm trying to come and see you. As soon as I get some stuff straight over here, I'm going to fly right out to be with you until, well, you know."

I couldn't even say it. She was dying, and I was worried about how I was going to feel. I gagged a couple of times, holding back vomit, because I had just pictured her in her casket. Cold, stiff, and dead. I wasn't ready to bury her or give her back to God.

In the few seconds of silence on the phone, I prayed to God to have mercy and spare my mama. I didn't pray much, but it was necessary for this situation.

"Baby, Mama lived her life. God has been good to me. It's just my time to go."

It was like she was dying right there on the phone.

"Mama, no!" I almost screamed. Tears and snot flowed freely. I was losing it I couldn't help but think this was payback for my malicious ways. This was the ultimate price. "You hold on, Mama. I'll be there soon. Real soon."

"I will, baby. Mama will." She hacked a couple more coughs. "Jerry, I'm over that. You never told me why you were locked up all them years."

I'd never really told my mother what had happened and why I'd ended up in jail for ten years. She had called me several times in jail and tried to pry it out of me, but I would immediately change the subject or fake like someone else urgently needed to use the phone. I just didn't think she could handle the truth. I was off the chain ever since I'd come to Maryland from California and still couldn't bring myself to let her know all about my life over here.

"I'm sorry, Mama. It's just complicated. Let's just say, I got mixed up with the wrong people, and things didn't work out for the best. I really don't want to bore you with the details. They're not flattering, but I'm better now. I have someone in my life that treats me right, and I'm looking forward to you meeting them really soon."

"So my baby found himself a man."

My mouth hit the floor. How did she know? "Huh?" was all that came out of my mouth.

"Yes, Mama knows." She giggled a little. "Jerry, you're my only baby. I know you inside and out. Make sure he loves you and you love him. Mama, don't believe in that type of livin', but you are my baby, and I love you, no matter what. That's all I am going to say about it."

"So, Mama . . . how is the family? Like Aunt Berta and them?"

"Oh, they fine, baby." She laughed. "They still crazy as ever, fighting and cussing and getting into all manners of trouble. Which reminds me, that crazy cousin of yours, Sherry, came by here with some cute little boy about three months ago asking about when you got out. She said she wanted to find out because she missed you and wanted to spend some time with you. She stayed with me for a week or so because she said she wanted to spend some time with me. She kept making phone calls all the time, blowing up Mama's phone and eating up my food, so I told her she had to go. I loved that little boy, but she was a pain in the butt."

"Ummm, did y'all ever talk about me or anything?" I asked, trying not to be obvious.

"Only when she asked me about where you were going to live and all that. I told her I didn't know where you were going to live, but I gave her your number instead. I knew you told her to stay away when she called you." Mama chuckled. "On her last day here, she asked me for some money to get her and the little boy back to Maryland. I went into my stash and gave her five hundred dollars and told her to never come back. She even had the nerve to tell me that that wasn't enough. That's when Sophie came out for a visit." She chuckled to herself.

I did as well. Mama was as sweet as pie, but catch her the wrong way and she will conveniently lose her religion and unleash Sophie, her alter ego. Sophie was like Tyler Perry's Madea character, but only worse. I could just imagine what she said to her or did to her. I was pretty sure she'd never set foot in my mom's house again.

"Oh, and, baby, she kept calling you James, for some reason."

"Ha-ha-ha." I laughed nervously. "Ma, you know she crazy as a bed bug. Ever since we were little and she fell off my swing set backwards and hit her head on cement, she's never been the same."

We both laughed at that one.

I heard Wallace getting out of the shower and had to cut the conversation short. "Well, all right, Ma. I have to go get in the shower and get into bed for tomorrow. I have a busy day tomorrow."

"Oh, okay, baby. Mama loves her some Jerry."

"And Jerry loves him some Mama." We both blew kisses into the phone and hung up.

Just as I did, I heard the bathroom door open and heard Wallace's footsteps going toward the bedroom.

I began to scramble around the kitchen, getting things together. My man was expecting a hot meal, and I was going to give it to him. I quickly threw some garlic sticks in the oven with the potatoes and green beans for the last couple of minutes and proceeded to take the now done steaks off the grill.

"Umm, boy!"

Wallace shuffled into the kitchen with a wife-beater and some boxers and some chocolate, furry-type slippers I'd bought him. "My baby got it banging up in here."

I smiled with delight because, every time he called me *baby*, my world seemed to light up.

"All right, baby, go into the dining room, and I will be right in with the food." He kissed me on the cheek and walked off toward the dining room.

I took out some candles and champagne glasses and put them on the dining room table, as well as our dinnerware. He had already turned on the digital music player, and the house filled with jazz and calypso. I fixed our plates and made my way to the dining room, where we sat across from each other. The lights were dimmed, and the light from the candle flickered on the walls.

As we both savored our meals, we sat and just gazed into each other's eyes. My shenanigans of the day faded away with each second of being in his presence. I felt safe and loved.

My mind temporarily drifted to Mama's sickness and how I was going to handle it. It seemed like I was losing one lover for another. I couldn't compare the two, but that's what it seemed like. I didn't want to lose either. I was brokenhearted by Mama's illness and awakened emotionally by Wallace's love toward me. I pushed it all back down inside and finished my meal with my man.

After we finished eating and playing footsie under the table, Wallace cleared the table while I went into the living room and started the fireplace. I moved the table back out of the way, spread out a fur-type blanket a foot or two away from the fire, and sat down Indian-style with my side to the fire.

Wallace walked in with a bowl of ice cream and two spoons and did the same. He began to feed me ice cream slowly by the spoonful. Chocolate peanut butter ice cream was one of my favorites, and he knew it. After he fed me a couple of spoonfuls, we then took turns feeding each other until it was all gone.

He sat the bowl on the table and crawled back over to me on his hands and knees and starting nibbling on my ear. He knew this was my spot. I was weak after his first lick.

He moved around to my mouth and kissed me deep and long. It was as if he was trying to take my breath away, lingering on my bottom lip for a few seconds. He slowly pushed me back and kissed my neck.

I had on a thin white wife-beater, which he ripped off slowly, exposing my slightly chiseled chest. He worked his way down to my navel, causing me to be tickled with laughter. He stopped there and took my hand in his and worked each finger into his mouth, sending me into a sexual fever. I was hot all over.

After that, Wallace pulled down my pajama shorts and worked my dick to a hard, stiff erection. He then pulled himself up to where I was and laid halfway on me and halfway off. He kissed me and jerked my dick at the same time.

My hands caressed his head and neck as he continued to work me to an orgasm. I came hard as he continued to kiss me all over.

He laid his head on my chest until my breathing had slowed down. "I love you," he whispered into my ear and kissed me on the cheek.

He got up and came back with a wet washcloth and cleaned me and himself up, and we drifted off to sleep right there on the floor.

Chapter 28

Shawn

Rock My World
December 15th, 2018, 1:23 P.M.

I was still seething hot when I walked into my office. I couldn't believe my father did that shit to his family. It was like he was still trying to hurt us from the grave. To top it off, the detective on my father's case just called and told me that James had a solid alibi for the night of my father's murder.

I flopped down in my chair and massaged my aching temples. I had a shitload of cases I was working on, and all this shit going on in my personal life. It was enough to make me wanna jump off the top of the building. I didn't know what I was going to do if anything else happened today. My ass just might go postal and kill everybody up in this muthafucka. I was thinking more and more irrationally as the days passed. Dealing with this faggot-ass James and all his bullshit was making me wanna say, "Fuck it!" and fuck him and get it over with. That's what he wanted anyways. *Why not go back to fucking him? Maybe he will leave me and Mona alone after I give him one last fuck.*

I couldn't blame him though. I was a good-looking man. Even at the age of forty-five I had no gray hair or wrinkles to be seen. I was toned and had a little muscle to flex with. Mona couldn't keep her hands off me at night. I was a wanted man, and I knew it. Too bad I couldn't have my cake and eat it too. I was so glad I had a stronger willpower than I had ten years ago, because I would have fucked James by now. Then again, I couldn't give all the credit to my willpower, because every time I looked at my wife and kids, I knew I would be worse off without them. Love for my family was holding me together.

Buzzz!

"Mr. Black, you have a call on line two. It's Mona."

"Hey, baby, I was just calling to see how your day was going."

This is my baby all day long. How can I think about messing around on her again? Here she is checking up on me at work. I couldn't ask for a better wife than her.

"Baby, everything is everything. I am so glad to hear your voice. I can't wait to marry you again."

I was genuinely excited about renewing our vows. I couldn't let the death of my father and all the shit James was dragging me through distract me from this any longer. "I was thinking about setting up a second honeymoon as well. You know it's always better the second time around."

"Oh, baby, can we go to Cancún or Paris?" Mona squealed into the phone like she was a kid getting ready to get a Happy Meal.

"Sure, baby. Whatever you want. It's going to be all about you."

"Wow! Baby, I can't believe in a couple of weeks we will be going away on a second honeymoon. I gotta tell Momma the good news. I will see you when you get home."

"Okay, snookums. See you then."

"Oh, and, Shawn, there will be something special waiting on you when you get here." Mona blew a kiss into the phone and then hung up.

I didn't have to be a rocket scientist to figure this one out. I was still a little apprehensive about the whole sex thing, but I again shrugged it off, because I knew Mona only called James' name out the other night because of the stress he was putting us through yet again. I was hoping.

I pushed the thought of James and his mess to the back of my mind and began to concentrate on my work.

As I was heading out of my office, my phone started to ring. I was going to ignore it, but something told me to answer it, it could be important.

"Mr. Black speaking."

"Well, well, well. You can't call nobody?" James sneered into the phone then laughed at the tired, played-out pimp line he just spat.

"I'm on my way home to *my* wife and kids. What do you want now? I hope it ain't sex, because that is out of the question." I decided I would take a stand and call his bluff. Maybe telling the kids the truth would make life a little easier.

"I was calling to ask you to meet me at The Stable."

"Fuck, no," I almost yelled into the phone. It was there that all this shit got me in trouble in the first place. I wasn't about to go there again.

"I wouldn't be so quick to say no. I have someone I want you to meet, and I don't think Mona would be happy if we pulled up at your house and introduced the two of you."

"Look, this better not be no game, James, because if it is, I will not hesitate in laying hands on you, if you know what I mean."

"Nigga, please! Your over-easy ass ain't gonna do shit. Meet me there in a half hour." *Click.*

I looked at the phone in disbelief. This dude was still crazy as ever. I didn't even know why I was shocked.

I pulled up to the parking lot beside the restaurant and paid the parking attendant. Just before I walked in, I called Mona and told her that I would be late coming home because of a very important case I was finishing up. Since I was now a partner at the firm, Mona knew I was really serious about my cases. She said she would wait up and be ready to rock my world. I was looking forward to it and couldn't wait to get my rocks off.

My mind was racing, trying to figure out who in the hell did James want me to meet. I walked in the restaurant and made my way to the table where he was seated. From the distance, I could see a lady with her back turned toward me and a little boy about the same age as Diana. I had to think he looked quite familiar.

When James waved me over, the lady at the table turned around, and so did the little boy. It was my old secretary, Sherry.

What in the hell is she doing here?

Then all of a sudden, the little boy jumped up and ran toward me screaming, "Daddy! Daddy!"

My facial expression said it all. I was in complete shock and awe. This little boy couldn't have been my son. Then it all hit me. I had fucked Sherry with a rubber that broke when we had sex in my office. It was the only way to get her to drop the charges she had against Mona.

I pulled out the chair and went to sit down, missing it completely. This news was rocking my world, and there was nothing I could do about it. James had a big smile on his face the whole time. Embarrassed and awestruck, I made another attempt to sit in my chair.

The waiter came over and asked if everything was okay.

No, muthafucka. I just found out I have a son I didn't know about. I just asked for a glass of water to refresh my now dry mouth and loosened my necktie, because it was getting increasingly hot in the place.

After a couple of seconds, Sherry said, "First, I wanna say I'm sorry. I would have and should have told you about Li'l Shawn a long time ago. I just couldn't bring myself to do it. I know it's selfish, but I wanted to leave you and your family alone."

I just glanced at her, Li'l Shawn, and James like I was in the twilight zone or something. I was totally gone. I couldn't believe this was happening to me. *Just when I thought shit in my life was bad, here comes something else.* "How do you know he's mine?"

I knew it sounded so cliché as it came out of my mouth. Here I was, another black man denying fatherhood. It came out so natural, but I truly didn't mean it that way. I was just in shock. He looked like me when I was a child, but I still wasn't sure. This shit is just too crazy.

"Um, um, I mean, are you sure?"

"Shawn, you are the only one I had sex with around the time I found out I was pregnant. Even though I did go about this the wrong way, I'm not a slut like you might think," she said, looking me in my eyes.

I looked at the little boy apologetically. "Well, I never said that. I'm just trying to get clarity."

"I don't blame you. If I was in your shoes, I probably would be asking the same questions too." She paused. "We can take a DNA test if you want to."

"Most definitely."

"Mommy, I need to go to the bathroom."

Immediately after Li'l Shawn and Sherry got up and made their way to the bathroom, James said, "Look, Shawn, you can make this easy on all of us. Just do what we ask, and Ms. Mona doesn't have to know a thing about Li'l Shawn."

"Are you serious? You are really willing to pimp me out for the sake of a kid and the happiness of my family?"

"Hell yeah." James laughed to himself.

I wanted to bash his face in right then and there.

"This shit is just too good to pass up on."

Again, my mind wandered to hurting him badly. I just sat there and pondered his proposition.

"Let's say I go for this deal, what does it consist of?" I folded my arms against my chest and sat back waiting for the details.

"All you have to do is make me happy with some sex and money every now and then. And Sherry is going to need two thousand in child support every month."

"I'll think about." I drank a little bit of my water.

"Well, don't think about it too long, because my fingers have a mind of their own and I would hate to slip up and call your house and let Li'l Shawn ask for his daddy himself."

Sherry, and Li'l Shawn came back from the bathroom, and again Li'l Shawn hugged me before he sat down beside his mom.

"Sherry, how did he know who I was when I got here?"

"Oh, I went online to your law firm's webpage and printed out your picture. I showed it to him, and he keeps it in his pocket every day, waiting for the chance to meet you."

I couldn't help but be touched by the sentiment. "Look, I don't want to be rude, but I need to be going. I have to be at work early in the morning." I scooted my chair back, preparing my exit. "I'll be in touch about the DNA test and the other things ASAP."

As I was leaving Li'l Shawn popped up and hugged me again. "Daddy, don't leave me! I want you to stay."

I picked him up and assured him that we would be seeing each other on a regular basis. I didn't know how I would pull it off, but I had to, until I was ready to tell Mona the truth.

I walked out of the restaurant and to my car shaking my head in awe of my new addition to my family. I was sure he was mine. He looked just like me, I just wanted to be a hundred percent sure by taking a DNA test.

I made my way into the house pretending I had a normal day. After I sexed Mona, I drifted off to sleep with yet again another full plate of deception and lies.

Chapter 29

Sherry

Getting the Juices Flowing
December 16th, 2018, 7:55 P.M.

Strangely, I was enjoying spending time with Keisha. She was actually pleasant to be around. When James asked me to help him keep an eye on her, he wanted me to pretend I was gay, which didn't sit right with me at first. Then again, I was using him as well. He just didn't know about it. His ass thought he was going to get away with taking Shawn away from me. Faggot-ass muthafucka.

When I saw Shawn at the restaurant the other day, I was like, *Damn! He's still fine as wine!* He had obviously aged, but it was hard to tell how much. I almost told James to go screw himself, and I would try to go after Shawn again, but I knew he would never leave Mona for me.

I pulled up in front of Keisha's house and parked the truck James let me use for a while.

"Hey, baby," I said to her as she greeted me at the door.

I kissed her on the lips, and surprisingly, I wasn't grossed out. I just mentally psyched myself out by thinking she was just a guy with different equipment.

"How you been doin'?" I asked as we walked into her living room and took seats together on the couch.

She had a Christmas tree up and a couple of gifts already underneath it. I noticed it was extremely quiet around her house. There were normally kids running around all over the place.

"Where the kids at?"

"Oh, they over my mom's house for the weekend."

Keisha was a good mom. It was just that the kids were bad as hell. She was living on public assistance again, after spending all the money that she stole from Kenny, her baby daddy, on fancy clothes and nights out on the town. We had been seeing each other for a couple of days now, and she was spilling her guts about everything, like how she set Kenny up and how she and his sister got romantically involved. She said she was tired of Kenny running the streets late at night and not coming home sometimes. That's when Antoinette would come over to visit her nephews, and they would talk for hours. One day when she was over and the kids were all asleep, Antoinette made a move on her, and they had been getting down ever since.

I was brought out of a daze by Keisha bursting out into tears.

"What's wrong?" I said, getting close to her and cradling her in my arms while she sobbed.

"I can't believe Antoinette is doing this to me. After all we have been through. How could she cheat on me and leave me home at night like this all by myself? First, Kenny, now her. I don't deserve this shit."

As she continued to sob in my arms, the nurturing mother in me started to stroke her hair and rock her like a baby.

"Everything is going to be all right," I said, lifting her chin up and looking into her eyes. "I'll hold you all night long, baby." I was laying it on thick. I almost felt sorry for what James was planning for her.

I kissed her on the forehead, and in return, she took me by surprise and kissed me on the lips and forced her tongue in my mouth. At first, I wanted to slap the hell out of her, until I noticed how gentle she was.

She continued to kiss me, slipping her tongue in my mouth even further. Not having sex for over six months was taking its toll, and I began kissing her back.

She slowly started unbuttoning my shirt, exposing my braless breasts. She took one in her mouth and started to suck on it as if she was nursing. I let out slight moans as the sensation she was giving me was making my pussy drip and soaked my panties.

She pushed me back on the chair and began undoing my pants. She removed my shoes, pants, and panties and threw them on the floor. She got up and ran into the kitchen and came back with a bowl of ice and a bottle of honey.

I watched as she took a cube of ice and placed it into her mouth and let it swirl around in her mouth. I had to admit, that shit was turning me on. I was ready to get it on.

With the ice still in her mouth, she made circles around my nipples, causing them to harden and become erect.

The ice and her tongue sent shivers down my back as the now melted ice ran down my chest. "Oh! My! Ahh!"

She worked her way down to my hairless kitty and began fingering it, first with one finger, and then with two.

I arched my back as she was working me overtime. I had masturbated before, but her shit was off the hook.

She took the honey, poured it on my pussy, and began lapping like a dog at a water dish.

I started twitching and shaking, and within minutes, I was screaming out her name.

She looked up at me with a wicked smile on her face. "We not finished yet."

I didn't know what she meant, until she pulled out her large veined dick from underneath her couch. I thought that was an odd place for a dildo, but I ignored it.

She poured honey on that as well, as she slowly eased the large fake dick in me. She pulled it out and licked it like she was licking a Bomb Pop.

Again, this shit was turning me on, and I wasn't used to women fucking me.

All of a sudden, she was fucking me like she was a nigga trying to get himself a good nut, and I was nutting all over the dildo as I came back to back. This bitch was good, and I was seriously thinking about jumping on this side of the fence for good. *Nah!*

She collapsed out of breath on top of me like she had really physically fucked me.

I had never been this exhausted after sex with a man and I loved it. We fell asleep on the couch cradled in each others' arms like we were lovers.

"What the fuck is this shit!"

We were awakened by the voice of a female standing over us with the dildo in her hand. We both jumped up like it was the police busting us for drugs. I immediately covered myself as the broad who I assumed was Antoinette stared me down.

I had to admit, Antoinette didn't look like a lesbian, but her ass sure fought like one. Before Keisha could get away, she sucker-punched her, dropping her to the floor instantly.

Damn! It's like that? I wasn't going out like that. I was still naked and I was scanning the room, looking for something to fight with, since she was a little bigger than me.

She charged me, tackling me to the floor. As I went down, we knocked over a table with a lamp on it.

She was on top of me getting ready to swing, when all of a sudden, Keisha came out of nowhere and jumped on her back. Keisha was clawing at her face from behind, and Antoinette was trying her best to shake her off.

I took the opportunity to grab the lamp and bash her in the head, sending her and Keisha flying backwards. Antoinette was out cold, and had a small gash on her forehead that was leaking blood.

I scrambled to get out of the house as fast as I could. I had my clothes in hand as I made a mad dash toward my car. It was the middle of the night on Greenmount Avenue, but I could have cared less.

Right before I darted out of the house, I told Keisha that we had to do it again, that I would call her to set it up. Nearly getting my ass whipped didn't deter me from getting another nut like she had given me. I had to admit, my adrenaline was pumping, and I was truly enjoying my trip back to Baltimore.

Chapter 30

James

Well, Well, Well
December 16th, 2018, 12:07 P.M.

I was in the house baby-sitting Li'l Shawn, because I had Sherry doing some of my dirty work today. Surprisingly, he was a very quiet kid who didn't require much attention, which was a plus for me. I strolled around the house doing chores like washing clothes and basic house cleaning, pretending to be a good man-wife and tend to my man's home—Correction, *our* home.

When I had brought home Li'l Shawn yesterday, I'd lied and told Wallace that I was baby-sitting for my cousin because she had to go out of state to handle some personal business. He ate it up because I was his baby and he knew I would never lie to him. I always wondered how I could get away with so much devious shit and still sleep good at night.

I decided I would take Li'l Shawn out for a little adventuring. I had some money to burn and didn't want to stay in the house all day waiting on Wallace to get in from running the streets.

"Hey, li'l man," I said to him, patting him on the head as I walked into the living room, where he was watching cartoons. "You wanna go shopping with me today?"

When he nodded his approval, I told him to get his jacket, since it was autumn and a little nippy outside. I told him it would be about fifteen minutes before I would be back.

I had already taken a shower, and all I had to do was get dressed. After I put on my jeans and nice button-up shirt, I finished shaping up my hair and made my way out the door, no destination in mind.

I decided to go to Columbia Mall and do some shopping for me, Li'l Shawn, and Wallace, but mainly me. We parked near the Nordstrom entrance and made our way inside. I was getting an adrenaline rush because I knew I was going to burn a lot of cash today.

As I browsed, I picked out a few Sean John outfits for Li'l Shawn and Wallace. I was also a cologne fanatic. I went crazy at the counter, sampling almost everything they had. I ended up buying about twenty different fragrances, because almost all of them smelled good on me. In fact, many people told me that "cologne mixed well with my body chemistry."

I made a quick trip to my car to drop off the bags I had already accumulated and continued on the shopping spree. We went from Eddie Bauer to Abercrombie & Fitch, to Rockport, to Abercrombie kids. I even made a trip inside Today's Pet to get some things for my cats. We again made a trip back to the car to unload the bags we accumulated.

In total, I think I spent about nine thousand in the mall in about three hours. A personal best.

We were both famished, so I decided I would take us to get some barbeque spare ribs from Famous Dave's in Owings Mills. I absolutely adored that place. The food was off the hook, especially their corn muffins.

As we were being seated, my eyes locked on to a person I was surely glad to see. I told Li'l Shawn to go and be seated while I go and have some fun. I didn't want him to be seen and have my plan foiled.

"Well, well, well," I said as I stood at the table where Mona and *my* two daughters, Ashley and Diana, were sitting.

"Oh, ah. Hey, James," she said, trying not to show her nervousness in front of the kids.

"Long time no see," I said, looking her straight in the eyes.

She had the look of fear that I liked on her face. Her ass probably was about to wet herself on the spot.

"Give me a hug and stop acting all shy and stuff."

As she hesitantly got up and gave me a hug, I pulled her toward me and whispered in her ear, "Daddy's back."

She went to sit back down and missed the chair, falling on the floor. It took everything in me not to laugh at her as she got up and sat in the chair.

Just to mess with her head again, I said, "So where's that buddy of mine?"

"He, uh, he at home," she stammered over her words once again. I was loving it.

"Oh, that's too bad. I was wondering if we could have a boys' night out again," I said, winking my eye, "you know, like we used to do."

"Yeah, sure. I'll tell him as soon as I get home," she said with a fake smile.

"These two young ladies must be Ashley and Diana."

She nodded her head.

"You two are so pretty, and y'all look just like your mom and dad." I smiled

Sweat was bristling at the top of Mona's forehead. I knew she wanted to get up and run, afraid I was going to spill the beans, of which I had no intentions. I was going to milk them once again for all I could, and then hang them out to dry.

I decided to let up and go about my business. She was suffering enough. But I made sure I made a mental note to get her on the phone and get some money out of her as well. Again.

I detoured to our assigned booth near them but not visible enough for Li'l Shawn to be seen and ordered our food. She glanced around from time to time, showing her uneasiness. I was enjoying torturing the Black family once again.

After about ten minutes of me and Li'l Shawn being there, they swiftly made their exit out of the restaurant. She looked like she was damn crazy as she sped out of the establishment. I couldn't help but laugh to myself.

Buzz. I felt my phone vibrating. I looked down and noticed a text message from a blocked number: Yo ass sure looked good in them jeans u are rocking. Too bad the paramedics might have to cut them off u. Safe ride home. lol.

I looked around trying to see if I could see anybody looking suspicious. Everybody was eating their food, minding their business. So it seemed. This shit did have me a little worried. Just a little, though. I just deleted it and continued to eat my meal.

Later on that day, I took Li'l Shawn back to his ghetto-ass momma, who informed me of her progress, saying, I would be able to exact my revenge any day now.

I walked in the house exhausted, yet ready to have me some try-to-break-the-headboard time with Wallace.

Chapter 31

Shawn

Testing the Waters
December 20th, 2018, 4:34 P.M.

I sat in my office and held the sheet of paper that showed I was 99% conclusively Li'l Shawn's biological father. I had a son? Flesh and blood that was mine? I was so excited to know this.

You're probably thinking, 'How can he feel this way when he already has three children at home?' Well, though I had been raising them as my own, technically, they were not mine.

I can remember the day I got the call that Mona went into labor. I was at work, and it was about ten o'clock at night. I was completely exhausted, because the case I was trying in court in a couple of weeks was whipping my butt. I had just made junior partner and was still trying to prove myself as a top-shelf lawyer.

Mona was due to give birth at any moment. I swore to myself I wouldn't be one of them husbands that acted a fool when his wife was going into labor, but I was fooling myself, because when I got the call, I completely lost my mind.

"Shawn, it's time." Mona breathed heavily into the phone. "They're coming!"

"Okay, Mona!" My breathing had become labored as well. "You call my mom or your mom? Is the suitcase in the car? How you gonna get to the hospital?"

"Shawn . . . Shawn . . . Shawn," Mona calmly spoke into the phone.

I heard her, but I kept on rambling. "Oh God! How am I going to get you to the hospital? Can I make it to the house in time? You call the doctor? Or am I supposed to call the doctor?"

I was now scrambling around my office, trying to find my car keys. Mona was talking, but I wasn't listening. My mind was racing, and I was already in the hospital in my mind. I raced to the elevator and pressed all of the down keys on the three elevators that stood before me. The way I was drenched in sweat, you would have thought I was a crackhead in need of a high.

"Shawn! Shawn!" She was yelling now, and that bro-ught me back around.

"Yeah, baby. Yeah, baby. I—I—I'm here. Just hold on, Mona. I'm coming."

In a flash I was out the building and practically running down the street toward the car garage a block and a half away.

It was winter, and I had left my coat in my office, but I didn't realize that until I got in the car. I sped out of the parking garage like I was Batman and the mayor had just flashed the bat in the sky.

"Shawn, baby, we on our way to the hospital now!" This time the voice of my mother-in-law played in my ear. "Just meet us at Northwest Hospital."

"How did you? Where is? Is she okay? Mama, I'm coming."

The hospital was about forty minutes away, but I made it there in twenty minutes. I should have been pulled over for reckless driving, because I was breaking all kinds of laws, running lights, passing stop signs, and I almost hit a pedestrian as well.

I ran into the hospital and up to the front desk, asking where my wife was. "My wife, here, er, pregnant, babies . . . miss them . . . no . . ."

The receptionist looked at me and laughed. I didn't see what was funny.

"This must be your first." She smiled.

I laughed slightly, sweating and breathing very hard.

"What's her name?"

"Who?"

"Your wife's?"

"My wife?"

"Yes, your wife's name?"

"She-she giving birth, having the babies, er, see her now." I rambled again. I thought I was having a panic attack.

"Okay, I understand that part." She looked at me like I was crazy. "But I will need to know her name to find her."

I heard her, but I didn't. I looked around and saw the double doors and ran toward them. I was totally gone. I didn't know anything: room number, floor, or ward, but I was running down the hall, calling her name out.

As I was running, I didn't see a patient with an oxygen tank, so I tripped and fell and hit my head on the side of a gurney. I was out for the count. I woke up in a hospital bed next to Mona and the twins. She was holding one, and my mom was holding the other.

I looked on in sheer embarrassment. Here I was in a hospital bed with a bandaged up head. Mona just looked at me and smiled, causing me to do the same.

My mother brought me over Alex and then Ashley, and I held my bundles of joy in my arms. The tears flowed freely. I was a father. A very proud father. I posed while my mom took pictures of me holding my babies. It was the proudest day of my life, bandaged head and all.

I laughed as I looked back on it, but that was then, and this is now. When Mona had called the day of the paternity results and told me that I wasn't their biological father, something in me changed. I really hadn't realized that until now.

I picked up a picture of my family off my desk. We had taken this picture about three months ago. All dressed in white, we all were smiling, showing our pearly whites.

I, on the other hand, wasn't smiling on the inside. I still had unrest in me. I was still a liar and I knew it. I wasn't happy that James had what I wanted all my life. Offspring. Children. Little versions of me.

The bad thing about it is, he didn't even want them. I couldn't prove it, but I was sure of it. He was a selfish SOB who only cared about materialistic gain, and that proved it for me.

I gently placed the picture back down on the desk where it belonged. I looked across my desk at the picture of my parents and frowned. I had suppressed so much anger and hurt over the years.

Some moments came across as good times, maybe even great times, but it was mostly just me and my mom doing our thing together. My father was always busy grading papers for his students and preparing assignments. Even in the summertime, he would teach school. I would ask if daddy was coming with us on our trips, and my mom would say he was making a living for us. I believed everything she told me, because she was my mom, and she never lied to me.

Truth was, the busier he was, the less I saw of him, which was a huge relief for me, knowing what we did when he did have the time to spend with me. That shit surely wasn't quality time to me. It was hell. I'll tell you that.

He's gone now. Dead. Worm food. He'd never apologized for any of it, but it's not like it would've helped me now anyway. I was fucked up for sure.

"It is what it is." I shrugged my shoulders in defeat. "Time for me to start looking ahead." I turned toward my computer and continued with my workday.

Two hours later, I was out again with Li'l Shawn after work and was enjoying spending time with him. Who could have thought I would actually have a child I didn't know about? I mean, I loved all my children, but there is just something about having a biological connection with your offspring that really made a difference to me.

I had taken him to the National Aquarium, the Science Center, National Great Blacks in Wax Museum, and various other attractions around Baltimore, and he was loving every minute of it.

I was asking him questions, and he was asking me questions too.

"Are you and my mom getting married? Do I have any brothers and sisters? Can I live with you? Why did you leave my mother?"

They were all so overwhelming, I didn't know how to respond. I told him I would explain it to him later on, and he reluctantly agreed. I was hoping he wouldn't pressure me anymore about it until I told Mona about him. I was still trying to figure that one out. How in the hell do you do that? I know I pulled back emotionally when she told me that none of our children were biologically mine. I just didn't know when to tell her or how. When is a good time to spring that kind of news on someone? I was still getting used to it my damn self.

I pulled up to the apartment complex where they were staying and called Sherry's phone, letting her know I was outside with Lil Shawn. I hated to see him go, but I had to mosey on home to my wife and kids. I so wanted him to be a part of the family I was leaving him to go home to. But I had to prep Mona first, just to see where her head was.

Sherry sashayed out of the house in slippers and rollers just like a ghetto queen. I handed her a check for two grand out of my car window with the promise of the rest the next week. Then I popped the trunk to my car, so she could also grab the Wal-Mart bags Li'l Shawn and I accumulated.

Christmas Day was just around the corner, so we had made a quick stop at Wal-Mart on Route 40. I let him go for it in the toy and electronic departments. He ended up spending about three hundred dollars. I was happy to see his smiling face. It must have been his first time really having a Christmas, because he was so fidgety, and he kept on thanking me. There was no telling who she had him around, and where she dragged him to.

I pulled up to the house with the hope that I could pick Mona's brain. I got out of the car and made my way into the house.

I noticed that the lights in the dining room were on, and soft R&B music was playing. I cautiously walked into the dining room, not knowing what to expect.

"Hey, baby," Mona said as she seductively walked up to me in a swaggered strut.

She was looking hot in a see-through pink robe that had fur around the edges. I could see she had on my favorite teddy, the one that exposed most of her breasts.

She took my briefcase out of my hand and placed it in a corner. She then pulled me by the hand and led me to the table, which was candle-lit. "I hope you will enjoy this night as much as I did planning it. I know you've had it hard this week at the office, and I wanted to reward you for all the hard work you do to keep this family together."

I just looked at her with the fake if-you-only-knew smile as she unveiled a dinner fit for a king. She had fried chicken, baked macaroni and cheese, candied yams, homemade rolls, collard greens, and my favorite dessert, Oreo cheesecake.

She made a plate, sat on my lap, and proceeded to feed it to me spoonful by spoonful.

I was enjoying the food and the view of her chest as she fed me my meal. I wasn't prepared for this. Now how can I bring up the idea of "adopting" a kid right now? It wasn't the right time.

Speaking of kids, she must've dropped the kids off at my mom's house. They usually went over her house to make cookies and help her decorate the house around this time.

After Mona finished feeding me, she led me upstairs, where she had me strip out of my clothes and step into our Jacuzzi tub that had been filled to the top and had scented candles around it.

I stepped in the tub and sat down. She disrobed and immediately did the same. She sat in front of me and took my feet into her hands and massaged each one, cracking my toes in the process. Then she began to work her way up to my calves, kneading them like dough. I lay my head back and enjoyed the treatment she was giving me.

After a couple intense minutes of that, she worked her way up to the most important muscle of them all. My dick.

I lifted my head up and watched as she massaged it till it was hard as steel. Her eyes met mine, and we drew together like two magnets, kissing hard and aggressively like it was our last night together.

She broke the kiss as she went down on my dick. Mind you, my lower half was underwater. She went down under the water and started giving me a blowjob that had me moaning loudly. She was doing a damn good job under the water, not coming up for long periods of time. I didn't know she could hold her breath for so long.

She came up just as I was about to cum. "Not yet, baby," she said, pulling herself up and positioning herself on my dick. "I wanna ride you home, daddy."

We'd never fucked in the tub, and I was enjoying this experience totally.

"Whatever, baby." I moaned as she started pumping up and down on me like a jackhammer. "Do the damn thing."

She was bouncing so hard, water was flying everywhere, even blowing some of the candles out. I was in heaven.

We came at two different times, her first, then me, and we collapsed in the tub, her on top of me.

"Damn, baby!" I said to her as her head lay on my chest. "We gotta do this shit again."

"Sure, Shawn. This is all yours." She opened her legs and rubbed herself feverishly.

We got out of the tub, dried each other off, made our way into the bedroom and lay in the bed, spooning like we always did. I decided to test the waters while she was in a loving mode.

"Baby," I whispered into her ear.

"Huh?"

"You ever think Diana is getting lonely?"

"What you mean, Shawn?"

"I was thinking today that maybe we should adopt a child around Diana's age. I've been noticing that Alex and Ashley are not paying her as much attention as they used to. I think it would be nice to adopt someone that Diana could play with."

"Baby, why are you thinking about this all of a sudden?"

"Well, it wasn't all of a sudden. I've been thinking about this for a while now. I know we're getting older, that you would probably not physically want to have another baby."

"Really?" She turned toward me, a puzzled look on her face. "Are you sure?"

"Yeah. With Alex and Ashley about to go off to college in two years, Diana is going to get quite lonely in the house by herself."

"Well, let's think about it." She kissed me on the lips. "We can talk about it more after we renew our vows and come back from our trip."

I was bursting inside with excitement. The only problem was getting Sherry to agree to give custody of Li'l Shawn to me and keep her maternity of him a secret.

I began kissing Mona again as the excitement had made me horny again. I mounted her again and proceeded to fuck her brains out.

Chapter 32

James

Questions
December 20th, 2018, 8:56 P.M.

I walked into the house, totally exhausted and ready to fuck or get fucked, whichever was fine with me. As soon as I got in the door, I noticed Wallace sitting in the living room listening to jazz music playing. He had brought a Christmas tree and everything while I was gone. Everything was so festive. It had been a minute since I'd experienced Christmas like this. It made me miss my mother, who I needed to call more often, since she was getting up there in age. I needed to take care of her more, maybe even bring her here to live with me. I know it seemed like I had no heart or feelings, but I was a human being. I had a heart. It was just caked under hurt and pain that I never dealt with. I was beginning to see that I was worthy of love and I was able to give it too.

Somehow, in a short time, Wallace began to break down this wall of anger that I had put up. This love stuff had caught me off guard, but I remembered the feeling well. My momma showed it to me all the time, yet I still went out searching for it in all the wrong places.

I stood a distance away and eyed my man sitting there on the couch. He was so fine, treated me so good. And here I was, a forty-five-year-old, running the streets, plotting and planning. I didn't deserve him. I needed to be home appreciating my man.

"Hey, Wallace, baby," I said, sitting down next to him and kissing him on the cheek.

He had a bottle of wine sitting on the table in front of him. It was obvious he had been drinking a little. He just turned and looked at me with a serious look on his face. "James, I'm not accustomed to having drama in my life or in my house."

"Huh?" I looked at him, confusion all over my face. I hadn't the slightest idea what he was talking about.

"And I definitely don't like threats being made at me by people I don't know."

"What are you talking about?" I said, now pissed off because he wasn't being clear. "What are you talking about, people threatening you?"

I began to wonder if Wallace was crazy, if that was the flaw he was hiding all this time. *I mean, it wouldn't be a surprise since I'm crazy as well.* I always believed what my momma used to say to me as a teenager all the time, "You attract who you are, not what you want."

"Someone called here today and left a message for you on my answering machine." He picked up the phone and proceeded to dial in the codes that played back the saved messages. He handed me the phone to let me listen.

It was distorted, and the voice was muffled, so you couldn't tell if it was a man or woman.

"This message is for James or Jerry. Whoever the fuck you are. Your time is drawing nigh, bitch, so watch yo back and yo front because payback is right around the corner. Your ass is as good as dead, muthafucka. So live it up now, you shit-chaser, because your life is in my hands, and I'm about to end it." Click

I was speechless for once. Again I had no clue who it was. I sat back for a minute as the message played over in my head again. For the first time in my life, I was a little afraid. Just a little though.

"I haven't the slightest idea what that was all about," I said, looking Wallace in the eyes. "That must be somebody playing a joke or something." I slightly chuckled and placed my hand on his manhood.

He took my hand off his dick and placed it on the chair beside him. "It didn't sound like a joke, James."

I looked at him in shock. I was hoping to avoid all of this with my signature blowjob.

"Whoever that was sounded pretty adamant about your demise. And, like I said before, I don't like or need any drama in my life." Wallace got up and picked the wine bottle up and proceeded to leave the room.

"Baby, I will look into this tomorrow, and I promise that it won't be happening again."

That was a lie that even I didn't believe. I had no clue what to do about this situation, but to let it play out and hope that whoever was after me gave up or brought it on face to face and got this shit over with. I wasn't going to let some crazy bastard mess up the only good relationship I had in my life. He or she wasn't going to scare me this easy. A few threats and the car incident weren't going to mess up the life I was destined to have.

I sat in the living room for a few more minutes, questions flowing through my mind.

Again, I shrugged it off and proceeded to go and please my man in the other room. I jumped in the shower and made sure I smelled oh so good when I got out.

I walked into our bedroom, with emphasis on *our*, with the

plan of seducing Wallace into forgetting about the threatening call. "I'm sorry, baby," I said as I crept onto the California king-size bed. I crawled across like I was a cat on the prowl. I was naked and dazzling.

He was watching *Madea Goes to Jail.* I could tell he was enjoying it. He had a smile on his face and chuckled as I made my way over to him. He was naked from the waist up, and I could see the glazed-over look he had from the wine he'd been drinking earlier.

"I don't wanna do anything to jeopardize our relationship, so maybe it's best for me to move back into my apartment."

He retrieved the remote that was beside him and muted the movie and turned to me. "I trust you, James, and I definitely don't want you to move out. You my baby." He touched my face, brushing my cheek with the back of his hand gently. "Just handle yo business about whatever is going on and make sure that it doesn't happen again." He pulled me in close by my shoulders and began to kiss me passionately, letting his tongue slip into my mouth. Then he pulled out and let his tongue trace the outline of my lips.

I let out a slight moan of pleasure. I reached over and tugged at his pajama pants, unleashing the monster within. It was pulsating and growing to full length fast. "Let me do what I do." I took him in my mouth and let him enjoy my gift.

He lay back as I did what I did best, and within minutes, he was coming all over my face. He cleaned himself up, and then he went back to watching his movie as I snuggled close to him with my head on his chest.

I can't believe the shit I did in the past was popping up now . . . right when I was thinking about throwing in the towel and settling down with my man. I drifted off to sleep, hoping this shit would end with me walking off into the sunset with Wallace.

***

The next morning, I awoke to the smell of fried bacon. I loved me some bacon. I simmered in bed for a few more minutes before I grabbed my chocolate silk robe and slipped into my Winnie the Pooh slippers. I sloshed my way into the bathroom to brush my teeth and wash my face before I made my way into the kitchen, where Wallace was.

I walked in the medium-sized kitchen and sat at the table, and once again, I watched my man make me a meal fit for a king. He had eggs going, bacon frying, and I could smell cinnamon rolls in the oven baking.

I shook my head. I didn't deserve such a man. A tear slid out of my eye, and I quickly wiped it away.

He had some calypso music playing and was swaying to the beat. So was I. He hadn't noticed me yet, because he was really into the music and cooking. It was so cute. He softened my heart, and I didn't even know it.

I eased back out of my chair and made my way over to him, careful not to be too loud. I snuck up behind him and slipped my hand in his robe pockets, squeezing him and rubbing up against him.

He wasn't surprised at all. He just continued to sway to the music with me attached to him.

I broke my embrace. "Ummmm!" I moaned. "Baby, it smells so good in here."

He turned around with a wooden spoon in his hand and guided it to my mouth.

Fluffy, well-seasoned eggs danced in my mouth. "Wow! You sure you not an undercover chef or something?"

He smiled and beamed with pride. "Well," he said, turning back toward his pots and turning them off, "sit down, baby, and I will tell you all about it while we eat."

I did as I was told and took my seat across from him. He loaded our plates, and he then sat down at the table. We held hands as he blessed the food.

"Okay, I'm ready." I dug into my plate of food.

He chuckled. "You always ready."

I laughed too. He was a comedian too. "No, seriously. I wanna know about my man." I just had to know what he was hiding.

He shoved a couple of forks full of eggs in his mouth before he began to speak. "Well, I am originally from Oakland, California, where I was raised by both parents. My dad was a doctor, and my mom pretty much stayed at home and raised me and my other two brothers. I was the oldest out of the three. My dad put in our minds a lot of pressure on being successful at an early age. He was superstrict and tolerated no foolishness, hence my no-drama policy."

He paused and dug into his plate once more and took a sip of his orange juice before continuing.

"From a very young age, I was a momma's boy and I clung to her like a boy shouldn't. My father wasn't happy at all when he caught me in the kitchen with my mom all the time helping her cook and prepare food. It was woman's work to him. I should have been out back with my younger brothers playing sports and getting into trouble.

"I, on the other hand, could care less about those things. I was a bright ten-year-old who was focused and knew what he wanted to be when he grew up. A chef. I liked to cook and see the smiles on people's faces as they savored the meal and delicacies that I prepared. My father tried to beat it out of me, but he was unsuccessful. I rebelled against him harder.

"Eventually, by the time I was the age of fifteen, I was cooking more meals than my mom. It seemed like my father had given in and all was well in my house. He even made special requests on some days."

Wallace paused again. He gulped down the last of his orange juice and the last two pieces of his bacon. I was astonished at the depth that he was going into about his life.

He wiped his mouth with a napkin. "At the age of eighteen, I already knew that I was gay and that girls didn't appeal to me, but I never let it show. I made sure I had girls calling me all the time, and I took my only girlfriend to my prom.

"After I graduated high school, I was all prepped to go to culinary school and begin my career as a master chef. I had big dreams, but my father cared nothing about any of that. One night, he came into my room with my mom by his side and gave me an ultimatum—Go to a four-year college and get a degree like a real man should, or get out of his house. The look on my mother's face spoke of disapproval, but she was always the loving wife, and she stood by her man.

"Without even thinking, I got up and packed my things and left. Before leaving, my mom secretly slipped me a wad of money. Five thousand dollars, to be exact. I will never forget the look on her face and my brothers' faces as I walked out the door looking back one more time at the house I vowed never to step back into again."

By this time, Wallace had shed a couple of tears, and I, too, had some threatening to fall.

I wanted to find his father's ass and kill him for putting my baby out on the street. "You okay, baby?" I got up and walked over to him and held his head against mine.

He cried even harder then. "Yeah, baby boy. I'll be all right." He wiped the tears away. "Sit down and let me finish."

I did as I was told and let him continue to purge himself.

"When I left that house, I had no clue as to what I was

going to do. My father was an only-child, and my mom's family didn't like my dad, so they disowned her. So going to live with a relative was out of the question. I was homeless. I decided then that the best thing for me to do was to get out of California. And that is what I did. I didn't know where to go, but in my research for culinary schools, Maryland had some promising ones, and that's where I flew to.

"When I got to Baltimore, I felt good about my new start. I had some change in my pocket and destiny in my heart, but it didn't quite work out the way I wanted it to. I was a sheltered child growing up, so I knew nothing about life and the streets. My father was busy providing, and my mom was busy raising, so I got a crash course within a week of moving into Baltimore. Five thousand dollars doesn't last long, and I was looking for a job within weeks.

"With no experience, a brother was as good as homeless. Nobody wanted to hire me. So I decided to try hustling drugs to make my come-up to pay for culinary school and my apartment, and maybe even get a car. That was twenty-eight years ago.

"I never made it through school, and keeping my apartment and my car became my priority. The money was coming in fast, and school was on the back burner. Permanently. I never got to see my dreams come true. I can't blame my pops though, even though I wanted to. He was only doing what he thought was right.

"When I look back on the whole situation, I shake my head, because now I know that a dream is only a reality to the person that holds that dream, and only they can kill it or live it."

Wallace's face was now in his hand, his arms propped up on the table. He rubbed his face and then got up and proceeded to clean up the table and load the dishwasher. It was like he snapped back right to the present.

His life story made me think about my potential and how I allowed some foolishness to hinder me.

"You satisfied now that you know all about your man?"

I got up as he walked up to me, and we embraced and hugged for what seemed like forever.

When we finally let go, it was because his Nextel went off. He had a call.

About an hour later, he was back on the street doing what he did. I, on the other hand, spent the day in the house all by myself.

Chapter 33

Mona

Confirmation
December 21ˢᵗ, 2018, 12:05 A.M.

I walked around my bedroom in a funk today because I was still thinking about the other night when I'd called out James' name during sex. How could I be thinking about his ass in that way again? *After all these years, I thought I would be over his crazy ass.* It also made me wonder if Shawn was having the same feeling about him as well. By the way he acted at the reading of his father's will, it was like he wanted to kill James dead.

It was Saturday afternoon, and I could hear the kids downstairs making a whole lot of noise as usual. I was usually out on a walk by this time on a Saturday, but I just couldn't get myself together.

My emotions were a raging mess. One minute I was happy, the next I was sad. It wasn't pretty. I kept having nightmares of James coming to claim the children that he fathered. I was trying to get this vow renewal ceremony together, and that too had become a task, making sure I didn't leave anybody off the guest list, and that the caterer was on point and the decorations all finished. I was going crazy.

Shawn was working more and more, and his talk of a new addition to the family was puzzling, to say the least. I didn't know what he was thinking about. I mean, don't get me wrong, I loved my kids and all, but adding another one would be putting a strain on my already heavy load.

I jumped in the shower then made my way downstairs to get something to eat.

"Hey, baby," I said to Diana as she sat on the couch watching Finding Nemo for the umpteenth time. I bent over and kissed her on the cheek. "You eat?" I asked, walking toward the kitchen.

"Yes, Mommy. Ashley fixed me some scrambled eggs and bacon before she left."

I paused at the entrance to the kitchen. "Did she say where she was going?"

"No, she just left out."

"Oh, okay," I said, continuing my way to the kitchen. She was always hanging out with her girlfriends on Saturdays. It was like she didn't want to be around her family. I shrugged it off as normal teenage behavior, because I too was just as wild.

I walked toward the refrigerator to see what I could fix myself to eat. Shawn had left me a note on the refrigerator.

> Hey love,
> Had a meeting with a client. Will be back soon.
>   Your hub
>   Shawn

I had to admit I was feeling a little neglected. Ashley was out, and now Shawn too. It seemed that everyone was off in their own little world.

I decided on a BLT, since it was lunchtime and I wanted something light. The dress I had picked out for the ceremony was absolutely stunning and I didn't want to risk overeating and gaining too much weight to the point where I couldn't fit into it.

After I ate, I decided to call my mom and see if she needed some company today. *Diana would love to see her nana today.* I picked up the phone and listened for the dial tone, like I always did when I heard a voice on the phone. It was Alex and a feminine-sounding, raspy-voiced boy on the other end of the phone. My last intent was to eavesdrop, but what I was hearing was blowing my mind.

"Yeah, baby, I was missing you too," Alex cooed into the phone.

"I can't wait to try that stuff we did with the dildo again soon."

I almost dropped the phone hearing this. I was wondering if they tried that shit here in my house. I was ready to run downstairs and whip ass for real.

The raspy-voiced boy snickered into the phone. "Next time, we need to use some of that jelly stuff to make it a lot less painful. I couldn't sit down for a couple of hours after that."

Again, I almost dropped the phone as I had just got confirmation of my son's sexuality. I slowly put the phone down on the hook, and tears slid out of my eyes freely. I leaned up against the refrigerator and sobbed a little.

I was so overwhelmed, I didn't even see Diana come in the kitchen.

"Mommy, what's wrong?" she said, startling me.

"Oh, ah, nothing, baby. I just hit my toe on the edge of the table really hard, and it hurts pretty bad." I wiped my eyes with my hands.

"Really?" she said, looking at me with sympathy in her eyes. "I know what you mean, Mommy. That happened to me too, and I cried too, but as soon as Daddy heard me crying, he picked me up and put me in the chair and kissed my feet and rubbed it until it stopped hurting." She pulled out the kitchen chair closest to her and sat down. "You want me to rub your feet?"

"Awww, that's sweet, baby, but Mommy will be just fine." I kissed her on the cheek again.

"You wanna go and see Nana today?"

"Oh, yeah! We going over Nana's!" she yelled, jumping up and down.

I was glad somebody was happy today, because it was shaping out to be a trying one for me. "Go upstairs and get cleaned up so we can go, okay?"

"Okay, Mommy," she said, skipping the whole way upstairs.

Just as I was getting ready to go upstairs, Alex came up out of the basement, a big Kool-Aid smile on his face.

"Hey, Mom." He walked up to me and kissed me on the cheek. "Y'all leaving out soon?"

"Yeah. Why you asked that?" I said in accusatory tone.

"Oh, no reason. I just wanted to know."

I knew what that meant. His nasty ass wanted to be in the house alone, so him and his friend could finish messing around in my house. Not.

"Well, we going over your Nana's, and I need you to come with me"

"Why?" he said with a little attitude.

"Because I said so." I countered with even more attitude. "Now go downstairs and get ready to go." I turned and left him standing there with a defeated look on his face. I, too, made my way to my bedroom to get dressed.

When we all got in the car, I noticed Alex was still in a funky mood. Before I pulled off, I turned around and looked at him. "You might as well get that smirk off your face because, last time I checked, I was the parent, and you were the child. And when we get to Nana's, you better act like you happy, or I'ma let her take you outside for a few rounds of boxing."

He smiled, knowing my mother was feisty and loved to play around with them in the backyard.

"That's better," I said, turning around and pulling off down the street.

Chapter 34

Sherry

Exposed
December 21st, 2018, 2:30 P.M.

"There they go right there," Keisha said, pointing in front of us as we drove two cars behind Antoinette in a car with some young-looking chick.

"All right, I see them," I said back, trying not to lose them.

I hadn't the slightest idea why I was helping her track down her cheating girlfriend. I would have thought she would have learned her lesson from the last time Antoinette knocked her on her butt.

My ass had to be a glutton for punishment as well, because I should have said no when she asked me to do this foolishness. I wanted to be home spending the holiday with my son. I shook my head in shame. Here I am running behind some chick I could care less about all because James wants this chick to pay for something she did to him a ways back.

I felt like I was on the television show *Cheaters*, following behind this broad, weaving in and out of traffic in the middle of the day. I had other things to do. *James needs to hurry his ass up and do whatever he got to do to this chick, and fast, so I can move ahead with my plans.*

We pulled into the Owings Mills Mall shopping center and watched them go into the movie theatre.

"Come on, let's go," Keisha said in a hurry as she exited the car and walked casually across the parking lot. "I don't want to lose them. I'ma catch this bitch and her little trick she has with her in the act."

"All right," I said, trailing behind Keisha, watching Antoinette and the little chick hold hands and walk into the theatre. It was still early, and there weren't a lot of people at the movies this early. "Don't walk too close," I said, pulling her back a little.

We walked up to the booth to buy tickets.

"Welcome to AMC Theatres. How can I help you?" the clerk asked.

"Yeah, um, what movie did the two chicks buy tickets for?" Keisha asked the clerk.

"Excuse me?" the clerk answered back, confused looking.

"Oh, I'm sorry," Keisha said apologizing. "My two girl-friends just came in here before us, and we were supposed to see a movie together. I forgot and was wondering if you could give me tickets for the same movie they purchased."

"Oh, sure, ma'am," she said with a smile.

I handed her the money and grabbed our tickets and entered the concession lobby.

We made our way into the appropriate theatre and sat about six rows behind Antoinette and her little friend.

About a half of an hour into the movie, Keisha got up with her soda and popcorn in hand.

"Where you going?"

"I'm going to say hi to Antoinette and her friend," she said, a sinister smile on her face. "You might wanna stand by the door, because it's about to get ugly up in this bitch."

As she made her way up to her former lover, I did as I was instructed and stood by the door.

Keisha threw her popcorn and then her soda on the two lovers, and she just wilded out on Antoinette. She wasn't doing too bad, because all I could see was her swinging and tagging Antoinette continually. The other chick just looked on with fear in her eyes.

When she had enough, she sprinted toward me, and we exited the movie and made a mad dash toward the car. We pulled off before Antoinette could catch up to us as we made a beeline back to Keisha's house.

Chapter 35

Ashley

Whipped Cream
December 21ˢᵗ, 2018, 5:32 P.M.

I just got back into the house from the movies and I was a total mess. Some chick had come in the theatre and just started going crazy on Tony as we sat and watched a movie I wanted to see really bad. It all happened so fast, I really couldn't do anything as the chick just up and started throwing punches. It was, "Bitch, this" and "Bitch, that" every time the crazy chick swung.

Tony was caught off guard and couldn't defend herself as the crazy chick tried to beat her into next week, and my little ass couldn't do anything but stand there and watch my girlfriend get her ass whupped. Then the chick sprinted off and left us there to get ourselves together. Tony was covered with popcorn and soda, and she had a busted lip and eye.

We quickly exited the theatre and made our way toward the car. The other chick was nowhere in sight. I wanted to know who the crazy bitch was.

Tony told me it was one of her exes that just couldn't let her go. I could believe her because her tongue work was the bomb. Then out of nowhere, she just hauled off and sucker-punched me in the eye.

I looked at her with hurt and shock in my eyes.

She followed up with a couple more blows as I tried my best to shield myself. I begged and pleaded as she continued to do me bodily harm. I just laid there and took it.

"Get the fuck out my car, you punk-ass bitch!"

I exited her car and watched her speed off like a bat out of hell. I broke down and sobbed right there in the middle of the parking lot, even as people passed me by. I couldn't care less. I was deeply hurt and dumbfounded as to why Tony would do this to me.

Then it hit me like a ton of bricks. I recalled just standing there as her ex wailed on her in the movie theatre. I stood there like a scared bitch and did nothing as she was getting fucked up royally.

I was so ashamed of myself. I pulled myself together and made my way to the bus stop to catch the bus home.

Thankfully, when I got home, the house was still empty, so I made my way to my room and sat on the bed and sobbed once again. I pulled a picture of me and Tony out of my teddy bear I'd hid it in.

I picked up the phone and dialed Tony again for like the tenth time since she'd left me. She never picked up, but I did leave a message pleading my case. But what could I say? I was wrong, and I knew it.

I got up and went to the bathroom to take a look at my face. My eyes weren't black, but I did have a cut over the top of my eye. I didn't even feel the pain of the cut until I looked at it just now.

The pain of Tony leaving me just hurt too bad. She was my first love, and I didn't want to lose her.

Chapter 36

James

Pleasure Principle
December 27th, 2018, 9:32 P.M.

Christmas had come and gone, and I was about to start the new year on a clean slate, so I had to get this one last person off my list. It was a little nippy when I walked out of the house, and the wind was brisk, so I had to zip up my thin Coach jacket. Having taken a shower no more than twenty minutes earlier didn't help either.

Wallace and I had just gotten finished breaking each other off, and his ass was half-asleep when I told him that I'd promised Sherry I would stop by to check on her and Li'l Shawn. He mumbled okay and rolled over and went to sleep.

I really needed to come clean with Wallace with some of this stuff I was doing. I didn't want to risk losing such a good man. *Who would have thought that I would fall in love again?* I still didn't believe that shit myself. Shit, love was nothing but trouble for me in the past.

As I walked to my car, I noticed a piece of paper underneath one of the windshield wipers. I hated when business folk put shit on your car, trying to advertise or sell you some useless crap. But none of the other cars on the parking lot had fliers except mine. That shit was odd.

I snatched it off the window with one swipe, ready to toss it to the ground, when I noticed my name etched out in magazine letters. *That shit was original!* I chuckled. *Somebody on some Cagney and Lacey type of shit!* I mumbled and chuckled again. My chuckle was short-lived because, when I got in the car and I opened the letter, my mouth hit the floor.

James/Jerry,
Your ass living on Nob Hill and shit. You think your shit don't stink don't you. You going to pay for what you did to me. I think you better leave that dread-wearing boyfriend of yours alone before he end up like the old man. Time is ticking, muthafucka. lol.
The Sandman

"Okay, this shit is getting ridiculous." I was heated and afraid at the same time. I didn't like being stalked, and I damn sure didn't like being afraid. This shit only made me madder at whoever was coming at me. They didn't want to fuck with me right about now. I was beginning to feel like a cornered animal ready to pounce at the next attack.

I put my car in drive and peeled out of the parking lot. I was steaming mad and was going to take it out on the next victim on my list.

I had gotten the call that I was waiting for all week. It was time to pay back the last victim for their betrayal. I was truly going to enjoy this. Sherry had called me and told me that she was just leaving the house and it was a perfect time for me to do my business.

It took me about forty minutes or so to get down to the east side where Keisha and her lover lived. It was late in the evening, probably about nine o'clock or so, and I was amped up and ready to strike.

I parked a couple of blocks up the street from the house, just to be safe. As I rode by, I saw that Antoinette bitch at the door going in. I loved getting two for one. Her ass was going to get hers just for messing over her brother, my ex-lover Kenny.

I got my supply bag and my gear, which included a gun and Taser, and exited my car. I went around the back into the alley so I could get in with ease. I was hoping I didn't have to pry the door open, not wanting to leave any evidence of forced entry or anything suspicious.

I crept up the alley and counted the house to make sure I was going to the right one. When I got to the yard, I quickly jumped the fence. I couldn't believe I was still so agile at forty-six. I loved it.

As soon as I landed, to my surprise, a pit bull ran out of nowhere and made a mad dash toward me. I scrambled around the yard, digging in my bag, trying to find something to subdue the dog. I knew I couldn't just shoot the dog because that would bring attention toward the yard.

Just in time, I reached my Taser gun and gave his ass a jolt that sent him careening toward the ground, as limp as an eighty-year-old man's dick without Viagra. I wiped my forehead as the perspiration dripped down my face from the short sprint around the yard.

I got myself together and made my way to the back door. I tried the door, but it was locked. *Shit!*

I quickly thought and felt around the border of the door, just in case they left a key in a crack or something. No luck.

Just as I reached down in my bag for something to pry the door open with, I noticed a flowerpot next to the steps, and sure enough, there was a key waiting for me to retrieve it.

I crept in the house, hoping this was going to be easy. I could hear sounds of pleasure coming from a nearby room. I couldn't figure out which one, so I pulled out my gun to catch whoever by surprise. I walked with my back toward the wall, after I left the kitchen, and through the hallway that led to the front of the house.

As I got closer, I could hear Janet Jackson's "The Pleasure Principle" playing softly. I stopped to listen to make sure the kids were nowhere around. It was quiet, so I assumed they were gone. Or, at least, I hoped so. *If these nasty tricks having sex out in the open with the kids in the house, that would be just plain trifling. And that's coming from me.*

I got to the living room and quickly glanced around the corner to see what was going on. These nasty-ass hoes was on the living room couch licking each other like they were eating Jell-O Pudding Pops. I almost lost my fucking lunch. I had to hold my hand over my mouth because I was gagging and shit. I barely could do one, so two was nauseating.

From what I saw, Keisha was sitting up on the couch, head tossed back, eyes closed, and her legs cocked up like she was getting a fucking pap smear exam. The other bitch, Antoinette, was laying between her legs, lapping and poking her pussy.

I pulled out my Taser, and I had the gun in my other hand. I walked up to the two lovers, a big smile on my face. Their asses were so into the sex, they didn't even hear me creep up on them. I quickly jabbed the cunt on the floor, and her ass flopped like a fish. It was lights out for her. She didn't even see it coming.

I kicked her with my foot, just to make sure she was out. At the same time, I had my gun pointed toward Keisha. She opened her mouth like she was about to scream.

"Bitch, scream, and I will blow your fuckin' head off!"

She stayed still and didn't let out a peep. She was petrified. I was her worst nightmare, and she knew it.

"What's up, Keisha? I bet you didn't see this shit coming. You forgot all about my ass, didn't you? You thought your ass was home free. You sent Kenny up river and thought you was going to run off with his money and live it up with this bitch." I darted my eyes toward her incapacitated lover.

She shook her head.

I slapped her ass with the gun. "That's for going through my pockets and taking the keys to my car, bitch! You thought I was going to forget about that shit, didn't you?"

I slapped her ass again. "That was for taking the money that was rightfully mine, bitch!"

She wiped the blood trickling down the edge of her lip.

"So how much money did you get me and Kenny for?"

She gave me a blank look, like she was afraid to speak.

"Bitch, answer me!" I roared, pacing in the middle of the room.

"A hundred thousand!" she muttered.

"Is it all gone?"

She nodded her head yes, tears rolling down her face.

"What the fuck!" I ran up to her and placed the gun to her temple. "You mean to tell me you blew through that much money and all you have to show for it is this shitty shack?"

I glanced over and noticed her dyke lover was off the floor and charging at me. I Tasered her ass, and she went down again. I leaned over and gave her ass another jolt, to make sure she would be out longer.

I prayed I didn't kill her ass. I remember hearing about police Tasering people and killing them. My ass surely didn't want to go back to jail. Before I entered the house, I had set the Taser to "low stun," so I knew she would be all right after a good night's rest.

I focused my attention back toward Keisha, my anger boiling.

This bitch had wasted the money I was going to steal from Kenny myself. *I gotta give it to her. A bitch is always three steps in front of a nigga.*

"You know you gotta pay for robbing me," I said, a smile on my face.

"Please, please . . . don't hurt me. I had no choice. I had to take the money. I needed it to take care of my kids."

This bitch must have thought I was a dummy. "Bitch, I know good and well you didn't spend that fucking money on those brats of yours, so cut the bullshit. You and this bitch over here probably blew that shit on trips and clothes. You know I wracked my brain trying to figure out what I was going to do to get back at you. I was stumped until I got in here and heard you two going at it like two alley cats in heat. It seems to me that you love getting your pussy licked, so your ass can twitch and shake. How about I give your ass an orgasm that your grandmother can feel?" I grabbed my crotch.

She looked at me and started shaking her head.

I laughed a hearty laugh as I looked at her contorted face. "Don't worry, bitch. I'm not going to fuck your greasy ass, even though I know your ass is probably in need of a good piece of dick."

"I heard you guys in here getting it on to one of my favorite songs, 'The Pleasure Principle,' and I am the one in need of pleasure right now. And you're going to give it to me. Open your legs and get ready to receive the best orgasm of your life."

She hesitantly opened her legs.

"Now close your eyes, bitch! And if you tell anybody about this shit, bitch, one of your little brats will end up on an AMBER Alert. You hear me?"

She nodded in agreement.

I moved in for the kill. I was going to love this, and she

was undoubtedly going to remember this for years to come. I cut my Taser on and raised the notch to "fry," then I slowly eased it toward her waiting womb. Sex for her would never be pleasurable again.

I covered her mouth with my hand, and with one quick jab, I gave her pussy the shock of its life. She was twitching and shaking, but I didn't let up until I saw her pussy sizzling like hot bacon.

After a couple of seconds, her ass was out cold. I removed the Taser, placed it on "safety," and put it back in my pocket. I couldn't risk the same shit happening to me. I needed my dick, like any other nigga.

I looked over at her lover, and her ass was still out. "You won't be enjoying that pussy no more." I laughed and exited the house the same way I came in.

I had a little more vengeance I had to get out before I could get back to my life with my man and live happily ever after.

When I got back home, it was a little after midnight. Wallace was still in the bed where I left him. I undressed and jumped in the shower for about twenty minutes to freshen up and get a good night's sleep.

"Hey, baby," I said as I slid under the covers and into the bed totally naked.

The flat-screen television was on, showing a marathon of *The Golden Girls*. Wallace and I were both hardcore Golden Girls fans. We had a lot in common.

Wallace was on his back. I could see him fighting sleep. I couldn't sleep without the television on, and neither could he. Even if we weren't watching it, it still had to be on.

I snuggled up to him, and he was naked as well. He liked to

sleep naked too. Our body heat mingled together as I wrapped one of my legs around his and laid my head on his chest.

He managed to mumble during one of his nods, "How is your cousin doing?"

"Oh, she is fine," I said half-heartedly. "I took her and Li'l Shawn to the movies and out to eat."

"You have fun?" He was fully awake now. He lifted my head by my chin toward his, and pecked me on the lips.

"Yeah, it was okay." I kissed him back.

I looked into his eyes. It was like they were dancing. It seemed like he instantly got excited about me every time we were apart for any length of time. I was getting the feeling that he truly did love me.

In those few moments, I wanted to spill out all of my secrets to him. I wanted to let him know about the pain I'd experienced in California and all the things I'd been getting myself into.

I knew I needed to release this anger and pain, and exchange it for this love he was offering so freely, but I just couldn't do it. I said I would never be vulnerable again.

Would he still be with me, or leave me if I told him about the true me? The evil me. The hurt me. The abused me. The little boy in me that just wanted to be loved. I could never tell him now. I was, no, we were too deep into this for me to go and risk losing it over the truth.

"I'm just glad to be back home with my man."

He smiled and pulled me on top of him.

I looked down at him and gazed into his eyes. "You miss me?"

"And you know this. Man!" he belted out.

I threw my head back and roared with laughter. It had been a long time since I laughed. It felt good, made me feel real. Too bad I was going to have to shut it off a little bit longer.

Chapter 37

Mona

Now or Never
December 27ᵗʰ, 2018, 12:13 P.M.

"What in the hell!" I belted out as I sat up of my living room sofa. The television was on, and James was sitting in the chair across from me, watching it like he lived there.

"How in the hell did you get in here?"

I'm sure I had the look of a mad woman on my face. My hair was a mess from sleeping on the couch. It was supposed to be a nap after I had dropped the kids off to my mom's house.

I looked at my watch. It was a little after twelve noon. I had cleaned up, and took down all the Christmas décor. I was beat. I must have been really tired to not hear him come in my damn house.

"Honey, I'm home." He chuckled. "You missed me, baby girl?"

"Missed you? Missed you?" I laughed. "I wish I would have missed you in the club in California, with your crazy ass. I probably wouldn't be in this shit I'm in now."

"Bitch, please. Your ass is as loose as a faggot's asshole after two years in prison." He laughed again.

I didn't find it funny. I had managed to keep my pants on

and not let them fall for another man since James. But here he was, bringing up the past, like I needed reminding.

He laughed again. "Mona, please . . . why can't we be civil, like adults?"

"Muthafucka, I asked you, 'How did you get in my house?'" My nose flared like a dragon getting ready to set something ablaze.

"Don't worry about that, Mona. I'm in here now." He smiled. His ass was bold as a muthafucka.

My eyes darted around the room to see if I could grab something to bash him in the head with. I wanted to kill the nigga for ruining my life.

Then it flashed in my head that I was a willing participant in both of the times we'd had sex. I immediately felt like a ho again. The time I let him fuck me like an animal on the very spot I was standing all came back to memory.

I crumbled back on the chair, my head fell, and shame embodied me once again. I still hadn't forgiven myself for my infidelities. Everybody else in my life had forgiven me, but me.

"Mona, look at you. You's a hot-ass mess."

I lifted my head up as he said that. I wasn't expecting this today.

"I can't believe you my baby mama." He shook his head like he was ashamed of me.

I shot back up off my chair. "Faggot, please! Your ass is lucky somebody wanted to fuck your sensitive ass."

His eyes got big as quarter pieces. He wasn't expecting a snappy comeback.

"Your ass wants to be a bitch, but my ass was born a real woman."

"Well, you fucked this faggot, and so did *your* husband. Now what does that say about you? I bet you and Shawn probably still dreaming about my ass at night."

"Nigga, please! No your ass is dreaming about me and all of this!" I did a little twirl to show him I still had a banging body.

"Whatever, Mona!" He waved his hand just like a woman would. "I just came by here to see how my kids were being raised."

"They have never been *your* kids, and their *father* and I are doing a very good job at it." I paused. "So you can carry your dick-sucking ass back to where you came from."

"Ho, say what!" He laughed. He then walked up toward me.

I stood my ground, in case he tried something.

James was about a foot from me when he grabbed my collar and pulled me close to him. "Mona, don't forget I know who your children's *real* father is and they don't. So, bitch, don't fuck with me if you want it to stay that way. I will have your ass stripping in a retirement home New Year's party if I want to and you could do nothing about it." He let my collar go and kissed me on the forehead. "Bye, boo." And, just like that, he was gone out of my back door.

I rushed to the back door and locked both the locks and peeped through the shades to make sure he was gone. I walked to the refrigerator and grabbed a Pepsi. I went to the cabinet and grabbed the bottle of Aleve for the headache that I now had and sat at the table.

My hands were shaking so bad, I felt like a crackhead. I couldn't even finish the soda. I went back to the living room and took another nap. I had to man up and break this to the kids ASAP. *I can't continue to live like this.*

I needed to get out of the house, so I decided to take a trip over Shawn's mother's house.

***

I pulled up to her house in Towson, which was only about a twenty-minute drive.

Knock! Knock! Knock!

After a minute, the door opened and Mother Black stood in the doorway with an inviting smile on her face.

"Well, what a nice surprise to see you here, Mona."

"Yeah, I thought you could use the company." I smiled back and walked in as she moved back out of the doorway to let me in.

It was such an ease of my mind to be here. Even after all that she went through with Shawn and her husband, she remained humbled and spiritual. *An hour or two over here would do my heart good.*

"Yes, baby. Mama sure could use the company today. And since we haven't been chatting like we used to, it will give us some time to catch up on you and my son."

"Sure thing, Mama. Let me go to the bathroom before we sit and talk."

I walked to the bathroom as slow as I could, which was only up one flight of stairs and around the corner. *I didn't come over here to talk about that. I was trying to get away from that by coming over here.* I sat on the bowl and prayed that I could find a way to distract her, or get her to talk about something other than Shawn and me. I stayed in the bathroom for about five minutes. I washed my hands and sprayed air freshener for effect.

I made my way down the stairs and into the living room, where Mother Black was. She had tea and cookies on the table for our little heart-to-heart.

"All right, Mama. I'm ready to talk." I picked up my mug and began to sip, trying to prolong the inevitable.

"So how are you and my son getting along?"

"Mama, what can I say? We are coming along."

"Umm-hmm." She nodded her head. "Are you guys talking and communicating?"

"Sure, Mama. We talk all the time." I smiled. It was true, but we limited what we talked about. Even though we were pretty much back to normal, we still had room for improvement.

Knock! Knock! Knock!

We were interrupted by a knock on the door. I breathed a sigh of relief. I knew she was going to grill me more. I really needed this out.

She put her finger up like she was excusing herself and went to answer the door. She came back with a husky African-American man and a thin, lanky Caucasian male.

I looked at her puzzled.

"Mona, these two detectives are working on my husband's murder case. Detectives, this is my daughter-in-law."

"How are you doing, ma'am?"

"I'm doing fine." I got up and shook both of their hands.

"Take a seat, young men." Mama Black pointed to her plaid sofa. "Is it okay if she stays here while we talk?"

They nodded their heads in agreement.

The African American officer spoke first. He said, "Mrs. Black, we would first like to give condolences about the death of your husband."

"Thank you so much, gentlemen."

"We have been working tirelessly trying to get this offender who murdered your husband off the streets. We need to know if there is anyone that you can think of that would have cause to kill your husband?"

"I'm sorry, detective, but I can't think of anyone I know that would want to harm him. I will say, though, that he did have some seedy type of acquaintances at the time of our separation."

"We have questioned a James Parks, since he was the last person to see him alive. We had to dismiss him as a possible suspect. He came back with a solid alibi for the night of the crime."

She looked at me, and then we both shook our heads. I guess we both wanted James to get some kind of payback for the way he had treated members of this family, but it was what it was.

He'll get his one day. Because I know karma very well, and she don't play.

"I think that's all we needed to ask you at this time. We have retrieved some evidence from the crime scene that is still being worked on. We will give you a call if anything definite comes up."

The two detectives got up, and we did the same.

"Here is my card. If you can think of anything, please call me ASAP. Anything you can remember will help."

"I sure will." Mama walked the detectives to the front door.

I quickly grabbed my coat and made my way toward the front door as well. "Mama, I really have to go." I hugged her and kissed her on the cheek. "I forgot I have a meeting with Diana's guidance counselor today." I lied.

As I sat in my car and started it up, I prayed to God for forgiveness for the lie I'd just told. I pulled off and made my way back home to wait until it was time to pick up the kids.

Later that evening, after picking up Alex and Diana from my mom's house. She was getting older and I wanted her to spend as much time with the "grands," as she called them, as she could.

I walked into the house with the kids in tow. It was so relaxing to get in the house and chill out. The kids had a marvelous time at my mom's house again. We had made several trips over to her house during this week. They were acting like straight fools, and my mom was right along with them.

They played everything from Charades to Scrabble. I, on the other hand, had other things on my mind. How was I going to tell Shawn about Alex being gay? He was still wrapped up in his own issues, so I was afraid this one just might push him over the edge.

Alex and Diana immediately went their separate ways when we got in the house. I was wondering if Ashley was back home after she darted out of the house again this morning, and what her and this Tony fellow were doing that had her leaving the house so early in the morning.

I walked up the steps and went to her room. As I got to the door, I could hear her crying. I knocked a couple of times to let her know I was there.

"Come in," she called out.

When I walked in, she was sprawled out across her bed with her face toward the wall.

"Are you okay?" I said as I walked over and sat on the bed. "I thought I heard you crying."

"I was," she said as she turned and positioned herself to face me.

I instantly saw a small cut above her eye, but it didn't look fresh. I didn't notice it until now, probably because I was so consumed with Alex's mess that I didn't notice the signs of my daughter being in an abusive relationship. It didn't help that I had never met this young man.

"Who did this to you?" I said, placing my hand right above the cut. "Did Tony do this to you?" I was boiling, ready to confront this bastard boy immediately. How dare he hit my baby!

"Well," she said, "me and Tony had a disagreement the other day, and I walked off. But Tony didn't hit me though. I did this when I got home and I hit my head on a cabinet door that I left open after I made something to eat."

"You sure?" I said, not believing her fully.

Her head was lowered, and I saw a few tears flow down her cheek.

"Ashley, baby," I said, lifting her head up with my hand. "Don't be fooled into thinking that this guy loves you and hits you out of love. You are a beautiful girl, and I am sure God will send the right boy along that will treat you right."

I'd always raised my children with the notion that if I validated them while they were young then they will already know their self-worth when they're looking for a mate. They won't stand for any abuse in any way and will love themselves before anyone can tell them different.

"Ma, I know that already. Daddy tells me that all the time. I just need to handle this on my own, okay." She wiped her face.

She gave me a great big hug, which let me know that she indeed was growing up, that I had to give her space to make mistakes, and learn from them as well. I kissed her on the forehead and walked out of the room.

It was almost time for me to start dinner, so I made my way down the stairs and into the kitchen to make a quick decision on what to fix. Just as I was getting ready to start, the phone rang, interrupting my flow.

"Hello," I said cheerfully.

"What's up with my baby mama?" James said comically into the phone.

I didn't find it funny. I hated the fact that he had such a link to me. "Hey, James."

"What's up with you? You don't sound too happy to hear the voice of the most important person in your life." He laughed a little.

"James, I don't have time for your shit right now. I have a family to take care of," I said as quietly as I could.

I don't know what I ever saw in him, because he now made my skin crawl every time I heard his voice. The liquor I was drinking in California must have been spiked with something for me to mess with his crazy ass. Just the thought of us being connected forever made my head spin.

"Look, *hoes 'r' us*, get your tone right when talking to big daddy. Remember the last time your ass popped off slick, I had your ass in an alley fucking the homeless. Don't make me take you down a notch. You hear me, cunt?"

I was angry and speechless at the same time. I didn't deserve this shit he was putting me through again. All I could do was tell the children who their father was and let the chips fall where they may. "Look, James, the children already know that you are their biological father, and they want nothing to do with a homewrecking faggot."

"Bitch, what do you take me for? A fucking dummy? They don't know shit, and if you wanna play Russian roulette, then it's a go, because I got both Ashley and Alex's cell phone numbers on speed dial. Now if you wanna play games, let's put one of them on three-way and see if they really know."

Shit! This muthafucka was good, and it seemed like he was always a step ahead of me. I breathed out a sigh of anguish. "Okay, James, what do you want?"

"Umm, the possiblities are numerous, but . . . I just wanted to check up on you again to make sure my number two ho was still in line. Holla." *Click.*

I sat with my back against a wall once again, literally and figuratively. I mulled over the possibility of what the children's response might be if they found out that Shawn wasn't their father. It was time to find out.

"Alex! Ashley!" I yelled out, calling them to the kitchen. "Come here for a minute."

Within seconds, they were in the kitchen standing on both sides of me. I looked at both of them several times. They were my babies, and I loved them so much. I hated that I was deceiving them. I had to get this over with.

"Come and give me a hug," I said, reaching out toward both of them.

Diana had entered the kitchen and proceeded to hug me as well.

It's now or never. "Hey, you guys. Sit down for a minute."

"Is everything okay?" Alex asked with an inquisitive look on his face.

"I just need to ask you guys something." I paused for a couple of seconds and walked around the room, stalling. "Um, well, er, this is very hard for me to do." I put my hand over my head and leaned up against the counter. "So I'm going to just out and ask you guys—What do you guys want to do, eat in or out?" I just couldn't do it. I just didn't have the courage to tell them yet. I knew that waiting and prolonging the situation was only going to make it worse. I just needed more time.

"Is that it, Mom?" Ashley said with a smile on her face. "We thought something was really wrong. Like Grandma was sick or something. You had me scared for a minute. I'ma little tired of eating out and would love if you make some of your homemade fried chicken with mashed potatoes and gravy."

Alex and Diana both agreed to the same as well.

"Sorry, you guys. I just wanted your input. You guys are important, and I want you to feel that way in every decision this family makes, okay."

"Okay." They all chimed in together as if they were in the army.

"I'll call you guys as soon as your father comes in, so we can eat together."

They all went their separate ways as I took out chicken from the refrigerator and prepared my family a home-cooked meal.

Chapter 38

Shawn

Family Time
December 28th, 2018, 5:43 P.M.

When I got home, it was about six o'clock or so. I walked into my house to the aroma of home cooking. My wife was such a good cook and mother. I knew when I went to work that my household was being cared for with a passion that only she could give. It was a shame that I still had some issues that I wouldn't talk about.

I looked at "my" children and knew that it was a blessing just to be in their lives. Even though my father wasn't the best example of fatherhood, one thing I can say, he did stay. He wasn't a deadbeat father, and neither was I. He and I had some of the same faults, but I had to take this thing to another level and man up. I wasn't going to let my family go down without a fight. Even with me having a son out of my marriage and me not telling my family, I wasn't going to allow my father's demons to destroy my life or the lives of his grandchildren.

With God's help, I knew this family could overcome all of this. That's why when I sat in my car after I'd dropped Li'l Shawn off, I prayed to God that He would bring resolution to this house and heal our family. I know that it seemed like I was asking for this help a little too late, but my mom always taught me to put my trust in God.

"Prayer changes things, baby" was what she would tell me during the time that I was just getting used to talking to her again. It was at times like this I felt like screaming to God, "Why me?"

On one of those Sundays, when I was actually paying attention in church, I remember the pastor preaching about trial and tribulations, about our tests not always being for us, but for somebody else's deliverance. Personally, I thought it was messed up to go through something, just so I could help somebody else. Selfish I know, but that was the way I felt.

"Hi, honey." I walked into the kitchen and squeezed my wife from behind. "You sure got it smelling good up in here." I nibbled on her ear.

"Baby, I'm so glad to see you," she said as she turned around and kissed me on the cheek. "I have something I wanna talk to you about."

With raised eyebrows, I said, "Oh, really."

I knew what that meant. I had fucked up and gotten caught in my game. *Shit! How did she know? Damn, I knew I should have just came out and told her. I am such a fucking dummy. I should have known that I could get away with hiding Li'l Shawn but for so long.*

"Uh, about what?"

"Later, baby," she said, patting me on my face, "later."

Oh, shit! It's one of them let's-talk-all-by-ourselves talks. What in the world am I going to do?

"Dinner!" she yelled out, alerting the children.

Diana ran me down and jumped in my arms. "Daddy!" she squealed.

I loved my little girl. She was my little princess. *How am I going to tell her about her new brother?*

She kissed me on the cheek multiple times, letting me know her adoration for me. It did my heart good. And gave me the strength to go on.

Ashley and Alex were a little laid-back and seemed like they were in their own worlds. I could understand they are sixteen-year-old twins with crazy mood swings.

"Hey, you guys!"

They both did their weak "Hey, Dad."

I took them both with a grain of salt. I noticed that Ashley had a little cut over her eye and made a mental note to get an answer later. "So how are you guys doing in school?" It was a question I should've been asking more often, but I was sure Mona was on top of things, including their schoolwork.

"Okay," they both said in unison.

I took their word for it, but again I made a mental note to call the school to set up a parent-teacher conference.

After that small interrogation, I let them eat, and they made their way back to their rooms.

I made my way to the shower, while Mona cleaned up the kitchen and put away the food. I stayed in the shower a little longer, just to prolong the inevitable, a conversation with my wife. Sometimes it was draining. I loved her, but she could go on and on.

I walked out of the shower after about twenty minutes and made my way to our room and sat down on the bed.

"Okay, babe, I'm ready to talk."

"Well, baby." She blew out some air. "James called me today."

"What!" I almost yelled. Just hearing the nigga's name sent me over. "Why in the hell is he calling here again?"

My mind wandered back to when she called out his name in bed the other day, but I knew better than that. I knew, after all the things that he put us through, she wasn't messing around with him anymore.

"He just called here to torment me and let me know that I was his baby mama." She put her head down.

"That bitch done lost his mind calling here. What if one of the kids answered the phone?"

"That's what I wanted to talk to you about. I think that it's time to tell the kids the truth."

When she said that, I felt my heart starting to race a little. I wasn't prepared or ready to do this yet. I had to find a way to stall her. At least until I could get the nerve to tell her about Li'l Shawn.

"Baby, it's not time yet. I think we should wait until after we renew our vows and go our trip. I just think that it's best to wait right now."

She stood up and fumbled with something on her vanity dresser. "Shawn, we have been prolonging this for too long, and I'm getting tired of James holding this over my head."

I got up and walked over to her and turned her around. Tears were streaming down her face, and she sobbed a little as I pulled her close to me.

"Baby, I know this is a lot right now." I kissed her tears and stroked her hair. "But, trust me, when the time is right, we will know it."

"You sure?" She looked up at me, pain in her eyes. She was carrying this secret for a long time.

"Yes, Mona, I'm sure," I replied, uncertainty dwelling in my heart. I was feeling my way through this. I just didn't want her to know.

I scooped her up in my arms and carried her over to our bed. Then I proceeded to strip her down and kiss every inch of her body.

Chapter 39

Ashley

I'm a Lover, Not a Fighter
December 28th, 2018, 9:43 P.M.

I had been sitting up in my bed for a long time just staring
out the window. I was emotionally drained. I wasn't expecting
for Tony to act like she did It was totally uncalled for her to
hit me the way she did. She never acted like that before, and
it was a complete turn-off. *I mean, yeah, I could have helped when*
that chick was beating her ass. But, hell, I'm too pretty for all that
fighting shit. Her ass could eat some mean pussy, but I wasn't
getting fucked up over that. There are plenty more tongues
where hers came from. Part of me still loved her, but her ass
was going to come back to me. I wasn't running back to her.

My phone began to vibrate on my bed. Guess who? Yep,
Tony! "Hello," I answered like I knew she was going to call
me.

"What are you doing?"

She asked me like nothing happened earlier this week. A
complete switch.

"Well, for starters, I'm here sitting with a cut over my eye,
trying to figure who the hell I was messing with."

"Excuse me?"

"You heard me."

I got up and pushed the dresser in front of my door over, so no one could just come in. I was about to light into her and didn't want anyone interrupting me.

"What gave you the right to hit me?"

"Ashley, I was raised in a tight-knit family that was taught to stick together in a fight. When you fight one of us, you fight all of us." She paused. "Once when I was in school, my sister got into a fight and I stood there watching her and didn't jump in. Well, after she got finished fighting, she was pissed that I didn't help her, so she beat my ass because I stood there and watched her fight. She won the fight nonetheless, but the point was, to stick together."

"Yeah, and! I'm not a part of your family."

"So you just going to get tough with me over the phone and you couldn't even check the girl's chin that was getting the ups on me."

"It wasn't my fight, so why should I have helped you?"

"Because I was your lover, bitch!" she yelled into the phone.

"You got that right—*was*!"

"Oh, it's like that?"

"Yep, ever since you decided to lay hands on me." I was standing and making hand gestures like I was sure enough through. The truth was, I was a lover, not a fighter.

"Oh, okay. I guess you will be ready to let your parents know about your little secret life."

I paused as soon as she said that shit. I wasn't ready to let the perfect couple, Mona and Shawn Black, know about their lesbian daughter. But she didn't know who she was fucking with. I had one up on her, and it was definitely a trump.

"Well, I guess you got me there," I said, letting her think she won.

"I thought so," she boasted.

"*Not.*" I paused for effect. "You must have thought you were dealing with an adolescent."

"Oh, wait a minute, you are!"

"You must have forgotten you were fucking a minor. In the state of Maryland, it is considered statutory rape. Punishable by time in jail." I had a huge-ass smile on my face.

Silence.

"Next time, know who the hell you dealing with when you want some young pussy. You dumb-ass trick!" *Click.*

I hung up on her silly ass. She really thought I was a dummy or something. Ashley one, Antoinette zero. *She will definitely have something to think about for the next couple of days.*

I went to the shower and cleaned myself up and hopped into bed.

As I lay back in my bed, I thought about how I got to where I was right now. A lesbian. Who would have thought I would turn out like this? I didn't even know what it was until I used to see the girls stripping down to their panties and bras in the locker room before and after gym class. There would be breasts and ass everywhere. If I was a guy, I would have had a very noticeable erection for hours.

I tried my best to hide my lust for womanly flesh, but it got harder and harder every single day that I had to watch the girls shower next to me. Most of the time I would wash my private area until I came.

Once, a girl noticed how much attention I was paying to myself down below and called me on it.

"Oh, my goodness! Ashley, girl, you gon' leave any pussy left down there? Because you been scrubbin' for days!" She laughed, and so did the other girls that occupied the shower with us.

"You betta leave something for the boys to lick down there."

Everybody was laughing pretty hard and loud after that comment.

I laughed nervously too because I didn't want to let on to what I was really doing. "Naw, y'all. I just like my stuff to be extra clean. I can't catch a man with funky pussy. If a nigga smell a funky pussy, his ass will be running for the hills. The last thing I need is to have a nigga spread some shit about I smell like a sewer or some shit."

They all laughed again. "Shit, in the yearbook, my ass going down as the girl with the cleanest pussy. Fuck the most successful or the prettiest. A clean pussy get you a house and a car, and I won't have to work a day in my life."

Everyone fell out laughing.

"And a nasty one will get you ass-stripping and sucking dick on the block."

Again, everyone fell out laughing.

They didn't know I had actually come in the shower twice in ten minutes, looking at all of the breasts and pussy walking around. My mind was racing as I saw several of the more attractive chicks bend over and scrub their ankles. I could see their pinkness, and it was driving me crazy. Mentally, my tongue was wagging and panting like a dog. Many times I would walk out of the shower wobbly-legged from coming so much, I would be famished by the time we got to lunch period.

The truth was, I couldn't beat the boys off of me, because I was far from an ugly sister. I wasn't model material, but I got more than my fair share of glances.

I would even go as far as hanging out with a boy every now and then, just to throw the snooping-ass chicks off my trail. A free dinner and a movie never hurt a sister, but that was as far as I would let that shit would go. No kissing or holding hands. I would hug you, but only when I knew some of the chicks from school was around. That mess was getting old quick.

It was cool up until a dude that drove me home one day tried to force me to have oral sex with him. His ass is damaged goods for sure. Let's just say, his ass needed a dick doctor when I was finished with him.

After that, I swore off men and started actively pursuing women. I stumbled onto Antoinette by chance and was in love ever since I met her. Up until now, that is.

I rolled over, shed a few tears and drifted off to sleep.

Chapter 40

James

A Dream Come True
December 28th, 2018, 11:15 A.M.

I was so glad that I was finished with that get-a-bitch-back shit. I was getting too old for that shit, and was about to retire as "king bitch." They all got what they deserved.

And I definitely got what I deserved. A well-endowed man with money, power, and he could cook his ass off too.

When I got in the house last night, Wallace wasn't in the house yet, and I was glad. I had to wash the smell of burnt fish off of me before he got home. It was only about ten o'clock when I got in the house. Wallace usually didn't get in the house until about one or two in the morning. Which left me enough time to shower and clean up and dispose of the Taser and the gun. I put all of the clothes I used for this last act of vengeance in the dumpster along with all of the hurt I had endured in my life. Wallace was a dream come true, and I loved and wanted him forever.

I must have been awfully tired, because I didn't realize I had slept through his coming in last night. *Damn, I must have been spent.* Again, I was glad to leave that beat-a-bitch-down shit alone.

Wallace had the house smelling good. He must have gotten up early this morning and started cooking breakfast.

Before I could get out of the bed, my baby was walking in the room with a tray of food and a huge smile on his face.

"Hey, baby," I said with an even bigger smile. It was a smile of love and adoration. I finally had a man that loved me and was always honest with me. "What do I owe this pleasure?"

He stopped in his tracks and did a little shimmy dance, all seductive, like he was a stripper with the tray in one hand. That really made me smile. He was so sexy, I wanted to pinch myself.

After his little dance, he instructed me to sit back as he placed the tray on the bed and pulled out an eating tray from under his bed. He pulled a silk napkin and placed it in the collar of my shirt, so I wouldn't mess up my silk pajamas.

"Baby, I don't know what I would do without you here when I come home from grinding in the streets." He looked at me with his sexy eyes, a tear sliding down his face.

I wasn't one for the mushy stuff, but the moment had me about to shed a tear or two. "I know it was wrong, the ways I went about trying to get you, but know I am glad that I did it, because we wouldn't be together now, if I didn't."

"I'ma go get my plate, so I can eat and talk to you about something." He walked out of the room.

After we both ate, he immediately went into the kitchen to clean up the dishes. I laid back in the bed and watched cable until he returned.

In less than ten minutes, he was back in the room, on my side of the bed. He leaned over and kissed me on the mouth with a wet, passionate kiss.

"What was that for?" I asked, my dick rising fast in my pants. I was always ready for some dick, and now was a good time. I could stand to work off that good breakfast he just cooked me.

"Because I love you."

"I—I love you too." It was the first time I had said it to anyone in a long time. It felt strange, but right.

"Sit up for me, baby." He looked deep into my eyes. "I don't know how to say this, so I'ma just do it."

I did what was asked, a puzzled look on his face. All kinds of crazy shit was flowing through my head. Was he about to tell me he had a wife, and I was his side piece? That shit would be uncanny and definitely shocking. Or maybe he was HIV positive and had given it to me? Shit, I hated not having control of any situation.

"Well, baby, it's been a couple of months, and my life has been all the better with you in it. It feels so good to have a man to come home to that I know I ain't got to worry about you cheating on me. I just want you to know that I want you in my life forever and I want you to be in my life forever."

When Wallace got down on one knee, like you see in the movies, and pulled out a black box, my eyes got as big as dollar coins. I was totally shocked, but I held my shit down. I wasn't going to be screaming like no bitch.

"James Parks, will you marry me?"

I immediately shook my head yes, and we embraced. It felt like, finally, my world was coming together. It was a dream come true.

He slid the ring on my finger and just gazed into the platinum band that fit perfectly on my ring finger.

"When we going to do this?" I said, a smile on my face.

"Well, I made reservations in Vermont at a bed-and-breakfast in two weeks, so we could get married and have a honeymoon all at once. I made my arrangements with my boys on the block to hold shit down while I was gone, so I could be with my boo. Here's some cash." He placed a knot of money in my hands. "Go and get us some clothes we could wear for the ceremony and the rest of the week." He kissed me on the cheek and left the house to take care of some business.

I walked around the house in a daze, excited and scared at the same time. Could I actually live with one person for a lifetime? I was willing to give it a try.

I was so amped up that morning, I had showered, shaved, and dressed within forty-five minutes and was out the door. I planned on getting the best clothes money could buy, because we were going to do it up in Vermont big time.

Two Weeks Later

The flight to Vermont was a very peaceful one. No turbulence or wild children crying out in displeasure. We had arrived at the bed-and-breakfast about twelve noon. I was taken aback by the wonderful décor of the plush close-to-the-mountains retreat. The air was fresh and crisp, unlike the stuffiness of Baltimore.

As soon as we walked into the room, it seemed like all my pain and fear was washed away. The thoughts of my past vanquished under the tranquility of the atmosphere. I was a little nervous about the ceremony, but that was probably the wedding morning jitters or something.

I went back outside and retrieved the last of the bags, while Wallace paid the taxi. I again stood in the middle of our cabin-like suite.

Wallace snuck up and grabbed me from behind. He put his arms around my waist and pulled me in. "You ready to make this happen?" He started blowing and licking in my ears, seriously turning me on.

"Of course, baby." I turned around and softly kissed him on his lips. They were so moist, I took another kiss.

I pulled away and walked toward what looked like the bedroom. He followed behind me as I grabbed a couple of bags along with me.

"Wow," I said in awe of the heart-shaped bed adorned with large pillows the top. On the bed was a big basket filled with fruit, wine, and chocolate. I really wasn't a fan of red, but it was only for two weeks.

A single tear slid down my face as I thought all about the pain my first lover caused me. It was now that I realized that all the hate and rage I perpetrated against other people was needless. Here I was now with the man of my dreams. I'd said I would never love again, and here I was, about to jump the broom and pledge to spend a lifetime with one man. I deserved this, and I was truly going to go through with this and be happy forever.

As I reminisced, Wallace drew me back to the present with a kiss on the lips.

"I love you," I whispered. It was true this time. I felt it deep down inside and I knew it was real, what I felt at that very moment. True love.

The ceremony went off without a hitch. It only lasted a couple of minutes, and we were out of there.

We spent almost the whole trip in our room fucking like rabbits and eating up a storm. I was going to enjoy life with him and I knew my being around made him the happiest man on earth.

Chapter 41

Mona

Shortcomings
December 29ᵗʰ, 2018, 11:30 P.M.

I was so emotionally exhausted when I woke up the next morning. I had mixed feelings about not talking to the kids about this whole paternity issue. I got up and walked around the house. It was Saturday, and everybody was gone out of the house.

I decided to do the same. I wasn't in the mood to be in the house cleaning and doing other various household things. I got dressed and made my way to the kitchen to grab a quick bite to eat. I noticed two notes on the table, one from Ashley, the other from Shawn.

Ashley had taken Diana to the mall, and Shawn wasn't specific about his whereabouts. I assumed he was somewhere trying to get himself together. After the talk we had last night, I knew he had a lot to think about. I couldn't blame him for wanting to be alone to sort things out. He deserved that much, since we went through so much in the last decade.

Alex didn't leave a note, so I assumed he was out with his friends, or boyfriend. I shook my head at that thought again. How was I supposed to deal with this? Give him his privacy, or expose him and force him to alienate himself from his family? This shit was too much to deal with at one time. *Good thing Diana and Ashley are doing good and have very little issues. I'm so glad my girls are stable and responsible.*

I decided I would go through my list of things that needed to be done just before the ceremony. I had to get my mind clear and get away just to cope with these things going on in my family.

I was out for about three hours before I had gotten tired and was ready to go home. When I got home, I was tired and hungry. Getting something to eat while I was out wasn't on my mind. I went straight toward the kitchen to get something to eat. It was about two o'clock in the afternoon, so everybody was still gone, or so I thought.

As I made my way toward the kitchen, I heard music coming from Alex's room in the basement. It wasn't that typical music that teens his age listen to, like rap and hip-hop, but some old-school music, like he was sure enough grooving.

"What in the hell is he doing down there?" I whispered to myself.

I leaned up against the door to see if I could hear anything. Nothing. The music was too loud to hear what was going on.

Against my gut feelings, I eased my hand around the doorknob, turned, and opened the door. The steps were carpeted, so I could not be heard coming down the stairs. There was a little hallway before I got to his room. I took my time, because I didn't know if I was ready to see what I hoped I wouldn't. It was now or never.

I peeked in his slightly open door, and what I saw blew my mind. My son was on the bed, pushing the large dildo I found in his dresser drawer into a girl on all fours, while he jerked on himself, and another girl was underneath the first girl as they performed oral sex on each other.

I could see the reason why he had to use the dildo on the two young girls. Let's just say, he had a shortcoming. He wasn't well endowed like either one of his "fathers."

I silently mouthed, "Thank You, Jesus," to myself. *My son isn't gay. He is just an under-endowed freak.*

I stood there still in shock. I was glad he wasn't gay, but I wasn't letting him have a fuck-fest up in my house. Me and his father were doing the only fucking in this house.

"Alex!" I yelled as I entered his room. "What in the world do you think you are doing? Have you lost your mind?" I wanted to go over and hug him and his girlfriends, but I had to put on the pissed-off-momma act, to show him I meant business.

"Um, uh, uh, Ma," he stuttered, trying to cover himself up. "I'm sorry. I—I—I thought you would be gone a little longer."

"Oh, really?" I said, my arms folded. "I think you and your little tricks need to get the heck upstairs before I start doing bodily harm to all of you, okay!"

I made my way upstairs as they scrambled to get themselves dressed.

After about five minutes, they were upstairs and in the kitchen, where I was waiting for them. I chastised them all and sent the young ladies home.

I didn't even bother punishing Alex, because I was too overjoyed about the whole not-being-gay thing. I told him I wouldn't tell his father if he promised not to repeat what I saw in the basement, until he was married and out of my house.

Chapter 42

James

Honey, I'm Home
January 11th, 2019, 11:59 A.M.

Ring! Ring! Ring!
I jumped up from a deep sleep. And I was sleeping really good, you know, slobber running down the side of my face. I squinted my eyes at the clock that showed that it was only twelve o'clock in the afternoon. *Shit.*
Ring! Ring! Ring!
"Who the fuck is it?" I moaned in disgust and pure laziness. I reached for the phone just to see who was ringing the hell out of it. I looked at it, pausing just to see if I wanted to deal with the caller, who I knew would call back again if I didn't answer it this time. I wasn't for it.

I was so tempted to roll back over and get me forty more winks of sleep that I so deserved. Well, not deserved. I didn't work, I just worked it, but nevertheless I was tired. Wallace and I had had a marvelous time in Vermont, and I was still reveling in the glory of it. It was a new year, and I wasn't for the foolishness. I was retired and was acting the part.

"Hello," I answered annoyed and groggy.

"James! James!" Sherry yelled into the phone in a panicky

tone. "Oh my God! James, I think Li'l Shawn is dead!" She said again even more exaggerated. "I gave him some Benadryl last night, and, and I think I gave him too much. I shook him this morning, and he didn't wake up. Oh, God! Oh, fuck! What am I going to do? I think I just killed my baby! Oh, God!" She burst into tears over the phone.

"You did what?" I yelled back at her. I couldn't believe this bitch done poisoned her kid. "Did you call the ambulance?" I said, calming down a little.

"No. I didn't know what to do. I don't want to go to jail, James. They gonna think I killed him on purpose. Oh my God!" She went back into her hysterics. "I can't go to jail! I'll kill myself first, James! I will!"

"Look, calm down," I said as I got off the bed and went to my closet and pulled out something to put on for the journey across town to her house. "I'll be there in a little bit. Don't do anything until I get there."

I hung up the phone, jumped in the shower, and made my way out the door to my car.

"Stupid bitch," I mumbled to myself as I sped toward Sherry's apartment. "How in the hell do you overdose a child with Benadryl? You got to be ten times dumb to do some shit like this."

Fifteen minutes later, I pulled up to the apartment complex and rushed in, hoping that her ass was lying and I could take my ass right back home.

I put my key in the door and walked in the apartment. It was totally quiet, except for a television I heard going in the bedroom. "Sherry?" I yelled out.

"I'm back hear, James!" she yelled back.

I walked to the bedroom in the back of the apartment. "So what in the-" *Wham!*

I felt a crushing blow to the back of my head and immediately felt myself passing out.

I woke up with my arms and my legs bound to a chair and my mouth duct-taped. I was still a little groggy, and my head hurt like hell. I focused my eyes on a person standing before me. It was Sherry, her arms folded, and a wide smile across her face.

"Hey, sleepyhead," she said, laughing in my face.

I didn't see anything funny. I was tied the hell up and wanted to know why.

"I guess you're wondering why in the hell you are tied up to a chair," she said, as if reading my thoughts. "Well, cousin, for a long time, I was pissed at you for stealing Shawn away from me. He was my man, and you had a nerve to go and fuck him and steal him away from me."

By this time, I was looking at the bitch like she was a certifiable lunatic. I even chuckled a little. I can't believe she thought I stole Shawn from her. Now I thought I was crazy, but she was crazy *and* delusional.

"I don't find a thing funny, muthafucka," she hissed at me.

Again I chuckled, because she was truly dysfunctional. She tried to steal a married man from me and lost. I guess I would be angry too. She was beat even before she tried. Dummy-ass whore.

"You gonna pay for making my son a bastard."

"Sherry, what in the hell is wrong with you? You done really gone off the deep edge this time. You's one crazy bitch."

"It's seems like crazy runs in the family, James or Jerry, whatever the fuck you going by now." She chuckled to herself.

"Girl, if you don't untie me right now, I won't be responsible for what I will do to you when I get loose. Besides, my man is

in the car, and if I take too long, he'll coming looking for me."
Wallace was already out on the strip, and I was beginning to
get a little scared, but I didn't let that shit show though.

"Ummmm-hmmm!" She let out a slight laugh. "You must
think you are the smartest person alive. But I was time enough
for you. No, *we* were time enough for you."

I raised my eyebrows. "We?" I said to myself out loud.

"You can come in now," she said out of nowhere. "Your ass
thought you could just fuck people over and get away with it.
Payback is here now, muthafucka."

I was puzzled because this broad was talking like there was
somebody else in here with us. I just shook my head in disgrace
and pity for her.

To my surprise, there was somebody else in the apartment
with her. Somebody I thought I would never see again. The
person who had been stalking me with nasty phone calls, the
notes on the car, the text messages, and trying to run me off
the road. I couldn't believe my eyes. It was Tyrone Jenkins, my
first love, and the first one to break my heart.

I was truly shook. I hadn't seen or heard from him since I
threw the brick through his living room window over thirteen
years ago.

My eyes bugged out as he walked up toward me with a gun in
hand. Tears began to swell up in my eyes. I feared this moment.
It was as if the dreams I was having in jail were coming to pass
and I could do nothing to stop it from happening.

"Hey, baby," he said as he walked up to me and kissed me
on the cheek.

I motioned my head the other way as tears of pain flowed
freely. I was still hurt from the pain he'd caused me all those
years back. I was quickly thrown into my past as pictures of
our escapades flooded my mind and heart.

"I've been looking for you for the longest time."

"Umm-hmm," Sherry hummed, seconding his comment.

"Sherry and I bumped into each other into each other back in California a couple of months back, and she helped me devise a plan to get your home-wrecking ass back."

Tyrone had an evil smile across his face. The hate was coming from his nostrils like a raging bull that had been seeing red for hours. He was ready to pounce, but I wasn't ready to die.

I vaguely remembered introducing him to Sherry one day when we were out at a restaurant on the other side of town from where he lived. We only did this a few times, when we felt like no one would recognize either one of us. To my surprise, she walked in the restaurant one day when we were out. I had no other choice than to introduce her to him as my friend. She knew I was gay, but I never let her know my business, especially who I was dating. I'd never thought that shit would come back to bite me in the ass today. Never.

Tyrone backed up and pointed the gun in his hand at me.

I pleaded with my eyes for him to spare me, but it seemed to be falling on deaf ears.

"Time's up!" He cocked the gun and added a silencer.

I closed my eyes tight, waiting for death.

Pop! Pop!

To my surprise, I felt my chest still pumping rapidly, but Sherry was dead. I looked at him in horror as blood covered the walls and some had managed to cover me as well. If I could have screamed, I would have, because his ass was truly heartless.

"*Mmm.*" I shook my head in fear.

"I don't need any witnesses," he said wiping the blood that had splattered on his face as well. "She was deadweight, and I didn't like her to start with."

He walked over to her and kicked her body to see if she was indeed dead. She didn't move once, confirming his plan, and my fear.

He began pacing the floor. It looked like he was thinking of what to do next. I started trembling. I knew he was going to do the same thing to me.

"Jerry, all you had to do was walk away and leave me and my family alone. Yeah, I was wrong for using you the way I did, but you got something out of the deal as well. You got my attention whenever I felt like it, and you got this meat in yo ass a couple of good times. What more could you have asked of me? I was your everything, and you go and fuck it up by spazzing out on a brotha, exposing me to my family and shit. Got me put out of my house I was providing for in my own way. I was homeless for years until I found me a job and got my shit together. To this day, my wife won't let me see my kids, and it's all your fault."

I couldn't believe he was so crazy to think I was to blame in this situation. He was cheating on his wife with me, lying to both of us, and I was to blame. Nutcase was all I could think of him right now. I don't know what I was thinking when I met him and decided to date him. I was indeed delusional for choosing his crazy ass. I couldn't blame no one but me.

"Why didn't you just walk away?"

No answer.

"Why?" he yelled.

He must have forgotten my mouth was taped up and I couldn't utter a single word.

"Why?" he yelled again, inches from my face.

I just shook my head in fear.

Wham!

He hit me across my face with the gun because I didn't answer his question. He hit me so hard, the chair fell over.

Tears again flowed out of my eyes. This time I felt a little deserving of the torture he was inflicting on me. My lip and my nose were now bleeding, and I looked back up at him, pleading with my eyes.

He walked away and turned quickly back toward me as if he was gonna take my life quickly. He hoisted me back up quickly and backhanded me until I saw stars. He stopped short, inches from my face, and ripped the tape from my mouth.

I started off with a plea with my first breath. "Tyrone, please don't do this. I'm truly sorry for the hurt I have caused you."

"Really?" he said, oozing disbelief. "It's amazing how sorrowful someone gets when they about to die. Isn't it?"

"I really am, Tyrone. I love you. I have always loved you," I lied. I hated his ass from the minute I found out my money was gone and he was married.

Wham! Wham!

"Bitch, stop lying!"

As blood trickled out of my mouth and nose, I decided to give it all I could, to save my life. It also flashed in my mind that he was probably the one who murdered Carl. I could see the look in his eyes that he was taking no prisoners and I was next on his shit list.

"Baby, I'm sorry if I hurt you. Come here so I can make it better." I cooed with as much seduction as I could muster up. "You know I can make you feel better. Just let me do what I do best, baby. You know I'll make you feel good."

He eased his way over to me slowly as he pulled out his Mini-Me dick and started yanking on it.

He stood in front of me, ready for me to work my magic. "You gonna make daddy feel good." He was hard within seconds and proceeded to press his warm dick in my mouth.

"Uhh," he moaned as I went to work. I tried to give him a

blowjob that would soften his heart a little and save my life as well.

"Oh, yeah, baby, suck this big dick." He grabbed the back of my head and fucked my face like a rabbit in heat.

I continued to suck as if my life depended on it, because it truly did. I couldn't fuck this up. I couldn't let this bastard end my life when it felt like I was just starting to live it.

He stopped abruptly, and I thought I saw a forgiving look. My heart skipped a beat, and fear made my stomach knot up.

He proceeded to untie me from the chair. Then he pulled me up and hugged me, embracing me with tenderness. He gently pulled me away and rubbed my face with the back of his hand.

I nuzzled it with as much affection as I could. It was now or never.

With the quickness, I kicked him in his balls and made a dash for the door, but somehow, he managed to aim the gun and shoot me in my right knee, sending me careening to the ground a few feet away from the door.

I was in so much pain, I couldn't even yell for help. I lay there helpless, trying to crawl toward the door. I looked up and saw him limping toward me, causing me to try a little harder to get to the door.

Just as I got to the door and was reaching up from the floor to turn the knob, I felt him pulling me back and dragging me across the carpeted floor toward the living room area of the apartment.

He bent down and hit me with the gun several more times to let me know he was serious.

"Ty—Ty—Tyrone. P—p—p—please don't do this." I was spitting out blood and teeth, and my eye felt like it was out of its socket.

"It's too late," he grumbled as he lifted me off the floor.

"You just tried to run out on me again. I'm going to have to end it for both us right here and now." He bent me over the couch and practically ripped my pants off of me.

I knew what he was about to do, and there was nothing I could do about it.

Tyrone forced himself in me and raped me, pumping and huffing and puffing for over ten minutes.

"Ahh! I'm about to cum." He pulled out and let his seed drench my back. He then collapsed on top of me, trying to catch his breath.

I screamed, "Yes," on the inside, knowing I had him where I wanted him. A man was at his weakest right after he climaxed.

"Didn't I tell you that I would make you feel better, daddy?" I said as docile and feminine as I could as I peered over my shoulder. "Baby, we don't have to part ever again. We can move to Canada and never look back." I was breathing hard from the pain in my legs, and the pressure of his near 280 pounds pressed up on me.

I was looking in his eyes pleading my case. He got himself together with the gun still in his hand.

"Seriously?" he said, pulling me up slowly. He turned me around again and started rubbing my face gently with his hand again. "So you still love daddy?"

"I never stopped," I said, nuzzling his hand back. I was getting the feeling he was falling for it. "You were my first love. My only one."

He started to kiss me passionately, and I kissed him back, knowing he had a change of heart. I had hope.

Suddenly, he pulled back with a hateful scowl on his face and aimed the gun at me. "It's too late, Jerry. You hurt me too bad, and now you have to pay with your life."

"No! Tyrone, please, please, please," was all I could get out before he fired the gun, shooting me in the head.

Unfortunately, the shot to the head wasn't fatal. My body had involuntarily slid off the couch and hit the floor with a thud.

I watched Tyrone walk away like the job was done. He ranted off a prayer to God with the gun to his head, and was crying and blubbering like he didn't want to do it. Then suddenly the gun went off.

Pop!

And his blood splattered the wall and carpet, and his heavy frame hit the ground with a loud thud.

I was drifting in and out of consciousness. My life flashed before me like I was watching a movie. I'd always thought that this sort of thing was fictional, until now. Flashes of me as a child blinked in and out.

One minute I was riding my bike in the park, the next, I was in my bed being molested by my uncle. Pictures of my mom and I eating dinner together at the dinning room table also played.

Tears flowed freely as my head was resting on the carpet facing the wall.

The brick through Tyrone's window, the look on his wife's face as I peeled off from in front of their home played. She was hurt too.

The hurt and pain on my face as I took a break from laughing on the plane to Baltimore, going to the bathroom to sob and cry.

All the bad things I did to the Black family.

The tormenting and the schemes played out again, only it was in fast-forward mode.

My jail time whizzed by.

Then my mother flashed into my head again. She'd made a trip to prison once, against my will. I cried hard at the visual of her walking through the prison gate. The look on her face was a proud one. She was always proud of me.

Here I was, lying on the floor, one family member and one ex-lover dead in the same room. All of this could have been avoided if I'd just walked away from Tyrone and moved on with my life.

I was looking for the love that I already had. My mother was the one that was appointed to love me, but I wanted more. I was greedy. My greed for love was my downfall. I had enough, but I wasn't satisfied.

I was sorry for my mistakes and the pain I'd caused others, but it was too late. I felt my feet getting cold, and coldness creeping up my legs. It was my time. I was dying.

"I'm sorry, God," I sobbed, my breathing labored. "Forgive me for my sins. Tell my momma I love her, God." The coldness was now at my ribcage. I squeezed out another plea. "Forgive me, God."

Chapter 43

Shawn

Full Custody
January 11ᵗʰ, 2019, 5:13 P.M.

I pulled up to Sherry's apartment building to drop Li'l Shawn off. I was a little reluctant about dropping him off. I was getting attached to him, and I wanted him in a home with a mother and a father. I couldn't continue this charade with Mona any longer. The only thing holding this back was, I didn't think Sherry was going to give him up without a fight or a large sum of money. I was willing to pay to get her to give me full custody of him, but I didn't think she was going to make it that easy. She was a relative of James, so I knew she would continue to try and milk me for all I was worth.

I pulled out my cell phone and dialed her phone, letting her know I was outside, dropping off Li'l Shawn. The phone just rang and rang. I hung up and decided to knock on the door because she was probably sleeping or something. I was paying her enough child support that she didn't need to work.

I knocked on the door with Li'l Shawn next to me. I knocked a little harder. Still there was no answer. I began to get frustrated because I needed to get home before Mona started calling my phone.

I picked up my cell phone, ready to call her phone again.

"Daddy, I have a key." Li'l Shawn smiled.

I was glad that I didn't have to take him home just yet. I still hadn't the slightest idea how I was going to tell Mona about him.

I put the key in the lock and opened the door. As I walked in, we both got hit with a foul odor that almost made my knees buckle.

"Stay right here," I said to my son as I continued to slowly walk through the house.

"Sherry!" I yelled out.

No answer.

I heard the television on, so I assumed she was 'sleep. I walked to the back bedroom, where I heard the television going. What I saw sent my stomach into convulsions. I had to hold my hand over my mouth just to keep everything down.

I immediately turned and headed back in the direction of the front door. Just as I got up to Li'l Shawn, my stomach emptied itself all over the carpet and floor.

"Daddy, what's wrong?" Li'l Shawn said looking at me with confusion and concern all over his face.

"Nothing. I need to go outside and make a phone call, okay." I looked at him with sorrow in my eyes. *How in the hell am I supposed to explain to him that his mother is dead?*

I walked outside and put him in my car and stood outside the car as I made the call to the police.

"Nine-one-one. What is the nature of your emergency?"

"Three people dead," was all I could get out before I threw up once again.

"Are you okay, sir? I need for you to calm down and tell me what is going on, so I can get you the help you need."

"Ma'am, I'm at Dunhill Village Apartments on Liberty

Road. I was dropping my son off at his mom's house. When I walked in, I found three people dead."

"Okay, sir, where are you now?" the operator asked.

"I'm standing outside in the parking lot with my son in the car."

"Okay, sir, stay where you are. I am dispatching the appropriate authorities within minutes.

"Okay, okay. Thank you."

I was a nervous wreck, and I wasn't prepared to explain to Li'l Shawn the details.

Within about five minutes, three police cars and an ambulance pulled up and approached me. I gave them the apartment number, and they raced in with guns drawn.

After about twenty minutes, the police came back out to question me. I told them I was a lawyer, that I knew two of the three people murdered in the apartment. I hadn't the slightest clue of who the third one was, and that could stay that way, for all I cared. My real problem was explaining to my family how I had an addition to the family waiting to meet them.

The police gave me permission to leave the premises after they took down my info. As I pulled off, I was thinking of a way to tell Mona about Li'l Shawn.

Li'l Shawn asked me about his mom as we drove up Liberty Road. I lied and told him she wasn't in the apartment and had left a note saying that she would be back later. I told him that I was going to take him to see someone special in the meantime.

I pulled up in front of the house and exited the car with Li'l Shawn in tow. I didn't know how she was going to react. It was all or nothing, so I put my key in the door and made my way in.

"Hey, son." My mom greeted me with a tight hug. She was still a vision of loveliness, even with her graying hair. She looked amazing and was the epitome of the phrase "black don't crack." She looked over at Li'l Shawn. "And who is this young man?"

I just looked at her, trying to gather my thoughts.

"This is my son."

"Son?" she said with raised eyebrows. "Boy, get in the living room and sit down so you can tell me what mess you have gotten yourself into now." She pointed toward the living room.

Li'l Shawn and I made our way to the living room as instructed and sat down. I purposely asked for something to drink for Li'l Shawn so I could get my thoughts together quickly. I didn't want to do this to my mother, I had no choice.

She made her way back in with a soda in hand. "Here you go, baby," she said, handing the drink to Li'l Shawn.

I instructed my son to go into the kitchen to drink his soda because I didn't want him to hear what I was about to say to my mom.

"Now back to you," she said, looking at me intently. "Spill it!"

"Okay." I breathed hard. "I have a son I didn't know about by the paralegal I slept with to drop the charges when Mona beat her up in front of my office building."

"So why are you here?"

"I need you to keep Li'l Shawn until I find the right time to tell Mona."

"Are you serious?" She looked at me with a smirk. "I have raised my children and I don't plan on raising any more. I'm an old woman, and I don't plan on chasing after any more children, Shawn."

"Look, Mom, I need this favor. All I am asking for is

another couple of weeks to get Mona ready, okay. Besides, you owe me this."

"Owe you?" she said, looking puzzled and offended.

"Yeah, Mom. It's the least you can do for not stopping Daddy from putting his hands on me."

She looked at me in shock, a single tear sliding down her face.

I couldn't believe I'd said it myself. How could I say such a thing to my mother?

Before I knew it, she had hauled off and smacked me so hard, I was seeing stars. My mom had never hit me before. Even as a child, she would just send me to my room.

I sat there as I rubbed my cheeks and took in the shock of the blow, mentally and physically.

"How dare you come into my house and tell me what I owe you?"

Her voice was a little above a whisper, but I could still hear the hurt loud and clear.

"I made my mistakes and done asked the Lord for forgiveness, and it was given so easily. Why can't you?"

"I didn't mean it like that, Momma." The tears welling up in my eyes flowed freely down my face. I was so ashamed of who I'd become at this moment, but I still pressed on with my plan. "I just need your help right now, and you're the only one that can help me." I got up out of my seat and made my way over to my mother and hugged and kissed her sagging cheeks. Tears still flowed from the pain of my past mistakes that were still fresh in my mind.

"Shawn, I know you're sorry, and I know that it was just the desperation talking. Just remember what happened the last time you let issues go unresolved in your life." She rubbed my face with her hands. "Shawn, I will do this for you, but don't let history repeat itself, because life is too short to do re-dos."

"Yes, ma'am," I said getting up and wiping my face at the same time.

She got up as well, and we embraced in a tight hug. I needed this hug. I savored this hug. It was the hug that only a mother could give. The one that says it's going to be okay, even when you feel like you're at your wits' end.

"Li'l Shawn!" I called out for my son, so I could formally introduce him to his grandmother.

He walked in and stood at my side, as if afraid I was going to leave him with a stranger.

"This is your grandmother. You will be staying with her for a little while, until I get things ready for you to come and live with me."

Still looking a little apprehensive, he nodded his head.

"Go on and hug her. She's not going to bite."

He did as instructed and embraced my mother.

I was so elated to see my son and my mom bond just for the short bit of time that they had met. "Okay, you guys, I have to go, but I will be back tomorrow." I hugged my mom and whispered another word of apology into her ear.

Li'l Shawn grabbed and hugged me and hung on for dear life. After a couple of minutes of reassuring him, I made my exit to my car.

As I drove home, I thought about what my mom said to me and how it rang in my ear over and over again. She was right, and I knew it. I just needed to follow through with it. I also had no clue how I was going to explain to Li'l Shawn that his mom was dead. The only plus was, James was finally out of my hair.

Chapter 44

Mona

Say What!
February 1ˢᵗ, 2019, 9:03 A.M.

Shawn was acting very sneaky lately, but I couldn't pinpoint what was wrong. I knew he was up to something. I was hoping and praying that he wasn't messing around with James again. I didn't know what I was going to do if it turned out that way.

I was in the house this Monday morning after I'd just dropped all the kids off and was about to start cleaning the house, like I normally did. Scrub this, polish that, you know, the usual. I was sitting at the kitchen table with a cup of coffee in my hand and looking over the seating arrangement for the reception after our renewal vows. I decided I was going to do it up, since this was going to be the second time around.

Knock! Knock! Knock!

I was expecting no one, so I was a little hesitant. My mind instantly flashed to James. I paused at the door, trying to gain my composure. I wasn't ready for this.

Knock! Knock! Knock!

"Oh, shit! What do I do?"

I wasn't afraid of him. I was afraid that I could be weak and give in to his charm and end up on the floor again with his dick in me.

I threw caution to the wind and reluctantly opened the door. It was FedEx delivering a certified package. I wondered what it was.

"Hello, ma'am. I have a package for a Mona and Shawn Black." The Caucasian man smiled a bright smile as he handed me his hand-held computer to sign for the package.

I had on some raggedy sweat shirt and pants, and my hair was slightly messy. I was a little ashamed. "Thank you, sir." I handed him back his portable computer, grabbed the package, and went back into the house.

I walked back slowly from the door to the kitchen, reading the envelope. "Sun Trust Insurance," I read aloud to myself. I sat down and opened the letter.

The Will and Testament of Jerry Parks.

I, Jerry Parks, of sound mind and body, hereby leave three checks in the amount of thirty thousand each to the following people, Diana Black, Alex Black, and Ashley Black upon my death.

My mouth was wide open. I was in complete shock. *Say what! James is dead.* I was relieved, but not happy. I wasn't heartless. I even felt a tear slide out of my left eye. I quickly wiped it away. I looked in the envelope, and sure enough, there were checks made out to all of the kids. I still couldn't believe James was dead. Gone. Forever.

I shook my head in disbelief. I sat back in the chair and absorbed it all. I noticed another piece of paper sticking out. I opened it. It was a letter from James addressed to his children.

To the children I never got to know,

If you are reading this, I must be dead. At first I wasn't going to write this, but I felt that all of you might want to know a little bit about me. Well, let me start by saying that it was never in my plans to father any children, but that doesn't mean I didn't care for you. In fact, I secretly loved all of you. I wish I could have gotten to know you better, but that was out of the question, since you already have a father in your life.

As your mother and father may have told you, I am a bi-sexual man. I was forty-five when I wrote this letter. I am pretty sure you are wondering how your mom and I got together. Well, your mom is a good woman, and I took advantage of her in a moment of weakness. Don't think anything bad of your mother. I was the one at fault.

To my two beautiful and precious daughters, Diana and Ashley, I have seen you both on several occasions. You were unaware that I watched each one of you as you waited outside of school waiting to be picked up. Both of you young ladies are very beautiful and spitting images of me. I love both of you.

To my energetic and strapping son, I prayed as I watched you during football practice. You never saw me watching you, but I was so proud of you, even from a distance. I can't tell you how proud of you I am.

I have made many mistakes in my life, but you three weren't any of them. I left you financial gifts, assured that you all will be accepted in college. I know it isn't a whole lot, but it is the best that I could do under the circumstances. Again wishing I could have gotten to know you all better, I wish you all the success in the world. You have good parents, so cherish them and make them and me proud.

Your Father,

James Parks

I folded the letter and placed it back inside the original envelope. Tears poured out of my eyes as I thought about what I had read. James had a heart. I didn't believe it until just now. He was secretly watching them and all. *He gave the impression that he could have cared less, and here it is in black and white.* He loved his children, but from a distance.

I sat in the chair for at least an hour pondering how I was going to tell Shawn that James was dead.

Chapter 45

Shawn

Case Closed
February 1st, 2019, 11:32 A.M.

I sat in my chair in my office, my door closed, and I had the obituaries of Jerry Parks and Sherry Adams in my hand. James' funeral was about two weeks after I had found him dead in the apartment with Sherry and the John Doe. The family had a double funeral, since they were killed together.

I had secretly taken the day off to go because I just had to see what his family was like. Were all of them as crazy as those two? I had snuck in the funereal and sat in the back row, hopefully unnoticed. I had gotten there just in time to see a couple of people at the caskets.

It was a closed casket for Sherry. From what I saw in the apartment, she was shot in the forehead at close range. James' casket was open because he was shot in the back of the head at an angle, so the hole in his head wasn't visible. I decided to get a quick look at him and make it back to my seat.

As I walked away from the casket, I saw an older, thin lady that James heavily favored in looks being consoled by various mourners as she sat in the front row. I also happened to notice a dude with dreads crying harder than most. You would have thought they were messing around or something.

I continued to walk away and passed my seat. I exited the chapel, deciding not to stay any longer. I felt kind of bad, though, because the way he died was horrific. Nobody needed to be murdered.

Buzz!

"Mr. Black, your wife is on line two." My paralegal, Renee, buzzed into my office, breaking me out of my recollection.

"Okay, I got it," I said, picking up the phone. "Hello."

"Shawn, do you have a minute?" Mona asked, a little shakiness in her voice.

"Sure. A couple." I sat up in my chair, ready for some bad news. *What else can go wrong?* "I don't have to be in court for another half-hour or so."

I was actually trial free today and planned on going to spend some time with my newfound son. It was getting harder and harder to look at him, knowing that I had to tell him soon that his mom was dead.

"Is everything okay?" I asked wearily.

"Well, ah, I don't know how to say this, so I'll just say it." She was breathing into the phone like she was blowing out candles on a cake or something. "James is dead."

"Oh, okay."

"Is that all you have to say?" she said, surprised by my reaction.

"Well . . . ah . . . yeah." I paused. "What should I be saying, Mona? This dude tried hard to wreck our lives, and you had two affairs with him. I'm glad he's gone and I surely don't miss him." I got up from my chair and walked toward the window. I wasn't ready for this conversation.

"Well, Shawn, you don't have to be so heartless about it."

She sounded like she was on the verge of tears. "He was a human being. And I told you that sleeping with him was something I regretted deeply."

"Look, Mona, baby, I apologize for bringing up you cheating on me with him. I said that I forgave you, and I meant it, but you still have to take into consideration what he did to me." I quickly wiped a tear that slid out of my eye.

"I know, Shawn. It's just too much right now, and I don't know how much more I can take of this."

"Don't worry, when James died, most of our problems died with him."

I didn't even believe that one myself, but I had to say something to calm her down. Shit. James' dying only left me with one thing to do—Get Li'l Shawn in my house without Mona giving up and leaving me. That wasn't going to be an easy pill for her to swallow, especially considering she and I didn't have any biological children together.

"Okay, Shawn, if you say so."

"All right, baby. I love you. I will see you when I get home."

"I love you too." She hung up the phone.

As soon as I hung up my office phone, my cell phone started ringing. The caller ID said that it was James calling me. *What kind of game is going on here? I know, the fuck, James didn't fake his death. And I know that was his grimy ass in that casket at the funeral.*

"Hello," I answered the phone, afraid of what I might hear. James pulling the ultimate stunt. Insurance Fraud. Then, again, I didn't think he'd be that dumb.

"Who am I speaking with?"

"Shawn Black. Who wants to know?" I said, putting on my authoritative voice.

"I'm a friend of James, and I, he was my"—The guy's voice

started to break up like he was about to cry. He continued, "James was my lover, and I found . . . he left his phone in the house the day . . . the day they found him murdered. They killed him, and they wouldn't even tell me who." He broke down again.

There was a long pause.

"I just needed to know who you were because your number was in his call log several times, and I figured you could tell me about my baby."

"Look, buddy, I am just James' lawyer, and I really don't know a whole lot about him."

"Oh, ah, his lawyer," he said, sounding a little happier. "Well, maybe you could tell me who did this to him."

"Look, ah, um, um—"

"Wallace."

"Okay, Wallace, that's something I can't do. I really don't know much." Well, I knew some stuff, but why should I help the nigga who was sleeping with my nemesis?

"Oh, okay," he said, disappointment in his voice.

I paused for a couple of seconds. "Look, ah, Wallace, let's meet somewhere. Maybe I can help you out."

"Great!"

"But, like I said, I don't know much."

We decided on a meeting place, and I headed out of the office.

I pulled up to Owings Mills Mall, parked my car, walked through Sears, and headed for the food court. I had described myself to him, and what I was wearing, so he could find me.

As I walked toward the table, I noticed a guy waving me over. *Shit! That dude was bawling his eyes out at the funeral.*

I sat down at the table across from him. This dude wasn't bad-looking. He was well dressed and had on some fly shit. His eyes were bloodshot red, and he had the look that said, "I just lost my best friend."

The James I knew was incapable of love, so how could this nigga be this fucked up over him being gone? *Well, the ass was good.*

"Ah. Hi, Wallace?"

"I'm just . . . sh-shocked mostly." He was falling all over his words again. Tears escaped his eyes and hit the table as he held his head down.

This nigga is fucked up. James musta put it on his ass good. There is no way I would be acting like this for no nigga. "Look, I'm sorry to hear about your loss." I had to say something semi-sympathetic to get this over with.

"Thanks," he said, now looking off into the distance, like he was in a trance.

"So, uh, anyway, you needed to ask me some stuff about James?" I said, reminding him why we were there. I still had to go and visit my mom and Li'l Shawn.

He slowly turned back around and stared at me for a minute.

I was getting uncomfortable by the second. For some reason, he started to look good to me. I knew I had to hurry up and get the hell out of here, not wanting to go down that road again.

Seriously, I wasn't, but he sure looked like he can ride it good. I felt my manhood rising.

"I really have somewhere to be soon, so can we make this fast? I'm not trying to be rude, I just have some stuff to take care of."

"I just needed to know if James ever talked about anyone from his past that might make someone want to hurt him? I went to the police, and they were like, since I wasn't family, they couldn't release the information about the killer."

"Oh, is that all you want to know?"

He shook his head yes.

"It seems like it was a double murder and suicide. They say whoever this dude was, he was crazy. He killed James and his cousin in a fit of rage. The motive seemed to be about some scorned-lover type of shit."

"Did they give you the name of the guy?" he said bright-eyed.

"Yeah, but he's dead."

"I just want to know," he said, a little furious that I was withholding information.

"His name was Tyrone Jenkins, and he was from California."

He looked at me, shock written all over his face. His fists balled up and he looked like he was about to explode. "My muthafuckin' cousin," he mumbled, his jaw twitching.

"He was your cousin?" I said, looking around. "You sure?"

"Yeah, man, his ass called me a couple of weeks ago saying he was going to be in town on business and shit. We even hung out a little bit. I can't believe this shit. My fuckin' cousin killed my baby." He just got up and walked away.

Just like that, he was gone. That's some messed up shit. His cousin, James' first love, killed his lover, James. Crazy. I got up and walked away myself, shaking my head in disbelief.

Chapter 46

Mona

Second Time Around
February 14th, 2019, 12:04 A.M.

This was it, the day I was waiting for. The day I was going to marry the man of my dreams again. Valentine's Day. And we had a packed house.

I know it seems cliché to be getting married on that day, but I thought it was the perfect time.

I was in the back dressing room in my off-white wedding gown, which was nontraditional but elegant. I wasn't about to drag a train down the aisle again.

Other than that, I was so happy to be closing the doors on some very ugly chapters in my life. James was dead. I was happy and sad. But I knew it was for the good of the kids. I could tell them now who their biological father was and not have to worry about them wanting to meet him. Well, they'd already met him, but they didn't really know who he was.

"Mom, you look *sooo* pretty in your dress," Diana said in a loving voice.

I loved my little angel. She was the flower girl, intent on being the best she could be. Many times I'd watched her have a play wedding with her dolls, and she'd walk around the house with a flower bouquet, practicing her little heart out.

I turned around to see what Ashley was doing. She looked radiant in the dress I had picked out for her to wear. She didn't seem too enthusiastic about being here, and she looked preoccupied with something, every so often talking on the phone.

"Ashley, baby, you okay over there?" I said as I pinned the veil onto my hair.

"Yeah, Ma," she said like she was annoyed or something. "I'm fine."

Ashley had been so moody lately, and I know it wasn't her time of the month, because ours usually ran around the same time. I had to make a mental note to have a one-on-one with her just to see if she wanted to talk. It was past due, and I was usually on top of my girls, but I was preoccupied with setting all this up, and running the house. My job was never done.

"All right, girls, go out there and head to your posts. It's almost time for me to come out."

As they walked out, my mom came in with a big smile on her face, just like she did the first time around.

"How's Mama's baby?" she said, tears flooding both our eyes.

"Well, Mama, I'm good. Just a little nervous," I said, though I remember being a wreck the day me and Shawn got married the first time, and today was just the same.

"Oh, baby," she said as she put out her arms and embraced me.

My mother's love was something I needed, and I was glad she was here to share this moment again.

Tears again flooded my eyes. I was marrying the man of my dreams again. I was so happy that things would be going back to normal now and I would be able to let the children know the truth.

"You are so beautiful, just like you were the first time."

"Thanks, Ma," I said, checking my makeup in the mirror. "All this crying gonna mess up my makeup."

"All right, baby. Let me get to my seat. I can hear the musicians warming up. I ain't trying to miss my baby come down the aisle again." She eased out the door.

I looked at myself in the mirror one last time, turned around, and made my exit out to the foyer of the church.

As I made it out, various family members were just arriving. They stopped and whipped out cameras and took a few quick shots. I took a couple then shooed them away.

I watched as the ringbearer made his way down the aisle, followed by the maid of honor. I know, I know. I overdid it. It was just supposed to be a renewal ceremony, but it was so good the first time, I had to do it up again.

Alex stood at the door, all smiles, even though he still couldn't quite look me in the eyes that long yet. He had some shame in his eyes ever since I'd seen him naked in the basement. I tried to reassure him a couple of times, but I was going to tell Shawn what happened, and let him deal with him. It was a man thing, as they say.

I had asked him to walk me down the aisle, since my father was dead.

"You ready, Ma?" he whispered into my ear.

"Yes, baby. And don't be trying to trip Momma up and have her fall in front of all of these people." I laughed lightly.

He laughed too. "Never that, Ma."

The music started for me to make my way down the aisle, and a smile crept across my face. Everybody stood up and turned toward us as we made our way down the aisle. Under my veil, I could see my husband-to-be smiling as he stood at the altar.

We finally made it down the aisle, and Alex handed me over to Shawn. I saw a couple of tears roll down his face. He, too, smiled that goofy-looking smile.

"That's my baby," I said to myself. With all the stuff we'd been through, I knew it was God keeping us together, and nothing could tear us apart.

We went through the ceremony in a breeze, but something happened that almost made me run out of the sanctuary and never look back.

When the minister got to "Does anybody here object to these two being together?" the room was silent.

I knew everyone here loved seeing me and Shawn together, and quite frankly, they couldn't do a thing about it because we were already married.

But, out of nowhere, a little boy pops up and yells, "No, Daddy, you were supposed to marry my mommy!"

It was like the movie, *The Matrix*. Everything stood still. The look of shock covered everyone's face as they turned around to see who this little boy was that had just dropped a bombshell on the ceremony.

I turned and looked at Shawn. He looked like he wanted to run. Then his mother quickly yanked the boy back down, as if the outburst didn't happen.

Okay, so now what the hell do I do? was the thought that flashed across my mind. *Run or stay? Or fuck him up for GP?* I stood there like a deer caught in the headlights of an oncoming car. I couldn't move, but staying in the spot felt like it was going to kill me.

"Baby," Shawn said as he shook my hand that he was still holding.

I looked at him with pain in my eyes. He was pleading with his eyes for me continue on with the service, but was I woman enough to handle this? How can I stay? Who is the mother? How long did he know? What in the hell? All of these questions floated through my head in those few seconds standing there.

I awaited Ashton Kutcher to pop out with his camera crew, telling me that I was being punked, that I could go on with the ceremony. But no Ashton, no camera crew. Just me, Shawn, and both of our families here staring at us.

Okay, so I turned back toward the minister and nodded my head, giving him the approval to continue. I know. How could I stay? But, then again, how could I leave? This family needed me, and I needed them. Walking away wasn't an option. The devil was a liar and a defeated foe. All those Sundays I spent on my knees in His house were not going to be in vain. This was one black family that was going all the way. Through hell and high water. We were going to make it.

The ceremony was sealed with a kiss. And, boy, did I kiss my husband! He was mine, and I wasn't giving up on him. Ever. God didn't, so why should I? We walked down the aisle and out of the church to the limo waiting for us outside.

Oh, don't get me wrong. I was mad as all get out. As soon as we closed the door to the car, I sat back with my arms folded. "So?"

He was sitting across from me, sorrow on his face. "Well, um, where do I start?" He paused.

I just looked at him. There was nothing for me to say.

"I have a son by James' cousin, Sherry. The condom must have broken when I had sex with her."

"How long did you plan on hiding him at your mother's house?"

"I was just buying time, trying to figure out a way to tell you. I just didn't want you to leave me, Mona. I put you through enough, and I thought this would be the straw that broke the camel's back." He broke down and started crying.

I got up and sat next to him and pulled him to my chest. There is nothing more heartbreaking than seeing a forty-five-year-old man cry. He was my baby. I couldn't stay mad at him.

"Shawn, all these secrets and lying have to stop right now. Our family is not going to make it if we can't be honest with each other. I love you, Shawn. There is nothing too big for us to handle, with God on our side. It's time for us to be examples for our children. All five of them."

He popped up with a smile on his face. "Five?"

"Yep, I'm pregnant again. I found out about a week ago, but I wanted to wait to tell you."

"Wow! I'm too old to be going through this again." He laughed.

I laughed along with him. "You sure are."

Shawn pinned me down on the seats of the stretch limo, and we made out, until the limo driver signaled us that we were at the reception hall.

After we spent about a half-hour in the hallway, some commotion broke out at the door, putting everything on pause.

Chapter 47

Ashley

Front and Center
February 14ᵗʰ, 2019, 1:33 P.M.

We were in the champagne room in Martin's West. I watched my parents as they were doing the last-dance thing in the middle of the reception hall. Everybody was watching them, and they were giggling, making the best of it, as if it was the first time. I could see my father whispering in her ear, and she was grinning from ear to ear.

Out of nowhere, there was a commotion at the front door, and I heard someone yell, "Ashley!"

Again, "Ashley! Where the fuck you at?"

It was Tony. Everybody looked at me, surprise in their eyes. I was mortified. How could she do this? She must have been following me the whole time.

"You thought you could just leave me, and that would be that?" she said as she walked up to my table. "I love you, girl."

By this time, my mom and dad were standing there next to my table as well. I could smell the liquor on her breath, and she was glassy-eyed and wobbly.

"Ha-ha, Tony, stop playing." I laughed, trying to play down

the situation. I looked at my parents' faces and lowered my head in shame.

"I thought Tony was a guy," my mom chimed in.

"I thought she was your mentor," my father said.

Then they both looked at each other, probably wondering how they could have missed this.

"Um-hmm." Tony nodded. "Your little princess likes to be licked by a bitch."

By this time, everything had stopped. The music, the dancing, the drinking. Everything.

I looked at my grandmothers across the room, and their mouths were flung open in shock.

Alex, who was sitting next to me, eased out an "Oh shit! You're a lick-'em girl." He chuckled.

I didn't find it funny. I felt the tears of shame flowing, and then the shaking and trembling came. I wanted to crawl underneath the table and disappear. My mind was spinning with excuses, but nothing could cover this one. My ass was caught red-handed, and I couldn't do anything about it.

I was threatening to run for the door, but my legs wouldn't cooperate with me. I was stuck. I had played the game and lost.

"Look, Tony, you gonna have to go, before I call the cops," my father said, walking up to Tony. "I'm pretty sure you don't want to go to jail tonight, and if you leave now, we won't press charges against you. You do know it's a crime to have relations with a minor."

Tony nodded. I could've sworn I saw a tear slide down her face, but I could care less. I had already come to the conclusion that sleeping with women was nothing but trouble.

She left without another word.

My parents looked at me, pain all over their faces, and just walked away. I knew this wasn't over, that I would be having a long talk with them ASAP.

The music was now back on, and everybody was back in party mode. After a few of my cousins got drunk, the focus was no longer on me.

I, on the other hand, sat in the back and made it my business to stay to myself.

Chapter 48

Shawn

The Black Family
February 18th, 2019, 2:54 P.M.

It was a few of days after the wedding ceremony. My entire family sat in the dining room around our large cherry oak buffet-style table. I looked around the table. Mona was at one end, I was at the other. To my left sat Alex and Ashley, and to the right sat Li'l Shawn and Diana, all with a look of wonder on their faces.

I was nervous. My palms were sweaty and I had no clue how I was going to say what I needed to say. I looked around at my family once again. *We made it!*

I broke down and cried right then and there. The tears and snot ran freely as I thought about the past ten years of my life. Not just what James put me through, but for what I allowed.

I could no longer blame him for my demons. In a way, he helped bring me to terms with myself. I was a fool to think I was going to get away with my deceitfulness.

I cried for me, my mom, my father, my whole family. Mona came to console me, but I politely shooed her away. I needed to get this out. I hadn't cried in a long time.

After a few minutes, I got myself together and cleared my throat. I was ready.

"I want to start off by saying I'm sorry for all that I put this family through. I was supposed to be the man of this house and I wasn't acting as such. I am asking you all for forgiveness, while I learn to forgive myself." I swallowed the lump in my throat, as my wife and children looked on attentively. I really didn't expect Li'l Shawn and Diana to understand, but I figured Alex and Ashley were old enough.

"I would like to confess to you all that I have been dealing with homosexuality for most of my life."

Alex and Ashley's eyes were big as saucers, and they said nothing.

"Ashley, you would not have had to deal with this if I had dealt with this the right way. I'm sorry. I knew I wasn't her biological father, but she still would have had a better chance at being as normal as possible if I would have dealt with my demons head-on. Her biological father did have the same issue, so she was predisposed to being sexually imbalanced.

"As the head of this household, I am declaring that from now on we share our feelings and problems as a family, like we should have been doing a long time ago."

Everybody nodded in agreement.

"Well, that was the easy part." I sighed and looked at Mona, who was in tears. "What I am about to tell you, Alex, Ashley, and Diana, will never change the way I have felt about you. From the moment I laid eyes on each one of you, I knew I was a blessed man. You are my crowning achievements and I love you all very much. I–I–I am not–"

Mona cut in, "What your father is trying to say is, Mommy messed up a long time ago." Her tears had stopped flowing, and she spoke with confidence. "Alex, Ashley, Diana"–She looked them in their eyes one at a time as she called out their names individually–"the man at the head of the table is not your biological father."

I looked at them all as she spoke. Their expressions didn't change one bit. I was sure they were going to get up and run out in a fit, but they stayed put. They were handling this much better than I thought.

"Ashley and Diana, you met your father at the restaurant we were eating at a couple of weeks ago. Do you remember the guy that came up to the table and hugged me?"

They nodded their heads yes.

"Well, he is your biological father."

"Alex, do you remember the guy at the funeral?"

He nodded.

"Well, that was your biological father."

"Look, you guys, what your mother did was a mistake, but I have forgiven her, and so should you." I looked at her, to reassure her.

Mona spoke again. "So, do you understand what I said?"

They all nodded. "Yeah, we understand."

Alex said, "But I don't care who our *biological* father is. All I know is that Dad"—He looked at me—"played sports with me, gave me baths, and helped me with my homework. He *is* my father, as far as I am concerned."

Ashley cosigned with a big smile. "He sure is."

"I love you too, Daddy." Diana got up and came over to me and gave me a big hug.

I was overwhelmed with emotion. "Okay, I'm not finished. There is something else I want to say." I looked at Li'l Shawn. "This little guy is your brother."

"Uh, Dad," Alex said, "we kinda figured that out already."

"Oh, really? How?"

Ashley laughed. "Well, he looks just like you."

She pointed across the room to a picture of me on the fireplace. I was about the same age as he was now. "Oh!" I let out a small chuckle.

Everyone else chuckled too.

It felt so much better to have all of this out in the open.

"Oh, one more thing," Mona said softly. "I have something for Alex, Ashley, and Diana." She pulled a large manila envelope from her lap. "Jerry Parks, your father, left each of you a letter. I want you to read this when you are alone, okay."

"Okay," they all chimed.

She handed them the letters, except for Diana. I figured, since she was only ten, Mona was going to sit down and read the letter with her.

"Okay, I think that's it." I clasped my hands in front of me. "Let's pray before we get up."

We bowed our heads as I gave a short prayer praising God for getting our family straight and on the right path.

"Everyone is dismissed, except for Li'l Shawn."

Each of them came and gave me a firm hug and left.

"Li'l Shawn . . ." I paused. I didn't know how to tell him that his mother was dead. How was he going to take it? "I'm sorry to tell you this, but your mom is in heaven. "Do you understand?"

"Yes, sir, I understand." He looked a little hurt. "Daddy, I'm not worried about Mommy, because I know that she is with Jesus."

I was shocked at his calmness and assurance.

"Mommy said when people die, they go to see God and they live forever. She said when we die and go to heaven, we take care of the people we loved here on earth until we go to heaven too. I know Mommy is looking down at me right now and smiling 'cuz I'm safe with my Daddy now."

Wow! Sherry was actually a great mother. She had her faults, but she sure did put her all into this son of ours. "Okay, we're finished now. You can run along and play."

Li'l Shawn hopped up like a jackrabbit and ran out of the room.

We made it! Thank you, Jesus! I looked up to heaven and truly thanked God for cleaning up our mess.

I knew I had a long way to go with healing, but I was going after all the help and support I could find. I wasn't looking back anymore. I was going back to counseling and seeking sessions from my pastor as well.

I got up and walked across the room to the mantle, where an obituary of my father was. I grabbed my coat off the back of the chair I was sitting in. "I'll be back in a few," I said to no one in particular as I left out the front door and headed to my car.

I pulled up at Woodlawn Cemetery and turned in. I had gotten a map of the location of my father's grave from my mother before I made my way here. She wanted to come, but I insisted that I do it alone. I needed this to be between just me and him. We had some things to resolve.

It was cold outside, and my black full-length pea coat almost wasn't cutting it. I bundled up and pressed on with my mission.

"Carl S. Black," I read aloud as I found his headstone. Shawn was his middle name. *Another thing I got from him,* I thought to myself.

I looked at his grave that still hadn't completely sunk into the ground yet. It was still fresh. As were the memories of my painful childhood.

"Well, Dad, here I am." I waited for a response that I knew would never come.

"It's me, Shawn, your only son. I'm here to ask you why, Why did you do those things to me? Why couldn't you just be a regular dad like all my friends had?

"You had to go and fuck up my life—No, no, no," I yelled out loud, squeezing my head. "I can't keep blaming you for this. I can't keep holding on to this pain.

"You let me down, Dad. I let you down, Dad. We weren't there for each other. I was supposed to be there for you when you died. You were supposed to be here for your grandkids. Why didn't you just let us help you?" I sobbed aloud like a lion roaring at night.

"I loved you, Dad, no matter what. I loved you, I loved you, I loved you, I loved you!" I fell to my knees, a broken man. "You were supposed to love me." I was now leaning on his headstone, weak and distraught. "Daddy! Daddy! Answer me! I forgive you Daddy! I forgive you! Please, Daddy! Please! I love you, Daddy! I love you!

I lay on the ground of his grave for what seemed like hours.

I eventually got up and made my way to my car and drove home with relief and hope. God had lifted the weight of my past off me. I felt like I could finally be the man of the house and know that the generational curses that plagued my family stopped at me. I was a free man.

To be continued . . .

BOOK CLUB DISCUSSION QUESTIONS

1. Is it possible to fall in love over a short period of time? Say one month?

2. Is it possible to know everything about your mate?

3. How long does it take to truly forgive someone?

4. Did any of the characters exhibit growth?

5. What character(s) stood out the most?

6. Did James have any good characteristics?

7. Which minor character would you like to have a story of their own?

8. Was there anything in the book that really shocked you?

9. Did this book end the way you wanted it to?

10. What did you like most about this book?

About the Author

M.T. Pope was born and raised in Baltimore, Md. He is an avid reader and manages a bookstore. He is also an aspiring singer/songwriter. He is a Christian and attends church services on a regular basis. He enjoys spending time with family and friends. He loves to travel and meet new people. He can be reached at chosen_97@hotmail.com,

www.myspace.com/mtpope
www.facebook.com/mtpope
www.twitter.com/mtpope
www.blackplanet.com/mtpope

He would love to hear your feedback.

ORDER FORM
URBAN BOOKS, LLC
78 E. Industry Ct
Deer Park, NY 11729

Name: (please print): _____

Address: _____

City/State: _____

Zip: _____

QTY	TITLES	PRICE
	16 ½ On The Block	$14.95
	16 On The Block	$14.95
	Betrayal	$14.95
	Both Sides Of The Fence	$14.95
	Cheesecake And Teardrops	$14.95
	Denim Diaries	$14.95
	Happily Ever Now	$14.95
	Hell Has No Fury	$14.95
	If It Isn't love	$14.95
	Last Breath	$14.95
	Loving Dasia	$14.95
	Say It Ain't So	$14.95

Shipping and handling - add $3.50 for 1st book, then $1.75 for each additional book.

Please send a check payable to:

Urban Books, LLC

Please allow 4 - 6 weeks for delivery

ORDER FORM
URBAN BOOKS, LLC
78 E. Industry Ct
Deer Park, NY 11729

Name: (please print): _____

Address: _____

City/State: _____

Zip: _____

QTY	TITLES	PRICE
	The Cartel	$14.95
	The Cartel#2	$14.95
	The Dopeman's Wife	$14.95
	The Prada Plan	$14.95
	Gunz And Roses	$14.95
	Snow White	$14.95
	A Pimp's Life	$14.95
	Hush	$14.95
	Little Black Girl Lost 1	$14.95
	Little Black Girl Lost 2	$14.95
	Little Black Girl Lost 3	$14.95
	Little Black Girl Lost 4	$14.95

Shipping and handling - add $3.50 for 1st book, then $1.75 for each additional book.

Please send a check payable to:

Urban Books, LLC

Please allow 4 - 6 weeks for delivery

ORDER FORM
URBAN BOOKS, LLC
78 E. Industry Ct
Deer Park, NY 11729

Name: (please print): _____

Address: _____

City/State: _____

Zip: _____

QTY	TITLES	PRICE
	A Man's Worth	$14.95
	Abundant Rain	$14.95
	Battle Of Jericho	$14.95
	By The Grace Of God	$14.95
	Dance Into Destiny	$14.95
	Divorcing The Devil	$14.95
	Forsaken	$14.95
	Grace And Mercy	$14.95
	Guilty & Not Guilty Of Love	$14.95
	His Woman, His Wife His Widow	$14.95
	Illusions	$14.95
	The LoveChild	$14.95

Shipping and handling - add $3.50 for 1st book, then $1.75 for each additional book.
Please send a check payable to:
Urban Books, LLC
Please allow 4 - 6 weeks for delivery

ORDER FORM
URBAN BOOKS, LLC
78 E. Industry Ct
Deer Park, NY 11729

Name:(please print):_____

Address: _____

City/State: _____

Zip: _____

QTY	TITLES	PRICE

Shipping and handling - add \$3.50 for 1st book, then \$1.75 for each additional book.
Please send a check payable to:
Urban Books, LLC
Please allow 4 - 6 weeks for delivery

Notes

Notes

Notes

Notes